Fatal Passion

by

Loretta C. Rogers

A Doc Holliday Mystery, Book 1

Fatal Passion

Cover Art by *Diana Carlile*

The Wild Rose Press, Inc.
PO Box 708
Adams Basin, NY 14410-0708
Visit us at www.thewildrosepress.com

Publishing History
First Edition, 2021
Trade Paperback ISBN 978-1-5092-3641-1
Digital ISBN 978-1-5092-3642-8

A Doc Holliday Mystery, Book 1
Published in the United States of America

I spoke to the horse and ran my hands down his silken neck, down his withers, and down to his wrapped knee. That's when I saw him. My breath hung in my throat for a second. I think I made that little humming sound you make when you're close to a shriek, but haven't yet committed yourself. "Cindi, quick, hand me the lead strap."

She did as I asked. "What is it...what's wrong?"

I snapped the end of the strap into the o-ring. "Whirligig won't hurt you. Trust me. Lead him out and put him in one of the empty stalls. And whatever you do, *don't* scream."

"Okay, but..." She did as I instructed and as soon as she turned I saw the look of horror on her face.

In a low harsh voice, I again cautioned, "*Don't* scream, otherwise you'll startle the horse, and he's liable to take off dragging you with him."

Her throat convulsed, and I was proud of her for swallowing the shriek. She immediately trotted the young stallion to an empty stall and secured him. I was on my knees checking for a pulse when she entered and squatted next to me. "Is...is he dead?"

I nodded as I pulled out my cellphone and hit the emergency number that goes straight to my dad's special line. "Tullah, you okay?"

I barely controlled the quiver in my voice. "Dad, I just found Forest Rakestraw in a horse stall at his farm. He's dead."

Praise for Loretta C. Rogers' Mysteries

"Fast moving, tightly written, with enough suspects and tricky solutions to keep the suspense high."

~Anonymous

**Other books by Loretta C. Rogers also available
from The Wild Rose Press**

Historical Romance
Isabelle and the Outlaw
McKenna's Woman
Bannon's Brides
Lady Adel's Captain
Cloud Woman's Spirit
Taming the Lyon
When Comes Forever
Fate Comes Softly
Bitter Autumn

Contemporary Romance
Forbidden Son
Christmas at Hope Ranch

Romantic Suspense
Murder in the Mist
Shadowed Reunion

Enigma Incident Report
Enigma Sheriff's Office
Town of Enigma, State of Kentucky

On March 15 the sheriff from Enigma was dispatched to an area of the Enigma County Civic Center at 315 2nd Street on an unintentional death. Responding sheriff, who was on the premises, found a white female in a sitting position, her head leaned against a wall, apparently dead from a heart attack. A vial of prescription nitroglycerin was clutched in her left hand. The victim was identified as the owner of the Freckled Fanny Horse Farm, and a mayoral candidate, by Sheriff Henry J. Holliday, who arrived on the scene at 7:35 p.m.

An on-premises physician pronounced the death at approximately 6:45 p.m. The sheriff and deputy observed no evidence of foul play.

A statement was taken from the witness and her grandmother, who found the body and immediately notified the sheriff. Witness had occasion to use the facility bathroom. She said she observed no other women in the restroom. She said she noted the victim's feet under the stall door and spoke to the victim. When victim did not reply, the witness noted the main ladies' room door opened and her grandmother entered. Witness said when she called the victim's name again and victim did not respond, she became concerned.

Witness used a trash receptacle to stand on to peer inside the stall and discovered the victim slumped against the metal wall. Witness leaned over the door and unlatched it from the inside. She being of the medical profession, i.e., a veterinarian, immediately checked for a pulse and determined the victim was deceased. A doctor on premises confirmed the victim was deceased. He, being the victim's physician, confirmed victim was not a smoker but had a known history of heart disease.

The deputy was dispatched to notify next of kin. Sheriff Holliday interviewed the witness who discovered the victim and the witness who notified him, and released them. Pending the coroner's determination of the death as unintentional with no legal causes for concern, the immediate family has the right to refuse or agree to a hospital autopsy of the deceased.

Chapter One

I didn't like Alma Tackett. I hadn't expected to find her dead, either. As karma would have it, the day after her funeral, I found another dead body. There are times when I think a dark cloud follows me around.

My name is Tullah Crow Holliday. There are things about me you should know. My mother was full-blooded Cherokee. Her maiden name was Crow. She died four years ago. I'll save the details of her death for another time.

I'm a veterinarian. And yes, according to my dad's genealogy, we are direct descendants of the infamous John Henry "Doc" Holliday. So you can well imagine how tiresome it gets when people wave and say, "Mornin', Doc, been in any gunfights lately?" Then snigger and go about their merry way as if such irritating comments somehow made their day. The other saying that gets my goat is, "Hey, Doc, I'm your huckleberry." What the heck is that supposed to mean?

But I digress.

I dislike parties. Making meaningless chit-chat gives me the hives. I despise getting *spiffed up*, as my grandmother calls it. You can believe it when I say an occasion has to be extra special for me to wear a dress, high heels, and makeup. My hair is black and straight and refuses to hold a curl no matter how much coaxing with a curling iron.

My insatiable curiosity often gets me into trouble, especially with my dad. On my days off I'm either catching up on sleep or paperwork, reading suspense novels, riding one of my horses, or hanging out at my dad's office or at the newspaper office. By the way, did I mention that my dad, John Henry Holliday, is the sheriff of Enigma?

Except for a small herd of beefalo, and three Quarter Horses that I keep for pleasure riding, and two house pets, I live alone. After my mother's death, Dad said he couldn't bear the memories, so he converted the old storage area above the sheriff's office into an apartment. It suits him, sort of. It's really a glorified man cave, and it puts him close to his work so he doesn't have to drive the ten miles into town if an emergency arises.

****

On the night in question, I heaved a sigh as I stood in front of the tall cheval mirror. It was one of those special nights where dressing in something other than jeans and boots was required.

I finished braiding my hair with nimble fingers and practiced speed. Alma Tackett was running for re-election against Forest Rakestraw. They would be debating their political views and soliciting votes. I personally don't like Forest, either. He's arrogant, a ladies' man, has more money than he has sense, and owns the Make My Day Horse Farm. Well, I should say his wife, Beverly, is the wallet that supports Forest's deep pockets.

Since neither Alma nor Forest would win any popularity contest, my guess was most folks would show up for the free food. Plus, in a small community like Enigma, any excuse for a little socializing and gossiping is seized upon.

I was rifling through my closet when my cell phone rang. I smiled at the face on the caller ID. "Hey, Dad, what's up?"

His voice sounded a bit frantic. "Where are you? I need help with this danged tie. What's wrong with wearing my everyday work clothes?"

I couldn't contain the smile as I envisioned my alpha male father, with his secret heart of gold, accidentally strangling himself. "Dad, you're a tough-as-nails sheriff who totes a forty-five on his hip. Just wear your bolo tie. The one Mom made you."

His voice stilled. I bit the inside of my jaw. I imagined the sorrow on his face, and tears welling in his eyes. For their twenty-fifth anniversary my mother had tanned the leather strands and braided them into a tie. She had also forged a sterling silver Celtic Knot, with turquoise embedded in the center of the knot, to honor my father's Irish heritage.

"Dad," I whispered, "Mom would want you to wear it. Your re-election is coming up soon. You need to look good for a little pre-election campaigning. Besides, you need her spirit with you."

He heaved a lengthy sigh. "Okay, Punkin. It's at the ranch in a blue velvet bag. There's a small knob behind the mirror I made for your mother. If you push it, a door will open. The bag is in there." His voice turned gruff. "Now, hurry up. I can see people beginning to arrive at the civic center."

"Okay, be there in ten minutes."

"Make it fifteen. I don't want you speeding. It's against the law. And you are wearing something besides boots and jeans?"

I laughed. "Don't worry, I won't speed, and no, I'm not wearing jeans. I would never intentionally embarrass you."

He answered with a polite cough. "Never thought you would."

A look at the clock told me I needed to hustle. Inside my closet I pushed dresses aside and opted for a casual look—dark gray slacks, a paler shade of gray sweater with a cowl neckline, and a new pair of black suede boots that zipped up the side. Since the weather was still chilly, I grabbed my black suede jacket. I also chose a long tasselled gold-chained necklace with a turquoise stone pendant, another of my mother's creations. I slapped on some lipstick, then decided it was too red, snatched a piece of toilet paper off the roll, and blotted my lips.

The clock seemed to mock me with its annoying tick-tock. All I could think of was a phrase from *Alice in Wonderland*—"I'm late...I'm late for a very important date."

Flying around like a mad woman, I rolled the mirror away from the corner and ran my fingers along the back edge as my father had instructed until I found a small round knob. It clicked when I pushed it. Much to my surprise, a door opened. Inside were several shelves, and on one shelf lay the blue velvet bag.

Although my curiosity was piqued by some envelopes and jewelry items, I closed the door and rolled the mirror back to its resting place. Why hadn't I known about the secret door? I'd think about that later. For now, I grabbed my phone off the bed, stuck it in my jacket pocket, and bounded down the stairs.

River and Rascal were curled on their favorite braided rug in front of the gas fireplace.

I lifted my keys off the front hall rack, latched onto my purse, and opened the door. "Okay, you two, no shenanigans while I'm gone." Before I shut the door and locked it, I called, "River...Rascal, guard the house." As if a seventy-pound black Labrador retriever and a ninety-pound gray teacup donkey could understand my words.

The time had sprung forward and it was still daylight. However, I flipped on the porch light as I shut the door. Out of habit, I glanced toward the security light that illuminated the wide barn doors at night. Not that I was afraid of someone stealing one of my animals; it just made sense. Instead of groping my way to the barn in the dark, or trying to find the flashlight that I always seem to misplace, if I had to attend to a sick animal the security light kept me from tripping over myself.

To move my practice from town to my property, I had hired a contractor to convert two of the horse stalls into an office and waiting room, with an attached bathroom and bedroom as well as an examination room and a surgical room.

I climbed into my pickup and set my phone in its cradle, then turned the ignition. Spring was in the air. Trees were budding out and winter brown grass was turning green. I turned up the volume on the radio, and as I drove down my long drive to the main road I sang along with Garth Brooks.

I thought about my town. Enigma didn't live up to its name. The town is neither a mystery nor a puzzle. History says that way back in the 1800s the two founders got into a fight because each wanted the town named for himself. One of the wives supposedly said it was an enigma trying to figure out how to put the two men's names together to form a name for the town. I guess a flashbulb went off—well, there weren't flashbulbs back then, but you get the idea—anyhow, Enigma became the official name.

Although it's not a real happening place, Enigma is a good place to live. It's horse country. Some of the finest thoroughbred horses are raised in our neck of the woods. The ladies' auxiliary meet every month to plan their booths for the September 4-H fair. The fair always includes a carnival and a horse auction which brings buyers far and wide, and there's a dance to end the occasion. Then, of course, there is Kentucky Derby week at the end of April. It's like a declared holiday when most of the business owners close shop and head to Louisville because it's one of the best times to experience live racing at Churchill Downs.

My grandmother, Tanti Crow, runs the local newspaper. She and Alma had known each other for ages. Those two women were like oil and water, if you get my meaning. Except no one really knows why they disliked each other, and their lips are sealed.

Saturdays, several of the horse breeders gather at the feed store, where they have their own coffee klatch. Then there's the usual clutch of shops, the bank, a couple of cafes, and two gas stations, but any major shopping is done either in Lexington or Louisville.

In my twenty-eight years there has never been a bank robbery, a kidnapping, or a murder. Except for a few speeding tickets, and an occasional fight down at the Lucky Horseshoe, there's very little excitement.

Well, there was that one time when Leroy Banks got drunk and rode his horse up to the drive-through window at the Crispy Chicken. Unfortunately, for the girl serving him, he threw up in the take-out window just as she was handing him his sack of food. Dad arrested Leroy for drunk riding and destruction of public property. As you can see, Enigma is pretty much crime free.

Chapter Two

Dad slipped the bolo tie over his head. I adjusted it under his crisp blue collar and slid the Celtic Knot in place. For a man two years shy of fifty, he wears his age well. The fringes of gray at his temples enhance his craggy good looks. Part of me wished he'd start dating again, and part of me thought I might be jealous of any woman who won his heart.

Several people greeted us as we strolled into the building. At the moment it was a scene of chaotic activity. Energetic men and women bustled about aligning chairs in straight rows. The Kentucky state flag and the American flag adorned the room, accompanied by enough *Elect Forest Rakestraw Mayor* and *Vote Alma Tackett for Mayor* placards to support a small printing press for a year.

"Waste of money, if you ask me." Dad despised politics.

I glanced at the gathering crowd. "Next year it'll be your turn to campaign, and you'll need billboards."

"Nope. Don't need 'em. I stand on the merits of thirteen years of protecting the community so folks can rest well at night. That ought to be good enough."

"Yes, but—" Before I finished my sentence, Talmadge Crandall approached. He isn't the most well-liked person. He's smug, pompous, and doesn't mind letting anyone who will listen know that his stallions produce more winners than any other thoroughbreds in Kentucky—or in the world, for that matter. In my opinion, he overly embellishes. Nevertheless, Dad shook the man's hand. "Arrest any bad guys lately, Henry?"

I could almost hear Dad's teeth grinding. "Nope."

Dad placed his hand in the small of my back to guide me farther inside the room when Crandall grabbed Dad's arm. "Just want you to know I'm coming to your office first thing in the morning to swear out a complaint against Alma Tackett."

That statement grabbed my attention. Talmadge Crandall swearing out a complaint against the mayor? That should be interesting.

"What for, Mr. Crandall?"

Dad gave me one of his *mind your own business* looks. "Tullah, why don't you see if your grandmother has arrived?"

Naturally, I ignored him. Curiosity always gets the better of me.

I didn't have to wait long. Crandall spoke with controlled vengeance. "Her so-called Gypsy Vanner stallion has no papers and no proof that he's a purebred, but she's passing the scrawny beast off as—"

Furrowing his brow, Dad interrupted. "Talmadge, there's no law that says all the horses in Enigma have to be thoroughbreds. Why, my own daughter owns Quarter Horses."

Crandall growled. He beat his fist against the palm of his hand. "Yeah, and none of 'em are stallions. That ugly beast was trying to break through my fence last night, and it isn't the first time. I personally put a halter on him and trailered him back to Alma's, and told her what I'd do to him if there's a next time."

Curiosity got the better of me. "What'd she say?"

Dad shook his head and shifted from one foot to the other.

Aggravation deepened Crandall's voice. "She said if I didn't get off her property she'd file a trespassing complaint against me. I figured I'd beat her to the punch."

Alma Tackett was loud, brassy, and sometimes used words that would cause a sailor to blush. "She actually *ordered* you?"

If looks could kill, I'd be dead. "That piece of crow-bait was back this morning." Crandall's voice rose as his anger increased. "I will *not* have my mares' bloodlines compromised. Before I wring Alma's hoity-toity neck, I want her arrested. Do you hear me, Henry?"

By the time he'd finished ranting, the veins in the sides of his neck bulged like blue balloons and his face had turned apple red. I feared Mr. Crandall might have a stroke right there on the spot. A knot twisted in my stomach, and I decided to stick close.

Dad never takes threats lightly. He spoke low and calmly. "First, I'd suggest you lower your voice, Talmadge. Second, I can't arrest Alma because her horse gets out. However, I will speak to her. If the horse continues to get out, the best I can do is cite her for keeping a nuisance animal. And third, you're hot under the collar, so I'm going to pretend I didn't hear you threaten to do Alma physical harm."

Crandall's upper lip lifted into a snarl. "If you expect my continued support, you'll do more than that, *Sheriff*!" With that, he stormed off.

I regarded Dad with concern and admiration. "Wow, he's really ticked off. You don't suppose he'll do something foolish?"

"Nah. He's just blowing off steam." Dad's warm hand patted my shoulder. He sighed. "I'm in desperate need of a strong cup of coffee before this show gets on the road. If I wasn't on duty, I'd lace it with a shot of good Kentucky bourbon."

I moistened my lips. "Dad, I'm about to add fuel to the fire."

He cocked an eyebrow. "Meaning?"

"I haven't had a chance to tell you this before. Oh, umm, this isn't good."

"Whatever it is, Punkin, spit it out." His expression sobered even more. "Wait, you're not...not in the family..."

I gasped. "Good heavens, no! I'm not even dating anyone. *Dad!*"

He shrugged. "Sorry. Didn't mean to jump to conclusions. What's the mystery?"

"Okay, so, a little before three o'clock yesterday morning, Denver March called me. His mother's favorite mare was down. He claims he didn't know she was in foal because due to her advanced age they keep her away from the studs. Anyhow, apparently the contractions were bad and the mare rolled—which, of course, repositioned the foal. Also, the foal was overly large. I ended up having to pull it out. Dad, it wasn't a thoroughbred, or at least not full-blooded."

His mouth tightened. "And?"

"It was a pied Gypsy Vanner. Worse, the mare was almost twenty. She wasn't able to handle the stress of birthing. Mrs. March is in Louisville on a buying trip.

Denver called her. If you think Talmadge Crandall is angry, *well*, I could hear Mrs. March screaming obscenities and threats through the phone. After Denver disconnected the call, he told me that Alma and his mother have had several heated arguments over her rambling Vanner stallion, among other things."

Dad's gaze darkened. "I'll approach Alma as soon as the rally is over." He harrumphed. "Tanti'll have a field day with this one. I can see the headlines now—Sheriff arrests Mayor over randy stud."

I laughed, hiding my mouth behind my hand.

Over Dad's shoulder, I spotted Wakefield Tackett crossing the room in our direction. From a distance he looked like he'd still be carded when he ordered an alcoholic beverage. Up close, the once-taut skin around his jaws had begun to loosen, and from the roundness of his belly it's obvious he enjoys the food at Patty's Sweet's 'n' Eats. Tonight he looked gray and drawn. Either way, I had no desire to feel his clammy hands clutching mine. "See you in a bit, Dad. I need to visit the ladies' room."

I'd turned to make my retreat when I heard, "Why, if it isn't Tullah Holliday," and Forest Rakestraw flashed one of his charming smiles. "I'm your huckleberry."

Tall, thin in the shoulders, good-looking but not handsome, arched eyebrows that matched his perfectly trimmed five o'clock shadow, mayoral candidate Forest Rakestraw thought of himself as God's gift to women.

It was on the tip of my tongue to say, *Gag me.* Instead, I offered a not-so-polite yawn. "Your antiquated witticisms are boring. You should get some new material."

His placed his hands over his heart. "You wound me to the depths, Doc Holliday. What about dinner and cocktails after the rally?"

"Oh, is your wife joining us?" I'd never date a married man. I do have scruples, plus everyone knows that Beverly Rakestraw has the personality of a barracuda.

His gall irritated me, and the scowl on Dad's face deepened. I leaned close and whispered, "It's okay, Dad. I can handle this."

Sam Rakestraw approached, beaming a Cheshire cat grin. He slapped Forest on the back. "My boy's gonna give Alma a run for her money, Henry. I hope we can count on your vote." He glanced around the large room at the gathering crowd. "In fact, my money says he'll be Enigma's new mayor come November."

"Are you buying votes?" My question apparently hit a nerve. Sam's jowls quivered. His face glowed beet red. "No, I-I-it was a joke. Can't you take a joke?"

Angela Teasdale approached. "Good evening, Sheriff. Hello, Doc Holliday."

Angela is the high school agriculture teacher and 4-H sponsor and had no way of knowing she had intervened at what was about to become an awkward moment. "Have any of you seen Mayor Tackett?" She touched Forest's arm. Her eyelashes fluttered. "We have about ten minutes before I introduce you. Please make your way to the stage."

I wondered if Angela was aware the tone in her voice had altered from casual to seductive-come-hither. I also didn't miss the slight flush to her cheeks when Forest winked at her and the inviting way she returned his smile.

Beverly Rakestraw sidled next to her husband. I took in the sight of her with a quick glance. Slim, long-legged, with those perfect-sized breasts that most women envy and men secretly drool over. Her hair was a paid-for shade of auburn, framing her face in a tumble of spiral curls. Hazel eyes, flawless skin. She had that clear, ageless look that comes with first-rate cosmetic surgery and the fawn-colored cashmere sweater dress she wore emphasized her lush body without being vulgar, unlike Angela Teasdale's blue jeans and boots. Beverly's manner was solemn and sincere, and struck me as false.

She placed a kiss on her husband's tanned cheek, leaving a red lipstick imprint. She pulled a neatly folded handkerchief from Forest's suit coat pocket and dabbed as she seared Angela and me with the evil eye. "My goodness, women seem to swarm around my husband like bees to honey." She patted him on the chest and pointed her glare at Angela. "Of course, my sweetie knows who butters his bread."

Rumor has it that although she disguises her age well, Beverly is at least ten years older than her husband.

At least Angela had the good sense not to counter-comment. Instead, she excused herself, saying she needed to make sure the microphones were working.

Now was a good time to make my exit. "I'll join you in a few, Dad. Why don't you grab us some coffee and a couple of Patty's donuts before they're all gone?" I excused myself. Soft and flaky, Patty Sweet's donuts are to die for. My personal favorites are the…well, all of them.

I felt Forest's eyes on me as I beat a hasty retreat.

Unfortunately, I stepped right into Wakefield Tackett's path. "Evening, Wakefield. Angela is looking for your mother."

I made sure to put my hands behind my back. Wakefield's are perpetually clammy. This evening his appearance looked a bit more grungy than usual, which wouldn't please his mother, since she was all about appearances.

"I-I think she's in the ladies' room. S-she isn't feeling well."

This gave me an excuse to escape. Don't get me wrong, Wakefield is nice enough. He doesn't have a lot of friends, so give him an inch and he becomes clingy. I'd already made that mistake once, to the point that he'd become a nuisance. "I'm on my way there. I'll tell your mother she's needed on stage."

His forlorn expression stopped me. I asked, "Where is your dad?"

Wakefield glanced about the large room. "I-I don't know."

"Why don't you grab a seat down front and save one for your father?" This time I patted him on the shoulder.

The bathroom door banged shut as I stepped into the ladies' room. There is only one toilet. The ladies' auxiliary promised the money from this year's festival would go to add two more stalls and another sink to make the bathroom more accommodating.

The stall door was closed. Occasionally teenage girls will prank users by locking the door from the inside and then crawling underneath it. I bent down to see if the cubicle was truly occupied, and recognized Alma Tackett's familiar pair of black pumps. I called out, "Evening, Alma. Nice weather we're having, isn't it?"

No answer.

I thought maybe she was concentrating on *business*, so I gave her to the count of ten before saying, "Alma, if you don't mind, I really need to use the toilet."

Reaching emergency status, I left with the intention of using the men's room. Thank goodness for Tanti's arrival. "Grandmother, please watch the door to the men's room? Alma is homesteading in the lady's room, and is…"

My grandmother made a shooing motion with her hands and said she would stand guard. She quipped, "Queen of the throne."

We both laughed.

I can't explain why, but while inside the men's stall, the hairs on the back of my neck prickled and the oddest sensation of dread swept over me. I hurriedly finished, washed my hands, and pushed open the door.

"Grandmother…" I grabbed her hand. "There was something odd about Alma."

"Like what?"

"Her feet didn't move when I spoke to her, and she didn't make a sound." I practically pulled Tanti into the bathroom. "Lean against the door, and don't let anyone in."

She nodded. Curiosity lit her newswoman's eyes. I pulled the trashcan over to the stall and turned it upside down. I gripped the top of the door as I stood on the receptacle and peered inside the cubicle. A macabre sight greeted me.

Alma's body had listed to one side. Her head

leaned against the gray metal wall. Her lavender skirt was hiked up to her thighs and red lace thongs were bunched around her knees. Her staring gaze reminded me of a doll's glassy eyes. Her mouth was pooched open much like a fish trying to suck air.

Although I'm a veterinarian and have seen many dead animals, the sight of a dead person is startling. At least I'm certain she's dead.

"You're awfully quiet, Tullah. What is it?"

"Quick! Go get Dad. I think she's dead."

"Alma?"

"Yes, who else?"

"Oh," Grandmother said rather flatly. She glanced up at me with a peculiar expression as if she'd misunderstood; and then her eyes widened. "Oh!"

Chapter Three

As soon as Grandmother left, I stepped down off the trashcan and in two quick strides locked the bathroom door. I didn't want anyone coming in. I could always say I was preserving the scene, or at least that's what the detectives say on television.

Except for an occasional drip from the sink's faucet, the bathroom was eerily quiet. After whipping out my cell phone and taking a series of pictures—another thing I learned from watching cop shows on TV—I reached inside my purse and pulled out a pair of disposable gloves.

Weird, right?

Nope, as a veterinarian I try to stay prepared. After all, you never know when the unexpected will happen. I needed to work fast.

The civic club building is old, and the walls are thin. I heard Dad's muffled voice and was certain he'd said, "Folks, there's been an emergency. My apologies. The rally is temporarily postponed."

Someone yelled loud enough for me to hear, "What's the emergency, Sheriff?"

Hesitation.

Dad had apparently ignored the question because he called out, "Doctor Gannon, are you in the room?"

My heart pitter-pattered. Rick Gannon is about the only bachelor in town who comes close to piquing my interest. The problem is he's too handsome and a little too citified to suit me. He looks as if he belongs on the cover of a male model magazine or a movie star news publication instead of being a cardiologist in Small Town USA. Although, I will admit that when I see him my deprived hormones cause my unmentionable body parts to sweat.

Silence. Or at least, I couldn't hear if the fine-looking doctor had answered or not.

Another voice boomed: Dad's deputy. Tiny Goodbody is the exact opposite of his name. His mother apparently had a warped sense of humor when she named him, because Tiny is six foot seven and built like a Viking, with a face that only a bulldog and a mother could love. Yet there isn't a mean bone in his body, until he's riled.

I could almost feel the walls vibrate when his bass voice boomed, "You folks heard the sheriff. Clear the building."

Stepping back on the trashcan, and being a tall woman, I leaned my nearly six-foot frame over the door, slid the bolt back, and swung the door wide. Careful not to disturb the body, I placed two fingers against the side of her neck to check for a pulse. Alma Tackett was stone cold dead.

Her purse hung from the door hook. It was expensive, one of those designer types with the initials all done in curlicues. Since it was unzipped, I did a quick search and continued clicking away with my phone camera.

I observed a packet of peppermints, ink pen, small notepad, lipstick, hand lotion, tissues, comb, tweezers, and receipts from various stores, and an open prescription bottle of nitroglycerin. I mused aloud. "Poor Alma. She never missed an opportunity to talk about her heart problem."

Don't ask me why I leaned closer to smell her breath. I mean, she wasn't breathing, so there wouldn't be anything to smell, except I detected the distinct aroma of honey. Since she had mints in her purse, I didn't give the matter a second thought.

I wondered if she had suffered chest pains and had opened the bottle. But why didn't she put the cap back on? Maybe she dropped it. I did a quick scan of the floor and spotted the cap, but not a pill. I had about concluded that the mayor, probably the most disliked citizen in Enigma, had the misfortune of suffering a fatal heart attack while sitting on the throne.

Footsteps alerted me that I needed to hurry my search and unlock the bathroom door. Being in the medical profession, albeit dealing with animals, though some people act like animals or worse, I could always account for opening the bathroom stall door by stating that I was checking for a pulse. Which is the truth.

I nearly jumped out of my skin when knuckles rapped loudly on the door with my dad demanding, "Tullah, open the door."

Two long steps and I unlocked and opened the door. The look on my father's face could have scalded coffee. "Where is she, and why was the door locked?"

I pointed. "To preserve the c-cri...um...the area. In case you need to look for clues."

His lips formed a stern line, and he gave me one of his *we'll talk later* looks.

I was surprised when old Doc Ritter skirted around me to the stall. For nearly sixty years, Paul Ritter was

Enigma's only doctor. He officially retired five years ago when Dr. Richard Gannon was hired as chief of staff of Enigma's new medical center. Doc Ritter is eighty-eight years young and still considers himself Enigma's top doc.

I babbled, "I've already checked. She's dead. Apparent heart attack."

Doc Ritter peered over his Ben Franklin glasses. His sarcasm was unmistakable. "I'll note your diagnosis, Tullah."

Dad stood behind the doctor, and I craned my neck to look over Dad's shoulder. "Tullah, you're not needed here. Go help your grandmother with Wakefield and his father."

I tried to appear surprised. "You haven't told them?"

He squinted. He does that when he's irritated. "Tullah, would you want to see your mother indisposed?"

His words stabbed my heart. I sighed, thinking about my mother's death. "Sorry, of course not."

There was a judgmental pause. Wakefield pushed past my grandmother and nearly bowled me over. Fortunately, before he fully entered the room I grabbed him by both arms and back-walked him away from the stall. His bottom lip quivered. "Is she...is she..."

I nodded. "I'm sorry." As much as I hated having his arms around me and crushing his pudgy body against mine, I swallowed my revulsion and did my best to comfort him. I counted to five and pushed him away. "Where's your dad?"

"H-he's...I-I don't know. H-he was here, and then he and M-Mother had one of their usual argu...arrr...sspats, and h-he left."

Most days Wakefield stutters. It gets worse and sometimes is unintelligible when he's stressed or overly excited.

"What did they argue about?" Geez, sometimes I could slap my brain for not controlling my tongue.

Wakefield gave me a doleful look and simply shook his head. "Y-you know…the u-usual."

The usual being Alma's not so secret life. "Listen, why don't you find your dad and break the news to him, then head over to the hospital." At least I was fairly certain Alma's body would be taken to the hospital rather than the morgue.

Poor Wakefield's stutter worsened when he was excited or upset. "I-I-I d-don't know w-where he is."

"Don't worry, Wakefield, we'll find him. You go sit down and wait."

As time ticked by, a siren wailed in the background, progressively getting louder. Enigma is fortunate to have a hospital and one ambulance. Within seconds, Bubba Dawson and Rita Graham arrived with a gurney.

Doc Ritter rubbed the bottom of his nose. "Bubba, take her on to the morgue. There's no need for an autopsy."

"Why's that, Doc?" I asked. My question caused Dad to mumble an ugly swear word under his breath.

Doc's bushy eyebrows reminded me of two caterpillars attacking each other as he waggled them toward me. "Tullah, not that I owe you an explanation, but I was Alma's doctor for more years than you are old. She was born with several holes in her heart. Sometimes they close up on their own. Sometimes not.

I encouraged her more than once to go to the cardiac center in Lexington, but she was too stubborn. Last week, she called saying her chest pains were coming more frequently."

"Oh. What did you tell her?"

He shot me an incredulous look. "I told her I'm retired and to go see Dr. Gannon."

"Did she?"

His voice increased in volume. "How should I know?" He scowled over at my dad. "Henry!"

"Enough, Tullah. You are not the medical examiner. If Doc says she died of heart failure, then so be it. Case closed!"

Even though I'm twenty-eight years old and can take care of myself, there are times when my dad can reduce me to feeling like a six-year-old. This was one of those times. I knew I had overstepped the bounds with my questions.

Coming to my rescue, Grandmother stepped forward. "All this excitement has made me hungry. Let's go to the Whitehorse Saloon for a hamburger."

Dad cleared his throat. "Not until I've taken yours, Tullah's, and Doc Ritter's official statements."

An hour later and as a way of making amends, I invited Doc to join us at the Whitehorse Saloon. I don't know if he turned down the invitation because he was annoyed with me or if he really wanted to go home and watch his favorite medical TV series. At any rate, Grandmother rode with me. Dad promised to meet us later.

The Whitehorse Saloon sits at the edge of town. Charlie Whitehorse and my dad have been friends since their Army days. The story goes that Charlie saved my dad's life. However, Charlie swears up and down that it was my dad who saved his life. Since both of them received purple hearts, maybe they saved each other.

Charlie doesn't like to talk about himself, and my dad is pretty tight-lipped about Charlie's personal life. All I know is he was born in Alaska and settled in Kentucky after he and Dad left the Army. I can tell you this—he's my godfather and like a member of our family. I believe he would lay down his life for any one of us if necessary.

Charlie gave me a hug and kissed the top of my head. "How's my favorite veterinarian?"

I laughed. "I'm on Dad's bad side, *again*."

Charlie walked behind the bar and poured merlot into a chilled stemmed glass and handed it to Tanti. He knows my grandmother too well. "I suppose you want burgers all around?" His coffee-brown eyes lit with humor.

Tanti said, "Yes, and don't forget—no onion on mine. Gives me heartburn."

My grandmother is seventy and still feisty. Strands of silver thread run through her black hair, which she wears like a braided tiara. She uses a walking stick with a horse head carved on it. Not that she's the least bit feeble. It just helps to steady her when she walks on uneven surfaces. Her comment about the onions unsettled me; especially after discovering Alma Tackett dead. "Grandmother, be honest. Do you have a problem with your heart?"

Tanti reached over and patted my hand. "You worry too much, Granddaughter. Just because onions give me heartburn doesn't mean I'm ready to meet the Spirit Father. In fact, I plan to live to the ripe old age of one hundred."

She does that all the time…talks around the question to avoid giving an answer. It infuriates me. Maybe that's what makes her a good news. Unappeased, I smiled. "And I bet you will, too."

"Tullah, you want a beer?"

"Not tonight, Charlie. A cola with lemon will do."

Charlie yelled out the order to the cook, and while we waited Tanti filled him in on Alma's death. "I'm wrestling with several ideas for tomorrow's headlines." Her face was completely deadpan. "How's this—Mayor Alma Tackett collapses on the throne, or…"

"Grandmother, you are perfectly awful."

Charlie smirked. "The old bag finally packed it in. Couldn't have happened to a nicer person. I reckon her death tickled Sam Rakestraw's funny bone, since he lost his bid at the office four years ago."

"Yeah, he lost the mayoral race to her, 'though I still don't understand how. It's common knowledge there was no love lost between him and Alma."

Charlie glanced up when the bar door opened. He waved and motioned my dad over. "That's for sure. As of now, Forest has no competition."

Tanti said, "This should prove interesting, since his opposition just bit the dust."

"What?" Charlie and I laughed when we responded in unison.

Tanti grabbed a napkin. "Lend me your pen, Charlie. I need to jot this down before I forget."

I could almost see the wheels turning in Grandmother's head when she said, "Mayoral candidate has no opposition. Will he win by default or will a new candidate qualify to give Forest Rakestraw a run for his money?"

I felt my eyebrows shoot upward. "Sam was practically bragging that he had enough money to buy votes for Forest."

Charlie leaned forward on his elbows. Mischief twinkled in his eyes. "As I hear it, it's the wife with the deep pockets."

I nearly choked on my soda. "You mean Beverly?"

Charlie waggled his eyebrows. "Just sayin'."

We were discussing Laci Shubert, Alma's secretary, when my cell phone rang. I answered, "Doc Holliday." I pressed a hand against my ear to filter out the noise while I listened to the hysterical voice on the other end. "Calm down. I can't understand what you're saying. Coyotes? Yeah, sure. I'll meet you at my place in ten minutes."

I pushed back from the table. "Cancel my order, Charlie. I've gotta go. Coyotes attacked Mrs. Connell's boxer. Sounds bad."

"Want me to go with you, Punkin?"

Dad strolled over and stood next to the booth.

"Thanks, no. Cindi's there."

"Make it fifteen minutes, Punkin. Speeding is…"

"I know, Dad. Speeding is against the law. In this case, it's an emergency."

Giving an all-around goodbye wave, I made a mad dash to my truck. I commanded the Bluetooth to call Cindi. Cindi Redfern is my veterinarian tech assistant, secretary, and bookkeeper, and worth more than she gets paid.

Pushing the speed limit, I arrived at my barn in ten minutes flat. Cindi met me at the door. She handed me a disposable white coat. "I've got the surgery ready."

"Thanks." I raced inside the room I had set up especially for small animal surgery and pulled on the coat.

Outside we heard the crunch of wheels and then the slamming of doors. Cindi hurried out to greet the couple. "Doctor Holliday is waiting for you. Follow me."

Bert Connell is an elderly, thin man who didn't look strong enough to carry his own weight. He and his wife live on the edge of town in a nice middle-class subdivision surrounded by woods. He struggled with the dog's dead weight. "His name is Brutus. We let him out to do his business and heard the most gawd-awful snarlin' and growlin'. They were all over him, a pack of coyotes tearin' at him. I couldn't shoot 'em for fear of hitting him."

He followed me into the small surgical room and laid the boxer on the metal table. "How did you get them off your dog?"

He glanced at his wife and rewarded her with a smile. "Eileen turned on the water hose and was squirtin' 'em while I grabbed a hoe and started whacking the daylights out of 'em. Finally, like the cowards they are, they gave up and ran off into the woods."

Mrs. Connell sobbed. "Brutus isn't going to die, is he?"

The dog was covered with multiple bloody lacerations and puncture wounds from bites. Although I knew the Connells, I had never treated their pets. "Is he up to date on his rabies shots?"

"Yes, we get the two-year kind," Mrs. Connell answered. "He's not due for another one until next

August."

I breathed a sigh of relief. I never liked having to euthanize an animal unless the odds of saving it are zero to none. "Ms. Redfern always keeps a pot of coffee brewing. I'll do my best to save Brutus, but stitching him up will take a couple of hours. Help yourself to the coffee and try not to worry."

The poor creature was a bloody mess. He'd lost part of an ear and had a gaping wound, with a flap of flesh hanging, at his left shoulder. He whimpered in pain. I stroked his neck. "It's okay, Brutus. We're going to fix you up good as new."

Cindi inserted the inhalant tube down the dog's trachea and started the general anesthesia. I said, "This dog is lucky to be alive. A pack of coyotes is nothing to mess with."

Cindi shuddered. "I shudder to think of what could happen if it was a child."

I shuddered, too. "I'll report this to animal control so they can check to see if the packs are living close to the houses. My biggest concern is rabies."

Three hours and over one hundred sutures later, Brutus was wearing a cone around his neck to keep him from licking his wounds or gnawing his stitches.

I removed my surgical gloves and tossed them into the hazardous material trashcan. While Cindi cleaned up, I walked out to talk to the Connells. They greeted me with anxiety written all over their faces.

I smiled. "Brutus is resting comfortably in a crate. We'll keep him overnight for observation. Cindi will give you a call in the morning to let you know if he's able to go home. There was extensive muscle damage to his shoulder, which might leave him with a slight limp. Otherwise, except for a few scars, Brutus should live a long life."

A teary Mrs. Connell gave me an unexpected hug. Mr. Connell pulled out his credit card and said, "We weren't blessed with children, Doc Holliday. Brutus and his sister, Queenie, and our two Maine Coon cats are extra special to us."

I nodded my understanding. A few minutes later, I walked them out to their car and stood for a moment before returning to the barn. "It's late. Go home, Cindi."

"Um, if you don't mind, I'd like to stay the night. I'll sleep on the cot."

"Things okay at home?"

"It's my dad. Since Mom divorced him—well— you know how he gets."

Earl Redfern is about as sorry as the day is long. There isn't one person in Enigma who would mourn his death; and no one thinks badly of Annie Redfern for packing her bags and leaving. Cindi is twenty-three and old enough to make her own decisions. She decided to stay in Enigma because she likes working with me and feels a certain obligation to look after her father. I've offered to help her find a position in Lexington or Louisville. I worry about her safety if Earl gets on one of his drinking binges.

"Sure, Cindi. Stay as long as you like. You don't need to sleep in the barn. I have a spare bedroom."

"No, that's okay, Tullah. I'd rather be out here with the animals. Plus, I can keep a check on Brutus. I'll be okay. Really."

I hadn't had anything substantial to eat since breakfast, and it was now past midnight. No wonder I felt lightheaded and a little woozy. "You know where the extra blankets are?"

She smiled and nodded. "You look dead on your feet. I'll see you in the morning."

After patching up a dog nearly chewed to death by coyotes, it was with trepidation that I let River and Rascal out to take care of their nighttime business. I knew they'd head for the barn, sniff around, explore the yard, then scamper back to the house.

I sent a text to Cindi:

—*Close and lock the barn doors*—

She replied with a thumbs-up emoji.

I opened the refrigerator and found a half-empty container of cottage cheese and a cup of applesauce. I mixed the two together in the container and scarfed it down while I dragged myself upstairs.

After unbraiding my hair and finger-brushing it, I changed into a pair of flannel pajamas and was falling asleep before I climbed into the bed and tucked the quilt under my chin.

That night I dreamed of my mother, coyotes, and Alma Tackett's staring eyes.

Chapter Four

On Monday, after a fitful night's sleep, I staggered to the kitchen and poured a cup of French roast, thankful for the automatic timer on my coffeepot. I cooked my favorite breakfast, sausage and egg scramble with buttered biscuit and strawberry jam. I made sure River's and Rascal's bowls were filled before going upstairs to shower and dress for Mayor Tackett's funeral.

The day was raw. The wind flapped the oak tree's leafless branches against my bedroom window. I cringed at the scratching against the glass pane that reminds me of nails on a chalkboard and vowed to either trim the branches or cut down the tree.

I sat on the edge of the bed and pulled on woolen socks, a pair of long underwear, and an ankle-length black velveteen dress with a high neckline, then slipped my feet inside a pair of knee-high boots.

At the front door, I checked the thermostat, hefted into my heavier coat, added gloves, and draped a blue hoodie scarf over my head, tied the ends, and tucked them inside my coat. A blast of frigid air nearly sucked my breath away when I opened the kitchen door. I raced to the truck, climbed in and turned the ignition, and shivered, waiting for the heat to kick in. While driving to the Cedar Hill Cemetery, I thought it odd that Mr. Tackett and Wakefield had decided to forego a viewing for Alma and instead opted for a no-frills graveside funeral. Mr. Tackett said it would be hypocrisy to hold a viewing when the majority of the citizens held little respect for his wife, and that he didn't need anyone's sympathy. He also said the only reason people would show up at the funeral home was for a free meal, and he'd already paid enough.

By the time I arrived at the cemetery, snow feathered down from the sky. Not unusual weather for March. The headstones were barely visible in the veil of white. Perhaps it was the miserably cold morning that caused such a small turnout. At least I hoped that was the reason. Alma would most certainly be disappointed.

The funeral home had provided a blue canopy and several rows of chairs, divided to create an aisle. At the front, the casket stood on a bier with wheels to eliminate the need for pallbearers. A spray of all-white oriental lilies, gladioli, and carnations, with a blend of fragrant green, draped the casket. Music that I didn't recognize played softly from a hidden cassette player.

I spotted Dad and Grandmother standing in what I supposed was the receiving line. In my lifetime, I have attended two funerals—that of Bryce Myers, my fiancé, who had been kicked in the head by a stallion, and my mother's. Bryce's family had held a viewing at the funeral home with friends and family members sharing tidbits and funnies about him. There was a large picture board of him and all the show horse awards he'd won, and a buffet meal was served.

My mother's funeral was different. Dad and Grandmother had honored her fully in both the Cherokee and the Christian way.

I believe Grandmother sensed I had arrived. She

turned and motioned me forward. I welcomed the warm hugs from her and Dad. Mr. Tackett and Wakefield stood at the front. While we inched forward, I listened to the snow's soft pelting upon the canopy, an appropriately lonely sound for this solemn occasion.

I had found Alma dead on Friday night. By Monday we were attending her funeral. Mr. Tackett was adamant that he did not see the necessity of an autopsy. She had died of a heart attack, and that was that.

From my observation, Mr. Tackett didn't strike me as the grieving husband. He stood emotionless, accepting each person's condolences. At one point, he turned a cold eye toward me before ducking his head so that the flabbiness of his chin rested on his chest.

Dressed in a double-breasted navy blue knee-length coat, Wakefield looked red from the cold, especially the tips of his ears. He looked at me uncomfortably, probably wishing he were someplace else. Well, I can't say that I blamed him. It struck me as odd that he didn't look particular saddened by his mother's death.

Reverend Chesterfield from the Baptist church materialized from nowhere and asked everyone to be seated. The two Tackett men seemed relieved to no longer be on display. The preacher cleared his throat and welcomed each and every one of us who turned out on this cold and snowy day. His voice droned, "Friends, we are gathered here to honor Alma Lewinger Tackett, beloved…"

I thought about the way I had found Alma in death. I thought about her in life—medium height, rounded hips, ample breasts, perfectly styled bleached blonde pageboy, perfectly applied makeup, manicured nails, expensive clothing, and rumored unfaithful to her husband on more than one occasion. I wondered if he'd gotten tired of the whispers behind his back, and I wondered if he had capitalized on her heart condition to hasten her death.

I've known Mr. Tackett my entire life. He's a year or two older than my dad. It's always mystified me that Alma Lewinger of the Lexington Lewingers had married Mr. Tackett. His name is George, but everyone calls him Mr. Tackett. As long as I've known him, he never was a handsome man. In fact, he's rather plain, with a comb-over to hide his baldness, bags under his eyes, a paunch that stretches the middle button on his shirts, and comes from a working middle-class family. He is the very opposite of Alma, who routinely traveled to Lexington for Botox treatments to keep her young-looking.

Wakefield is their only child, and a bachelor. I glanced from him to his father and found little resemblance. I remembered how Alma bragged to the entire town that Wakefield was attending the University of Kentucky's College of Pharmacy. When he dropped out, she made excuses that due to his sensitive nature he needed time away from his studies. Wakefield confided to me a long time ago that due to his grades he'd flunked out, and that what he really wanted was to be a writer. Without telling his mother, he'd changed his curriculum to creative arts, but he hadn't succeeded at that either. In truth, he'd had a nervous breakdown and spent several years in a behavioral health institution in Lexington. I feel badly that he hasn't found his true niche in life.

Something itched in the back of my mind. It aggravated me that I couldn't call it forward. I didn't care what the death certificate stated. Perhaps it was my vivid curiosity that had me thinking that Alma did not die of a heart attack.

The preacher's loud "Amen," shook me from my reverie. I had drifted so deep in thought that I'd missed the entire eulogy.

A gust of wind blew snow flurries under the canopy. The small group of mourners did not linger, and I didn't blame them. They pulled their coats closer to their bodies and hustled to their vehicles.

Dad said, "Tullah, take your grandmother home."

I didn't ask questions or scold that he shouldn't linger in this weather. I knew his need to visit my mother's grave. I wrapped my arms around him and laid my head on his shoulder. He patted my back. Tanti, too, hugged him. He caught her tear on the tip of his gloved finger.

I held Grandmother's arm tight to keep her from slipping on the slick ground. For a seventy-year-old woman, she is still spry and needed no assistance climbing inside my truck. I started the motor. Cold air from the heater quickly heated, and we relished the warmth. I followed the small parade of vehicles out of the cemetery and to the main road. "Grandmother, I would like it if you spent the night with me."

She reached over and patted my cheek. A wistful expression captured her face. "Your father visits Josie's grave to be close to her. I wish to hear the silence. You understand."

Tears filled her eyes, and I knew her heart ached for the daughter she had lost. She would spend the evening going through photo albums and revisiting my mother's life.

I nodded my understanding. No words were needed. Heaviness burdened my own heart.

After a while, I said, "Grandmother, do you truly believe Alma died from a heart attack?"

The corners of her eyes crinkled into crow's feet when she smiled. "I believe you want to believe foul play is involved."

"You know me too well, Grandmother."

She turned to face me. "Ever since you were a little girl you have always had an insatiable curiosity and a love for solving puzzles and riddles."

Concern filled her chocolate-brown eyes. "You are the sum of many parts, Granddaughter." I watched the struggle to control her emotions. The tragedy of my mother's death still haunts her, as it does my father and me. "From your mother you inherited the love for all creatures, and like my Josie, you have a beautiful soul."

I pulled into the parking space of her ground-floor apartment and shifted the truck into neutral. My hand was on the door handle when she said, "I'll see myself in. Promise to drive careful, and call me when you get home so I won't worry." Before opening the door, she said, "Tullah, although he died before his time, your grandfather was a man given of visions." She chuckled. "With Henry's ancestral history, he could be a great lawman if he chose to leave Enigma. He, too, is intuitive. From them you inherited an inner sense."

"And from you, Grandmother, I inherited my love of books, and *snooping*." I meant the snooping part as a joke because in her younger days, when she was a reporter for the *Louisville Times*, Tanti won numerous awards for her crime articles.

"Yes, and that, too." She opened the door and stepped to the ground. This time her brows furrowed. "Ever since the tragic way your mother died, you have become obsessed with solving mysteries." She pretended to think something over. "Never forget—curiosity killed the cat, Tullah."

I waited until she was inside and a light shone through the living room curtains before I backed out and headed toward home. The ten miles felt like a hundred. Although it was two o'clock in the afternoon, the day was gray, and falling snow kept the windshield wipers working on high. I didn't realize I'd been holding my breath until I pulled under the carport. I prayed no one called in with an emergency, because I dreaded driving in snow.

Cindi's blue truck was parked under the tractor shelter. The barn doors were closed, and a light shone in the office. I sent her a text.

—*U need anything?*—

She answered:

—*All OK. Will let R&R out*—

I sent her a smiley face. I hustled up the steps, unlocked the kitchen door, and flipped on the light. I bent to slide the security door up on the doggie door. Shrugging out of my coat, I heated water in the microwave for a mug of hot chocolate, and then raced upstairs to change out of my dress and into a pair of blue sweats and my favorite fuzzy green turtle slippers. Back in the kitchen, I made myself a plate of buttered saltine crackers, stirred hot chocolate mix into the water, and added a splash of half 'n' half for extra richness. Grandmother is always complaining I'm skin and bones. I figured the extra calories wouldn't hurt me.

In moments, the doggie door flapped back and forth. My pets wiggle-waggled into the living room. Satisfied with sufficient hugs and scratching behind their ears, River and Rascal curled on their favorite braided rug in front of the flickering fireplace.

I settled in my recliner and switched on the television, hoping to catch the weather, before I sent Grandmother a text letting her know I'd made it home. She replied with a double hearts emoji.

I knew Dad would either send me a text or call. Since my mother's tragic death, the three of us check in with each other often.

Wrapping a red-white-and-blue crocheted afghan around me, I sipped my cocoa, letting its sweet heat warm me, and while I nibbled on the saltines, watched the weather, satisfied the next weeks would bring a warming trend.

Clicking off the TV, I grabbed a spiral-bound notebook. Sure, the weather is miserable, and who would trade warm and cozy for driving in the snow and shivering under a canopy to attend the funeral of someone you didn't particularly respect? Still, I was compelled to jot down the names of the attendees: the bereaved, George and Wakefield Tackett; the Baptist preacher and his wife—well, it was mandatory for them to show up; Sam and Forest Rakestraw—naturally they'd show up; Laci Shubert, Alma's personal secretary; Judy and Dave Clemson—Judy was Alma's beautician; Delbert Simms, one of the county commissioners—he said he came representing the other four commissioners and all sent their condolences; and four of the five city council members.

Including Tanti, my dad and me, sixteen people out of a population of sixteen thousand was sad. I tapped the pen against my lips.

Question one: Did Alma really die of a heart attack, or was she murdered? Question two: If she was murdered—why and who?

My brain told me to make a list of who should have attended the funeral but didn't, and possible whys.

Talmadge Crandall—actually threatened to hurt Alma. Side note: he was at the rally when he made the threat.

Evelyn March—had several run-ins with Alma about her Gypsy Vanner stallion. She was in Lexington on the night of the murder. Side note: TC had the same complaint.

Charlie Whitehorse—he'd called Alma an old bag and seemed glad she'd died. Side note: shame on me for including Charlie. Also, he was at the saloon when we arrived.

Dr. Paul Ritter—weather conditions possibly kept him home due to his advanced age.

Dr. Richard Gannon—probably busy at the hospital.

Except for Tanti, none of the ladies' auxiliary. Side note: most of them are elderly and don't like to drive after dark or in bad weather.

Sid Haskell—works for E M. Side note: he once managed Alma's horse farm. Rumor has it he didn't like the way she treated her horses. Rumor also has it that he and Alma had a fling and he was angry when she broke it off. Maybe that's the real reason he quit.

Patty West—councilwoman. Side note: Rumor has

it that Everett West was another of Alma's conquests.

There are others I considered. In mulling over the names, most of them were inconsequential, like Mr. and Mrs. Connell, who live in the county and have no dealings with the mayor's office, or Cindi Redfern, even though her father once worked for Alma. I wasn't sure about Sue Sweet. She didn't attend the funeral even though Alma has, well, had a standing order for two dozen glazed donuts for the weekly council meetings.

My cell phone rang. Dad's face popped up on the caller ID. "Hey, Dad, you okay?"

"Sure. Just checking in. 'Night, Punkin." He ended the call. That was my dad—a man of few words.

My bladder said it was time to get out of the chair. On the way to the bathroom, another question popped into my brain—Did Alma leave a will? She never minded flaunting her wealth. Note, I said *her* wealth. She didn't mind relating that Mr. Tackett came to the marriage with empty pockets. Who would inherit—Mr. Tackett or Wakefield or both equally?

It's not unusual for me to receive numerous phone calls per day. For this reason, I have a soothing musical ring tone. That way my teeth don't grind together every time the phone rings. I was headed to the kitchen when Beethoven's *Für Elise* played.

"Doc Holliday."

"Tullah, this is Forest Rakestraw."

Instantly, my guard went up. "Forest, how many times do I need to tell you—"

He chuckled. "Don't worry; I'm not calling to proposition you."

"Then what?"

This time he sounded serious. "Listen, Beverly bought a new two-year-old stallion. Great bloodlines. Has all the makings of a winner."

"Okay, so what's the problem?"

"He had a good workout this morning, rub down, legs wrapped, warming blanket, the usual. About an hour ago, our barn manager called up to the house to say he'd found the colt standing in the stall with his left foreleg swollen and feverish. When can you come out and look him over?"

Alarms went up. Forest had a reputation for using all kinds of malarkey to lure women to the barn and other places. "Have your stable manager apply cold compresses on and off for two hours. You have some essential balm, right?"

"I don't doctor the animals, Tullah. That's Joe's job."

Joe Belcher is the best. He knows how to take care of horses. "Then tell Joe what I said. I'm not your regular vet. Call him if the leg doesn't improve."

Forest chuckled. "C'mon, Tullah. Lighten up. I promise to keep my hands to myself."

"Goodnight, Forest." I disconnected the call.

An hour later I heard from Joe Belcher. "Sorry to bother you so late, Doc. Mr. Rakestraw relayed your message." He faltered. "I, ah, understand why you hesitate to come out. Here's the thing, the colt's leg is badly swollen and he's lethargic. I'd appreciate it if you'd come out and take a look."

"You could call Dr. Cooper. He's your regular vet."

"Yeah, sure, but he's also two hours away; and with this weather it'd add another hour to his travel time. I can't risk it, Doc. Mrs. Rakestraw paid a fortune for this colt."

The desperation in his voice compelled me to say, "Okay. I'll drive out in the morning."

Grandmother was right—I have a love for all creatures. "Joe, if the roads are still icy, it may take me a while to get there. Hold off on giving the colt anything for pain."

Joe thanked me and hung up.

I opened to Cindi's number.

She answered on the first ring. "Hey, Tullah, how was the funeral?"

"Frigid and unusual."

"Frigid I can understand. Unusual? You'll need to explain that one."

"Yeah, later. Listen, Joe Belcher at the Make My Day farm has a colt with an inflamed leg. I'll explain about the funeral if you don't mind riding along with me."

"Absolutely. What time?"

"Come for breakfast at seven-thirty. We'll load the truck and plan to leave by nine. I figure if the roads are slick, it'll take us about an hour to get there."

"Sure thing, Tullah. I'll get everything we'll need ready tonight."

"You really should go back to school and get your degree in veterinary medicine. You're wasting your talents being a vet tech."

Cindi sounded a bit wistful when she said, "Maybe someday. For now, I'm happy where I am."

I left it at that and said goodnight.

Chapter Five

On the way to Forest Rakestraw's Make My Day farm, I received a call from Denver March asking me to swing by and check on a week-old foal. The one that Mayor Tackett's Gypsy Vanner wandering stud had sired. Denver had the baby on a lactating mare but was certain it had developed colic.

A colicky foal, in my mind, took precedence over a two-year-old colt with a swollen knee, especially since the barn manager was already treating the swelling.

Besides, the March farm was on the way. Of course, I could have stopped by after I'd finished at the Rakestraws'. Mainly, I wasn't in the mood to fend off Forest's intolerable flirtations.

Gravel crunched under the wheels as my truck rolled to a stop. Denver met us at the entrance of the barn. His office was off the right entrance. The aisle was wide and clean; the walls were painted bright white over cinder blocks. Wide doors closed at both ends of the barn.

Denver clapped his hands together against the cold. His breath misted when he greeted us. "Sure am ready for warm weather."

Denver was a couple of years older than me. For as long as I'd known him, he'd never married. Not because of his looks or personality. He was handsome enough, pleasant and easy-going, and moderately wealthy. His marital status was none of my business. "I totally agree. Why the frown, Denver? Has the foal's condition worsened?"

"Tullah, my mother hates Blue Belle just about as much as she despised Alma Tackett. When BB is old enough to wean, will you find a home for her or at least board her until you can find someone who'll take her? She's free just as long as she goes to a caring home."

Cindi and I followed Denver down the wide aisle. Thoroughbred broodmares thrust their long necks over the high gates and welcomed us with nickers.

We entered a stall with a bay mare and a foal lying in a pile of fresh straw. A blue roan filly. The name certainly suited her. I knelt down to exam the baby. "I'd take her myself except I don't need another mouth to feed." I thought for a moment. Gypsy Vanners are known for their calm demeanor and are often referred to as adult-sized draft horses. "Call me as soon as she's weaned. I'm certain the Happy Hooves Equestrian Center will be the perfect place for Blue Belle. She'll be loved and given the best of care."

A wide grin spread over Denver's face. "A riding stable for disabled children and adults. Of course. Now why didn't I think of that?"

Cindi prepped the foal while I prepared a warm soapy solution and administered a soapy water enema to Blue Belle. "All done. This should do the trick."

As much as I hated to ask, I felt compelled. "Denver, other than the Vanner stallion mishap, is there another reason why Miss Evelyn and Alma didn't like each other?"

He stared off into space and seemed lost. I gathered my bag and motioned to Cindi that we should leave.

"Of course, it's none of my business. I shouldn't have asked."

He glanced at my assistant, who took the cue. Cindi said, "Nice seeing you, Denver. I'll meet you in the truck, Tullah."

He waited until Cindi was out of earshot. I wasn't sure if the tone I detected was bitterness or deep concern. "It's no secret that Mother hated Alma. Now that she's dead, I guess it doesn't make any difference for you to know. Just...just keep it to yourself."

I nodded. "You have my word."

He heaved a sigh and blew it out. "Years ago, Mother suspected my father was seeing someone on the sly. She hired a private investigator. The day I was born is the day the PI showed her pictures of Alma and my father. In fact, he wasn't even home when she went into labor with me. He was with *her*."

Denver was quiet as if collecting his thoughts. "I won't belabor all that happened, because it's all secondhand from my mother. Anyhow, fast forwarding, she forgave him, and he promised to toe the line. Which I guess he did...until a car crash years later. I believe I was fifteen years old. Since alcohol was involved, there had to be an investigation. Mother paid handsomely to keep it out of the newspapers that my dad was driving and Alma was the passenger. Alma lived. My father didn't."

"Is that why Alma walked with a slight limp?"

"I suppose."

"I'm sorry, Denver. I don't know what to say except why didn't Miss Evelyn use this to keep Alma from becoming mayor?" Especially since she was making noises about moving on up the political ladder.

He escorted me to my truck. His voice sarcastic, he asked, "Would you want people to know about your husband's sordid past, and that he didn't even have the decency to be at the hospital for his son's birth, or how many birthdays and anniversaries he'd missed to be with another woman?"

I opened the door and welcomed the heater's warm air. Once again, I apologized. "I didn't mean to dredge up hurtful memories."

He offered me a weak smile. I climbed inside the truck. "Call me if Blue Belle needs further attention."

He simply nodded and turned back toward the barn.

Shifting into drive, I shot forward toward the highway.

"What was all of that about, Tullah?"

"Some things are better left unsaid." I knew I'd protect Denver and Miss Evelyn's secret forever.

Cindi's eyebrows went up. "Okay, but does this mean you're not going to tell me about the funeral?"

"No, silly." I related about the lack of attendance, giving her the names of those who attended and those who didn't.

"Yesterday's weather wasn't fit for man or beast. Still, you'd think out of a show of respect for Wakefield and Mr. Tackett that more people would have shown up." Cindi shook her head. "I still can't get over the mayor's death. I mean, she was what—in her late forties?"

"Fifty-two to be exact."

"Wow."

I swallowed the lump growing in my throat and wondered if Grandmother had a similar reason for despising Alma. The age difference between Alma and my grandmother didn't point to marital indiscretion. It was common knowledge that my grandfather had died in Vietnam. A sudden thought had me gripping the steering wheel. Surely not my dad! My brain screamed, *No...no...no!*

"Tullah, you just missed the turn to the Rakestraws'." Cindi looked at me with a puzzled expression on her face.

Gently pressing the brake, I slowed to a snail's pace and carefully maneuvered a U-turn. "Sorry." I gave her a reassuring smile.

"I don't blame you. I've had my own experience with Forest Rakestraw. He's like a twelve-legged octopus. I'm not a violent person, but I'd like to slap him silly. He seems to think women should fall at his feet grateful for rewarding them with his arrogant smile."

I was glad Cindi had misread my reason for missing the turn. True, I didn't like Forest or his wife. I still had Denver's heart-wrenching confession on my mind.

"Wow, oh, wow." Cindi sat forward in the seat, craning her neck. "Would you look at this place?"

Since the Rakestraws had never required my services, I'd never before had occasion to visit their horse farm. Like most of the thoroughbred farms around here, pristine white rail fences lined each side of the long drive that seemed too remote to be seen by passing motorists. We passed through a wide entrance with a gatehouse that hinted at a statelier dwelling ahead. The asphalt-paved drive wandered through groves of budding live oak with nothing more on its mind than soaking up the dappled sunlight. It was now a few minutes before one o'clock. Don't ask me why, but a brief uneasiness settled over me. Except for not being excited about encountering Forest Rakestraw, I couldn't think of a reason why I suddenly felt edgy. Joe Belcher had assured me I'd meet with him and not Forest. Besides, Cindi was with me. What could happen—right? Girl power.

The lane opened up, and I whispered, "Holi...Moli!"

Just ahead was the barn. In bold black letters above the expansive gaping doors was *Make My Day*. "If this is the barn, I can't imagine what the house looks like." The building was the size of a football field and resembled a picture from a magazine. Painted bright white and trimmed in forest green, it had to be at least five thousand square feet. It featured a drive-through canopy wide enough to accommodate two horse trailers, and its beige metal roof sported cupolas that included copper spires. Miniature red maples inside large white planter boxes lined the front of the structure.

I rolled the truck to stop in front of the barn. We opened the crew-cab doors and grabbed our rubber boots and coveralls along with the medical kit. It only took a moment to swap our regular boots for the knee-high rubbers. With the brisk wind, I was surprised to see the front entrance wide open.

Arch after arch after arch was supported by graceful columns. Cedar lined the ceiling, cinder block walls with matching cedar wainscoting separated each stall, and the stalls had metal sliding doors framed with heavy-gauge mesh for the stallions to see through but not break through. Above each stall was a rolled venetian blind. Most stallions are fractious, especially around other studs. The blinds would be pulled down when a stallion was brought out of its stall or into the barn. Large lighted globes lined the entire length of the barn. At the end of the aisle were three wash-and-groom stations. From where we stood, the infra-red heaters were visible. There were tack rooms and a door labeled "Blanket Closet."

"Tullah, feel that? The floors are heated."

"I'm totally impressed. In fact, I almost feel underdressed." And then I called out, "Joe?"

"Yeah, me too. I guess this is what money can buy."

I expected Joe Belcher to answer from one of the stalls. When he didn't, I balled my fist and rapped on the door marked "Office." Getting no response, I tried the knob and found the door locked.

I glanced around. "That's a mystery. Joe said he'd meet us here."

"What do you suggest, Tullah?"

I looked about, half expecting to see one of the trainers or exercise boys. Given Forest's reputation with women, I was certain Beverly Rakestraw wouldn't allow exercise girls or any females on the premises. Except for the horses, it seemed the barn was empty. "C'mon, let's walk down the aisle. We'll look for a gray two-year-old with a bandaged knee. After I treat him, I'll leave a note for Joe instructing him to call me, and then we'll head to town for a burger at the Whitehorse."

"Okay, you're the boss."

We strolled down the wide aisle padded with

rubber matting, admiring the regal thoroughbred stallions with names like Powerhouse Slew, Flying Ebony, Highland's Atta Boy, and then we came to a magnificent dappled gray's stall. The horse's left front knee was wrapped.

"This is it." I read the embossed nameplate. "Montezuma's Whirligig. Who comes up with these crazy names?"

"Gosh, he's every bit of seventeen hands, Tullah. You think we should enter his stall? After all, he is a stallion."

Cindi stood about five foot two and probably weighed all of a hundred pounds soaking wet. I certainly understood her concern.

I also understood her fear. Stallions are prone to aggressive behavior. The gray struck me as different. "He doesn't have a mean bone in his body."

Doubt filled her face. "How do you know?"

I slid the bolt back to open the door. "It's in his eyes."

I spoke to the horse and ran my hands down his silken neck, down his withers, and down to his wrapped knee. That's when I saw him. My breath hung in my throat for a second. I think I made that little humming sound you make when you're close to a shriek, but haven't yet committed yourself. "Cindi, quick, hand me the lead strap."

She did as I asked. "What is it…what's wrong?"

I snapped the end of the strap into the o-ring. "Whirligig won't hurt you. Trust me. Lead him out and put him in one of the empty stalls. And whatever you do, *don't* scream."

"Okay, but…" She did as I instructed, and as soon

as she turned I saw the look of horror on her face.

In a low harsh voice, I again cautioned, *"Don't* scream, otherwise you'll startle the horse and he's liable to take off dragging you with him."

Her throat convulsed, and I was proud of her for swallowing the shriek. She immediately trotted the young stallion to an empty stall and secured him. I was on my knees checking for a pulse when she entered and squatted next to me. "Is…is he dead?"

I nodded as I pulled out my cellphone and hit the emergency number that goes straight to my dad's special line. "Tullah, you okay?"

I barely controlled the quiver in my voice. "Dad, I just found Forest Rakestraw in a horse stall at his farm. He's dead."

"Confound it, Tullah. Have you touched anything? Who's with you?"

"Cindi, and no, I've only checked for a pulse, and well, I did open the stall door, before I saw him."

"Is Joe Belcher around?"

"No. That's just it, Dad. Joe was supposed to meet me. Should I call the house to notify Mrs. Rakestraw?"

"Hold off until you hear my siren. Tell her I'm on my way. I don't want you dealing with hysteria. I'll notify Dr. Gannon and get an ambulance dispatched. You hang tight, and don't let anyone near the body. Not even Mrs. Rakestraw."

Dad knew me too well. I was far better with animals than with people.

We disconnected. I decided to examine the body before I notified anyone else. "Cindi, keep an eye on the entrance door. If any of the hands come in, do whatever it takes to keep them away from the stall."

"Gotcha."

While she kept a look out, I knelt over Forest and rechecked for a pulse. My heart banged away. The body was cool but not cold. There was no sign of trauma, such as being kicked in the head or stomped. Except for several piles of fresh horse pucks, I found no evidence of a struggle. I reached in my coat pocket and removed my phone and scrolled to the pictures I'd taken of Alma. I did a silent *aha.* Forest sat on a bucket with his head leaned against the stall's cement block wall, his eyes wide and staring and his mouth pooched like he had gasped for air. Very similar to the way I'd found Alma. And just like Alma, he was stone cold dead.

Cindi spoke in a loud whisper. "Tullah, what are you doing?"

"Smelling his breath."

"He's dead. Dead people don't breathe."

"Never mind. I'll be finished in a minute. Is anyone coming?" I snapped photos from different angles of the stall. That's when it occurred to me—bathroom stall—horse stall. Was *stall* the common denominator? Instinct told me this was no coincidence. All I had to do now was convince my dad we had two possible murders on our hands.

"No. All clear." She added, "He's not so handsome now, is he?"

I left poor Forest where he sat, his once fine-looking face twisted in agony, and waited, dreading the call to Beverly Rackstraw.

Chapter Six

Off in the distance, a faint but distinctive siren wailed. I immediately scrolled down the screen of my cellphone to the Rakestraws' number.

Grandmother always said I was intuitive. My intuition was telling me to put my phone on speaker. "Stay close enough to listen in, Cindi."

Oh, snap. I dread making this call.

Her voice effervesced. "Beverly Rakestraw speaking."

"Hello, Mrs. Rakestraw, this is Doctor Holliday. I'm at your stud barn, and—"

Her voice immediately changed from pleasant to surly. "Joe Belcher has strict orders to only use Dr. Cooper."

"Joe isn't here, and—"

"I know he isn't. He had a family emergency in California and left early this morning to drive to the airport. Put Forest on the phone—this minute!"

Cindi and I exchanged shrugs. She made a slap-your-face motion with her hand which almost caused me to laugh.

Beverly reiterated, "Your services are not needed. Send me a bill for your time, and tell Forest to call me."

I said, calmer than I felt, "Mrs. Rakestraw... Beverly...did Forest have a bad heart?"

My question obviously took her by surprise

because she sputtered, "You're a veterinarian. Why would you ask such a question? I demand to speak to my husband. Now!"

I blurted, "Forest can't come to the phone because he's dead in the gray colt's stall. And—"

My dire announcement was met with a cackle. "Come off it, Tullah. I don't know what you're up to, but that's not funny." She emphasized each word. "Put Forest on the phone."

Cindi motioned for me to hand her the phone. She said, "Mrs. Rakestraw, this is Cindi Redfern. I'm standing next to Tullah. I was with her when she found your husband."

Beverly screamed. "Then why are you idiots talking to me? Call nine-one-one!"

Cindi returned the phone. I said, "I've already called. They're on the way."

"Okay, I hear them. The sirens. Oh, my gosh, I'll be there in a minute."

"Beverly, was Forest ill?"

She sounded addled. "No…yes…well, not really. He'd complained of chest pains."

"Do you know when the chest pains started?"

This time her tone changed to impatient. "Ah-um, Tullah, I can't think. I-I believe shortly after the rally. What does this have to do with anything?" She disconnected the call.

Dad's 4Runner screeched to a stop. I stood at the barn's opening. He sprinted toward me. "Where is he?"

I pointed. "Stall number seven."

Dr. Rick Gannon barreled out of the ambulance. Bubba and Rita removed the gurney and rolled it down the corridor, its wheels swiveling like a grocery cart's.

Believe me, I was hot on the heels of the doctor and my dad. Dr. Gannon wore a white lab coat over a crisp white shirt, expensive-looking black gabardine slacks, and blue pin-striped tie. I took notice of his black loafers with vents cut in the leather. Richard Gannon isn't a native Kentuckian, nor is he from the country, and he doesn't ride horses. I'd often wondered why he'd traded New York for a country doctor position. "Um, Doctor, I hope you have a pair of disposable shoe covers."

I didn't use them and didn't keep shoe covers in my medical bag. Rubber boots served the purpose when I needed to muck around in a corral or a stall. Besides, hosing off rubber boots is more economical.

He frowned. "I'm not performing surgery. Why do I need them?"

Dad offered me a *he'll find out* look.

"Okay, at least be careful where you step."

We arrived at stall number seven. Doctor Gannon paused at the door, his nose wrinkled against the pungent odor. He looked down at his polished loafers, then at me. "It's filled with piles of horse sh...poop."

"Uh-huh. That's generally what happens on a horse farm. The horse eats, and what goes in must come out, and it lands wherever the horse is standing."

The expression on Gannon's face was priceless when he said, "These are Italian leather."

I widened my hands and shrugged. "If I had an extra pair of boots, I'd lend them to you."

Dr. Gannon bent down and rolled the cuffs of his trouser legs up to his ankles, all the time muttering oaths under his breath.

When he's on the job, my dad is all business, and

not the least bit squeamish about blood and gore. To him there's nothing funny about death. In this case, he excused himself. His shoulders were shaking with silent laughter as he hot-footed it out of the stall. He yanked a handkerchief from his coat pocket to cover his mouth. Even Bubba and Rita were having problems containing themselves.

Beverly Rakestraw barreled down the aisle in her golf cart, screaming, "Get out of the way." She halted the cart within a hair of running over Bubba. She propelled herself forward with such force she practically bounced off his chest. He had the wherewithal to grab hold of her to keep her from entering the stall.

"Get your hands off me, you hairy bear."

Bubba held tight. "Calm down. There's nothing you can do for your husband. Let Dr. Gannon examine him first, and then I'll let you go."

It appeared she was beginning to hyperventilate. Dr. Gannon said, "Take her to the ambulance and administer oxygen."

Gannon heaved a breath, trying his best to tiptoe around the piles of manure, and expelling sounds of disgust each time he missed. Finally, reaching the deceased, he looked around for a place to set his medical bag. I relieved him of it. "Tell me what you need."

"Disposable gloves and my stethoscope."

"I checked the moment I found his body. There was no pulse and no heartbeat." I looked at my watch. "Cindi and I arrived at approximately one o'clock. It's now one-thirty. From the temperature of his body, I'd say he's been dead for more than three hours."

When the handsome doctor swiveled to look up at me, he wobbled, and to catch his balance he put his hand down. What oozed between his fingers wasn't pretty. The four-letter words spewing from his mouth were unrepeatable.

"Of course he's dead," Gannon spat. "If all you need is for me to pronounce him dead, I can certainly do that."

He held his hand out and splayed his fingers. He growled, "Ms. Graham, Mr. Dawson, you may remove the body."

I unfastened his medical kit and spotted a large packet of wet wipes, which I opened and extracted several. He was not a happy man as he cleansed his hand and in between his fingers. Not once but several times. His nose wrinkled in disgust as he mumbled, "Gads, and to think I turned down a position in Australia for Podunk USA."

Having gained control of his laughter, Dad stood hands on hips. He coughed and cleared his throat as if trying to swallow another round of laughter. "What's your opinion, Doc? Heart attack?"

Gannon asked for more wipes. "Without a formal autopsy, Sheriff, I can only speculate. Of course, the horse could have stomped him to death."

"No way," I interjected. "There's no blood, no hoof impressions or bruising on the head, no bite marks on the hands, no torn clothing, nothing to indicate Forest Rakestraw was attacked by the colt. If the colt had attacked him, Forest wouldn't be sitting on a bucket. He'd be lying in a heap."

I despise when anyone speaks to me in a superior tone. "I beg your pardon, Ms. Holliday, but you are not a medical examiner."

When Dad speaks between his teeth, my advice is to back off. He stepped almost nose to nose to the good doctor. "My daughter's a first-rate veterinarian. She knows all the signs of animal attack on a human or on another animal, *and* because she has an additional degree in forensics medicine she's qualified to deliver more than kittens and puppies." He lowered his voice. "Don't ever look down your imperial nose at her. And from now on you will address her as *Doctor* Holliday."

Gannon's face suffused a deep red. "Of course, I misspoke. My apologies, Doctor Holliday."

Recovering from the insult, I nodded. "If you step more in that direction, there aren't as many piles to avoid."

We had all seemingly forgotten about Beverly Rakestraw. Rita helped her out of the ambulance. She pulled the sheet back. Beverly wrung her hands and sniffled. All of her beauty was gone. She reminded me of how we must all look under fluorescent lighting— tired, sallow, and shop worn.

Dad touched her on the elbow. "Did Forest have a heart problem?"

She rubbed her forehead. "Not to my knowledge," she said, struggling to maintain her composure. "I've already told Tullah that he complained of shortness of breath and twinges in his chest and stomach."

Dad said, "Was this recent?"

I answered for her. "A couple of hours after the rally."

Dr. Gannon approached. "I'm sorry for your loss, Mrs. Rakestraw. Although we can't rule out a heart attack, we'll need to perform an autopsy to determine the exact cause of death."

Beverly wiped her eyes. Her expression remained somber. "Of course, whatever it takes."

A small crowd of employees had gathered at the barn's entrance. Dad met them. Questions abounded.

"What's going on?"

"Did somebody get hurt?"

"Mrs. Rakestraw, is everything okay?"

"Where's Joe?"

Dad fielded all the questions. "Mr. Rakestraw has suffered an apparent fatal heart attack."

Someone said, "He was healthy as a horse."

I'm sure there was no pun intended.

Dad answered, "We'll know more after an autopsy is performed." He instructed them to go about their chores as usual.

It was almost as if Beverly didn't know what to do next. I felt badly for her and stepped forward. "Is there someone you would like me to call—a relative or a friend—to stay with you?"

Her voiced cracked as she replied, "I'm sorry I yelled at you, Tullah. I'll make the calls myself. Except...I dread telling Sam."

Everyone knew Sam Rakestraw doted on his son, who'd been a high school jock drafted to the Dallas Cowboys and played a season before suffering a lacerated spleen and chest contusions, total hip replacement, and rehabilitation for prescription opioid addiction. Basically, Forest was a screw-up. "What about Janie?"

Beverly made a pfft sound. "Sam disinherited her when she married what's-his-name. Everyone knows that."

Janie is Forest's younger sister by two years. Ten years ago, she had married Hari Nadisu, an oncologist who practices at a top oncology hospital in Texas. "It doesn't matter, Beverly. Regardless of how Sam feels, Janie is still Forest's sister and deserves to know."

"Then you call her. Let it be you who suffers Sam's wrath."

Temper caused my scalp to prickle. "Shame on you and shame on Sam. Yeah, I don't have a problem contacting Janie, and if you still prefer Dr. Cooper to tend to the colt, I'll contact him, too."

Beverly's perfectly arched eyebrows shot up, and her brown eyes filled with tears. She sniffled. "Nothing against you, Tullah, at least not now that Forest is d-dead. You know how he was with women. Dan Cooper tends to all my horses and has for years." She climbed in the golf cart, did an about-turn, and stopped long enough to speak to the small group of farm hands.

Fuming, I jammed my hands inside my coverall pockets and listened to Doctor Gannon quibbling to himself. He did the best he could to clean his Italian loafers with the wet wipes before he climbed into the ambulance next to Rita Graham. The engine roared to life. Rita turned on the siren and gave it a couple of woop-woops warning people to clear the way.

Giggles beset Cindi. "I nearly popped my seams when *Dr. Arrogant* sank up to his ankles in manure."

Her laughter was contagious. At least it erased most of my anger. "Dad, I nearly lost it when you had to excuse yourself to go outside."

"Got to admit it was funny. Dr. Gannon has been duly initiated." Dad sobered. "Where're you headed from here, Punkin?"

"I promised Cindi a burger at the Whitehorse. How 'bout joining us?"

"Can't—paperwork. After you've had lunch, come by the office, I'll need formal statements from both of you."

He turned to leave.

"Dad?"

He lifted his eyebrows.

"Thanks." No explanation was needed.

Touching my cheek, he replied, "Nobody tromps on my girl." He added, "I'll follow you out."

"Not just yet, Dad. I don't care how Beverly Rakestraw feels about me. I'm not leaving until I've examined Whirligig's leg."

****

The Whitehorse Saloon was dimly lit, warm, and filled with chatter. A country song played on an old-fashioned jukebox Charlie had bought at an auction house. At his usual place behind the bar, he waved. "Where's Henry?"

"Paperwork. You know how it is."

"Yep, tell me about it." He grinned. "I've got a large pot of chili simmering. Made it fresh this morning. Guaranteed to cure what ails you."

A cold chill riffled through me, almost like someone had walked over my grave. Suddenly, I was teeth-chattering cold. I slid into the booth and ordered a cup of hot chocolate.

Charlie's chili is the best. In fact, he's won the state fair chili cook-off contest five years in a row. Cindi and I placed our orders. "Fix a container to go, Charlie. Dad'll be working late tonight, and as usual he'll forget to eat."

Charlie delivered the bowls himself. Flora, his waitress, followed with two mugs of steaming hot chocolate topped with marshmallows, and a cup of coffee for Charlie. After Flora left, I asked, "Charlie, why are you still a bachelor?"

He scooted in beside me and wrapped his hands around his steaming cup. He grinned and winked. "Because your grandmother is too young and you're too old."

"Funny, Charlie." It felt good to laugh. Still I couldn't shake the vision of Forest Rakestraw sitting on an overturned bucket, slumped like a ragdoll.

"So what's new in the world of animals?"

I gave Charlie the abbreviated version of Denver March's colicky filly followed by a long sigh. Between spoonful's of spicy chili, toasted buttery garlic saltines, and sips of cocoa, I explained about finding Forest Rakestraw's body the unpleasant encounter with Beverly, and Dr. Gannon's hilarious episode with fresh manure, deliberately omitting how Dad had taken Gannon to task over his not-so-subtle diss. Where I was concerned, Charlie was almost as bad as my dad about jumping to my defense.

Charlie guffawed and quickly covered his mouth with a napkin to keep from spewing coffee all over Cindi. "Man, I'd've given my right arm to've seen that."

Charlie leaned back. His forehead scrunched into serious thought. "Mayor and mayoral candidate both dead in the same week. Seems more than a coincidence."

Charlie had voiced what I'd been thinking. My brain was working overtime, and I was anxious to get the meeting with my father over so I could get home and start making notes of my suspicions.

Scraping my bowl clean and finishing off the last of my drink, I asked Cindi if she was ready to go. Charlie collected our dishes and wandered off to the kitchen. We hefted into our jackets. I accepted the sack of goodies for my dad and kissed Charlie on the cheek.

Ten minutes later, Cindi and I parked in front of Dad's office and strolled inside. "Afternoon, Joyce," we greeted Dad's secretary. I held up the bag. "Is he in?"

Joyce sniffed. "Charlie's chili. I sure wish he'd share his recipe."

"Keep on wishing, Joyce. Besides, you're his only real competition."

"If I could wrap my taste buds around whatever his secret ingredient is, I'd take this year's championship away from him."

"How is the computer class going, Joyce?" She's old-school and hasn't quite caught up with new technology.

"Some of it boggles my mind. There are days when I'm reminded of the saying you can't teach an old dame new tricks."

"You're not nearly as old as my grandmother."

"That's not much consolation. I'm about ready to slide into—" She coughed. "—my sixties."

Cindi volunteered, "Whenever Tullah doesn't need me, I'll be happy to help with whatever is confusing you." She looked at me, and I nodded.

"Oh, would you? I'd be eternally grateful."

Deputy Tiny Goodbody strolled out. He's the biggest man I've ever seen. The gun strapped around his waist looks small in relation to his body. In spite of his size, he's a gentle giant, most of the time. "Your dad's in his office." He thumbed over his shoulder. "Too bad about Forest. Sam is pretty torn up about it."

"I guess Dad told him?"

"Yep, Henry stopped by the feed store. Beverly had already called and broke the news." He sniffed; his stomach growled. "I don't mean to sound callous. I've known Forest since he was a sprout and can't say I really liked the kid. Spoiled, overly indulged." He shrugged. "Anyhow, it's been a long time since breakfast. Can I bring you back some, Joyce?"

"You betcha." She lifted the old-fashioned phone receiver and punched a button. "Henry, Tullah and Cindi are here."

Dad opened his office door and instructed Joyce to give each of us a volunteer statement form. He pointed and said, "Cindi, sit at Deputy Goodbody's desk. Tullah, you'll be there." He indicated a small table and chair by a window overlooking the town. "It's important your statements don't sound identical or scripted. Take your time, stick to the facts."

I almost felt like I was taking a written exam. "We understand, Dad."

It took a few minutes to collect my thoughts. An hour later, Dad escorted Cindi out of his office as I was handing my form to Joyce. To say I was mentally drained is an understatement. The expression on Cindi's face indicated she felt the same way.

I stretched the kinks out of my back. "It's after five. Unless there's an emergency, we're done for the day."

Cindi's voice was thoughtful. "I second that."

We said goodnight to Joyce. Dad walked us out to

my truck. He hugged me. "I'll check on you later, Punkin."

Chapter Seven

Eventually I pulled into the yard and under my carport. The moment we walked into the house Cindi and I were assailed by two happy pets. There's nothing like warding off slobbery kisses from a black Lab or keeping upright and not bowled over by an exuberant hundred-pound teacup donkey. I filled the kettle with water for tea while Cindi removed cups from the cabinet.

"Wow, what a day," she said as she placed a teabag in each cup.

"So much has happened," I said, "I'm having trouble wrapping my brain around it, from the death of Mayor Tackett, the funeral where almost no one showed up, and now finding Forest Rakestraw dead." *Not to mention Denver March's shocking confession about his mother and Alma.*

Cindi leaned against the kitchen counter. She let out a sigh. "Yeah, and dealing with Mrs. Rakestraw's hysteria. Geez, I thought the most exciting thing in a veterinarian's life would be delivering twin foals or calves."

I poured steaming water over the teabags. "There are thin mints in the cookie jar." I pointed to the top of the refrigerator.

"Cindi, do you think Beverly Rakestraw's hysterics was genuine or fake?"

"Hmm." She gave me a questioning look. "I'm not sure. Some people react differently than others. I'd like to think she wasn't putting on an act." She reached up for the horse-shaped cookie jar and removed the head.

That surely wasn't the answer I was hoping for. My grandmother hadn't been hysterical or even cried when my mother died. Yet my dad went on a three-day bender. It took him a week to sober up. As for me, I'd rather not talk about her death.

"Perhaps you're right."

River and Rascal had automatic feeders and waterer. Satisfied they had plenty of food, I suggested we take our tea and cookies to the living room. I grabbed the remote, pointed it toward the gas fireplace, and wah-lah, instant flame. The animals settled on the braided rug in front of the fire.

Cindi sat in the wing-backed chair. She mused, "I wonder how things will end up with the election."

The entire day had been upsetting. I sipped my tea and pondered Cindi's question. "I'm sure the election committee has policy for this sort of thing. Well, not this *exact* sort of thing."

Cindi didn't respond except to say, "Let's enjoy our tea. Maybe it'll relax us. I hope I don't dream about dead bodies tonight."

Her reassurances about the tea's soothing qualities didn't make them real. She fidgeted with the teabag.

"What's on your mind, Cindi—are you still upset over our finding Forest—dead?"

"Maybe, a little. It's really, well, Tullah, I appreciate your letting me stay here. I'll pay rent or you can deduct it from my pay. It's only fair."

I knew she adored animals, and I considered

myself lucky to have her. She certainly couldn't count on her deadbeat father to help her. It would be difficult to find someone as competent, as willing, or as good with animals, who could also type, deal with frantic pet owners, had a two-year degree as a veterinarian technician, and answer the telephone.

She misread my silence and said, "It's okay. I knew it was a long shot before I asked." She straightened her shoulders and rose to leave.

I kept my voice quiet. "Sit down, Cindi." I leaned forward, resting my elbows on my knees. "Sleeping on a cot in a cracker-box room in a barn is no place to live. Once upon a time I had high aspirations of becoming a traveling veterinarian and following the race track circuit." I shrugged. "That didn't pan out, so the travel trailer behind the barn is collecting cobwebs and dust. I'll get the electrician, plumber, and septic company out tomorrow to hook everything up. No rent. Call the power company and have the utilities put in your name."

She clapped her hands together like an excited child. I hated to burst her bubble. "There is a condition attached to this. Earl is your father, and I understand that, no matter the wrongs he does, you love him." I paused because I despise giving ultimatums. "He's not welcome here, nor are you to ever give him shelter."

Her expression saddened a little. "I understand, and you have my word. If he sets foot on the place, I'll call you or your daddy. There's no helping Earl. Mama tried. I tried. One day he'll end up dead in a ditch and I'll probably cry at his funeral." She blinked back tears. "I think he's hated me since the day I was born."

She swiped her eyes, her voice almost a whisper.

"I'm not crying for myself. It's what he did to Mama…to both of us."

Her shoulders sagged. I searched for words to give her some comfort. "You are a good person, Cindi, and don't you ever forget it."

And then, trying to lighten the mood, I set my empty teacup aside. "C'mon, let's go look at your new home."

We hefted into our jackets and walked across the yard. I said, "We can leave it where it is or move it a little farther from the barn." I pointed to a cluster of oak trees. "Over there might be nice."

She laughed as she pulled the jacket closer to ward off the evening chill. "One thing for sure, I'll never have an excuse for being late to work."

I inserted the key and opened the heavy metal door and screen door. An old mustiness greeted us. There was still enough light to get a good look inside. "Here it is, all two hundred square feet."

Cindi gushed as she explored. "It's perfect. A kitchen, bedroom, bathroom with a shower, a dining-sitting area with a place for a TV." Her eyes widened. "There's even an air conditioner and plenty of storage. I can't wait to move in."

You'd have thought I had given her keys to a mansion. "I'll help you clean it, and feel free to put your own touches on it."

She gave me an unexpected hug. "You're the best, Tullah."

We said goodnight, and I sprinted back to the house. Forest Rakestraw's death was on my mind as I rinsed the cups and saucers and set them in the dishwasher.

Since this wasn't an emergency, I phoned my dad on his regular line.

"What's on your mind, Punkin?"

"How do you know I'm not calling just to chit-chat?"

"Because you're too much like me. Small talk isn't your thing."

"Ah, Dad, you know me too well."

"Okay, out with it."

Enigma County isn't big enough to warrant an official medical examiner, and our small hospital doesn't have the proper facilities to perform autopsies. Because of this, any deaths determined questionable or with possible criminal cause attached are prepped and sent to Lexington.

"When's the corpse being sent to Lexington?"

"Day after tomorrow."

"I'd like to catch a ride with you."

"There's no reason for me to go, Tullah."

"But, Dad, listen. You have to be there. I'd stake my life that we're looking at murder."

"Tullah…" I almost felt the breath from his exasperated sigh. "You read too many mystery novels. It's a simple case of heart attack or cerebral hemorrhage. The ME in Lexington will email the official report when it's finished."

"Oh, so that's what Dr. Gannon is proposing? He's wrong, Dad."

"All right, what are you basing your notion on?"

My mind raced as I struggled to present my theory. I drew a deep breath and blew it out. "The night of the rally, Wakefield said his mother wasn't feeling well, that she'd been having chest pains, and today, Beverly said Forest was also experiencing shortness of breath, chest pains, and stomach twinges. Also, I'm certain I smelled some kind of floral scent on both of them. Something like honey."

He snorted. "That's it? That's all you've got?"

"Dad—"

"No, listen to me. It was public knowledge that Alma had a heart condition. Even Doc Ritter confirmed that. An open nitroglycerin bottle was found in her purse. As for Forest, maybe it was his soap or his wife's perfume you smelled. At any rate, we'll find out when the autopsy results are in. Until then, I don't want to hear any more nonsense about murders. Go to bed. It's late."

Silence stretched between us until I conceded. "'Night, Dad."

I slept fitfully—until my eyes flew open with my brain wide awake. The hands on the clock indicated it was two in the morning. Moonlight filtered through the venetian blind slats, casting bright rays across the bed.

In my head I heard my grandmother's words, the ones she said to me after Alma's funeral. It was almost as if she were standing in the kitchen shouting at me. *Never forget—curiosity killed the cat, Tullah.*

I wrapped a chenille housecoat around my shoulders and padded barefoot downstairs to where I'd left my laptop. One part of my brain said it would remember what I wanted to notate in my "Enigma Deaths" file, and to go back to bed. The other part obsessively needed to get the bees humming inside my head on paper.

I typed: *I am certain I detected the aroma of honey on both Alma and Forest. However, Alma did have tic tac®s in her purse. Note to self: why didn't I check to see what flavor they were? Also, Dad is correct about Forest. The sweet odor might be perfume from a secret meeting or even from his wife. Note to self: buy several jars of honey to see if I can match the smell. The big question: if it is murder, who killed them, and what was their motive?*

It almost felt as if someone was watching me. Silly, I know, right?

I closed the laptop and raced back to the bedroom. I removed my robe and crawled into bed. My mind was made up. Come hell or high water, I would attend the autopsy. I could call my former professor, Dr. Claire Delaney, Chief of Pathology, in Lexington, to arrange it.

****

I wasn't aware I'd fallen to sleep until two wet noses nudged my hand. I squinted against the sunlight. Holi Moli, the hands on the clock read seven.

I hustled into a clean pair of jeans, an undershirt, and a flannel shirt, and raced downstairs in my socks to slide the doggie door's security panel open. The animals dashed out, ready to begin their day.

My cellphone rang. "Don't tell me we have an emergency."

Cindi said, "Ms. Sterns thinks her Chihuahua is dying. She's on her way."

"Yikes, I overslept. I haven't even had coffee."

"I've got a pot brewing. It'll be ready by the time you get here."

I raced back upstairs. Normal office hours begin at eight and end at five. It isn't unusual for my days to begin early and run late. I brushed my teeth, swished with mouthwash, ran a brush through my thick mop of hair, and pulled it into a ponytail.

Back in the kitchen, I grabbed a bran muffin from the fridge, stepped into my boots, and while holding the muffin between my teeth, hefted into my jacket, praying for a cup of coffee before my patient arrived.

Hustling from the house to the barn, my eyes went straight to the growing pile of horse manure. It's unbelievable how much poop three horses can generate in a day, and how tired I am every evening when I have to muck out the stalls. On behalf of myself and my horses, I looked heavenward and sent up a silent prayer for warmer weather. Turning the horses to pasture would save me a lot of work. I made a mental note to call Benefield Pooper-Scoopers to come haul away the Mt. Everest of meadow muffins.

I had barely washed down the last of my breakfast when Luanne Sterns rushed in. Tears glittered on her pallid cheeks. "Oh, Doctor, you must save her! Gigi's all I have in the world. I'm almost certain she has a tumor. I'm so afraid it's about to rupture. Poor little girl is in agony."

I knew little about Luanne Sterns except that she was the priest's old maid sister and new to our community. Nice enough, although she looked anorexic. Frail arms, all the veins visible in her hands like a diagram with a celluloid overlay. She was a member of the ladies' auxiliary, and Grandmother once mentioned Luanne had a green thumb and created beautiful flower arrangements.

I accepted the wicker basket holding a little dog wrapped in a pink crocheted blanket, and invited the tearful owner to follow me to the exam room. The sweet, fawn-colored dog looked up with baleful eyes and whimpered as I lifted her from the warm nest and placed her on the examination table. I cooed her name as I leaned over to place the stethoscope to her chest. That's when I saw the contraction. I moved the stethoscope to the dog's stomach and smiled.

"Ms. Sterns, you are about to become a doggie grandmother."

She twisted her hands together like two corkscrews. "Please, call me Luanne." Her scarecrow face flushed pink, and her eyes lit like two blue globes. She burbled, "Oh, my, but how? I mean, I know *how*, I just don't know when. I keep such a close watch over her."

I winked. "Well, it's quite obvious that little Gigi slipped out and met up with a secret lover." I ran my hands over the little dog's extended abdomen and checked her dilation.

Luanne's complexion changed from pasty white to sunburn red. I wondered if the idea of her precious little dog being promiscuous was embarrassing. Surely Luanne Sterns wasn't a puritan—not at her age.

"What is it, Doctor? Why is your forehead wrinkled?"

So much for hiding my concern. I offered my best reassurance. "Gigi is tiny and the puppies are large. I feel at least two. There may be a third. I'll need to deliver them by cesarean."

Luanne clutched her bony hands to the base of her throat. "Do whatever it takes."

I nodded and pointed to the chair in the waiting room. "Help yourself to the coffee. If you prefer, there's juice in the refrigerator. Please make yourself comfortable. Barring complications, we should have puppies in an hour."

Luanne paced about before pouring a cup of coffee. She settled in a brown leather chair, picked up a magazine, and crossed her bony legs.

Before closing the door to the surgery, Luanne blurted, "I want her fixed."

I nodded. "As soon as the puppies are weaned you can bring Gigi in and I'll spay her."

"How long will that take—the weaning, I mean?"

"Five or six weeks."

"I don't mean to sound crass, Doctor." She picked at her thumbnail. "My brother, you see, isn't as fond of animals as I."

An hour later I invited Luanne into the recovery room. "Gigi and pups are doing well."

Luanne smiled down at the two tiny brown-and-white puppies. "They are adorable. What are they?"

"Both are males, and it appears the sire might be a Jack Russell."

She emitted a throaty growl. "If I told *her* once, I told her numerous times to do something about that dog. He's continuously digging under the fence and getting into our back yard. Digs in my garden, sends dirt everywhere."

Cindi and I exchanged looks and said in unison, "Who?"

Luanne's lips trembled. She almost shouted the name. "Alma Tackett. Since she's dead, I suppose my brother and I will need to deal with her nincompoop husband or son."

I hadn't expected such vehemence. It is true that while the Tacketts own a horse farm in the country,

Alma maintains a residence inside the city limits. It was news to me that she and the Sterns were neighbors.

The way she shook her body, Luanne reminded me of an indignant hen ruffling her feathers. There was something about her that didn't jibe. Sort of like a kid whose conscience is clear because she doesn't have one. She removed a tissue from her purse and blew her nose without making a sound. It was just a sort of squeezing process. She inhaled deeply. "I'm sorry. I shouldn't have raised my voice, and it was unchristian of me to speak ill of the dead. Do I take Gigi and the puppies home, or should I leave them here?" No one could accuse Luanne Sterns of making small talk.

"We'll keep her overnight for observation. Otherwise, your new little family can go home tomorrow afternoon, say about three."

"Fine. Thank you. Thank you both." She stopped, her hand on the doorknob. Her smile appeared contrived, as if she was trying to hide the sadness in her eyes. "The puppies are cute. Please find homes for them." And she whirled out the door.

I muttered an expletive under my breath. "I'm a veterinarian. Why do people assume I'm an adoption service?"

Cindi patted me on the shoulder. "Now that I have my own home, I'll take both of them. In fact, I think I'll name them Ozzy and Pogo. How's that?"

"Then Ozzy and Pogo are two very lucky pups."

We finished cleaning the surgery and prepared for the ensuing appointments. I had a few minutes before the next patient's arrival. Needing privacy, I excused myself on the pretense of making a sandwich and asking Cindi if she wanted one. In truth, I was starving.

My heart skittered as I dialed Dr. Claire Delaney's number.

"University Hospital...Pathology...how may I direct your call?"

"Hi, this is Dr. Tullah Holliday. May I speak to Dr. Delaney?"

"Please hold. I believe she's in the lab."

While I waited, I opened the refrigerator and removed a package of ham, along with bread, sweet pickles, mayo, and cheese.

"Hello, Tullah, is that really you?"

"Yes, ma'am. I'm glad you remember me."

"How could I forget my best and brightest student? What can I do for you?"

I gave her the annotated version of why I wanted to attend the autopsy, and was operating on the hope that she'd be intrigued. I ended with, "Of course, I totally understand if you say no."

There was a cautious silence. "Hold on while I check to see if I'm scheduled for this particular cadaver."

While I waited, I laid out four slices of bread, spread them with mayonnaise, and added cheese, pickles, and several slices of ham. I was beginning to worry Dr. Delaney had forgotten about me.

"Hello, Tullah, are you there?"

"Yes...I'm here."

"Sorry to leave you holding. The Rakestraw autopsy was assigned to another pathologist and a group of third-year students for observation. We did some schedule swapping. I traded him my cancer victim for your suspected heart attack. Can you be here Thursday morning, ten sharp?"

"Yes, ma'am, and thank you. I'll treat you to lunch. As I recall, Szechuan chicken was your favorite."

I could hear the pleasure in her voice. "It still is. I'll look forward to seeing you."

I was almost giddy with excitement when we hung up. I wrapped the sandwiches in plastic wrap and returned to the office. Cindi and I barely had enough time to wolf down our lunch before our next patient arrived.

Compared to finding two dead bodies almost back to back, the day was fairly mundane—spaying and neutering, clipping toenails, and amputating an eagle's badly mangled wing.

Chapter Eight

Calling it a day, I showered, washed my hair, and changed into my sweatpants. After a microwaveable TV dinner and two cups of coffee, I settled in my recliner with a glass of merlot and my laptop to type in the notes that I'd earlier scrawled on a notepad, and to create a list of suspects with possible motives for both Alma's and Forest's deaths. I reread what I'd written about the detectable odor on Alma and Forest, and corrected several typos.

I stayed up far past my usual bedtime, yesterday's events whirling in my mind like a windstorm. What was supposed to be a routine day had turned into something far removed from that. I thought about a quote from Agatha Christie—"If you place your head in a lion's mouth, then you cannot complain one day when he bites it off."

There was a solid truth behind it because I feared I was about to stick my head in the lion's mouth by proving those two deaths were not from natural causes.

I read through all the notes I'd written, just to give myself an overview, and then I highlighted the details that interested me the most. I let River and Rascal in for the night and slid the security panel in place.

My grandmother's ringtone sounded on my cellphone. "Hello, Grandmother, are you well?"

"I am. The reason I'm calling is to ask a favor."

"If it's within my power."

"You are a good granddaughter. My favor is small. I need you to drive me to Lexington."

My heart fluttered. Had my grandmother suddenly become a clairvoyant? I didn't want anyone to know about my trip to Lexington to participate in an autopsy, especially since Dad would accuse me of meddling where my nose didn't belong.

"Are you ill, Grandmother? Do you need to see a specialist?"

She groused, "Do I have to be sick to want to get out of Enigma for a day? No, I am not sick. You have been working way too hard. I thought we might spend the weekend with my cousin Uma Hoktochee, eat fancy food, and do a little shopping."

My body automatically cringed. "Grandmother, Uma speaks to me as if I'm ten years old, plus all those annoying digs about why I'm still single at my age. Also, my sex life, even if I had one, is none of her business. Besides, she has only one bedroom."

"Tul...lah." I hate it when she breaks my name into syllables. "A few hours won't hurt. She's almost ninety-two. Consider her age. She called to say she needed to talk to me about something important and that she didn't want to tell me over the phone."

I sighed and measured what to say. "Okay, I've already planned a trip to Lexington on Thursday because I'm short on medical supplies, plus I promised to have lunch with one of my med school professors." I fudged the truth, since I was the one who did the inviting. "I'll drop you off at Uma's. The two of you can spend the day together, and if you wish to spend the weekend, I'll drive back on Sunday to get you."

"What time will you pick me up Thursday morning?"

"Seven-thirty." That would give me enough time to drive the sixty miles, drop Grandmother off, and arrive at the hospital. "And Grandmother, my Friday schedule is filled with appointments. Don't expect me to spend the night at Uma's."

****

Between appointments, Cindi and I spent Wednesday doing inventory and making a list of needed supplies. We shifted all the large animal appointments to Friday. She was more than capable of handling the clinic for minor things. If there were any emergencies, she was to refer them to Dr. Cooper. I also emailed my list to the veterinarian medical supply house, stating that I would pick up my order before closing time Thursday.

Grandmother was literally standing outside her apartment door when I pulled up. I've learned many things from her, and one of them is that there is no excuse for tardiness unless you are dead or dying. I was actually thankful not to see a suitcase, although her purse meets airport regulation standards for a carryon. It wouldn't surprise me if she'd packed a nightgown and a change of clothing and would announce that she planned to stay with Uma for a few days. Don't get me wrong, I adore my grandmother even though she tends to forget that I'm an adult with a business to run.

The drive was made more pleasant by the chit-chat. Of course, I was careful not to divulge my true reason for making a trip to the big city. However, Grandmother revealed her own surprise.

"You seem upset, Grandmother. Is this why you

want to visit Uma?"

"I am upset, and no, it has nothing to do with my cousin." She turned to face me. "The newspaper is closing. The big conglomerate that owns it is closing all the small-town papers, stating there aren't enough subscriptions to keep us open." She pshawed. "May lightning strike them in their overstuffed pocketbooks."

When my grandmother wishes a hex on something, I know she's really upset. "Actually, I can see their point. Most people read the news on their cellphones or computers. If it's a matter of losing your income, you can always move back to the house with me. I'd love it."

She waved her hand as if swatting a mosquito. "No, no. I have my pension and Social Security. It's just that I'm still young. Seventy isn't so old. What will I do with myself? It's not like Enigma is a happening metropolis, you know. Our Enigmians deserve to hold a paper in their hands, stain their fingers with ink, and then roll it up like cord wood for the fireplace."

I knew better than to smile. "Let me think on this, Grandmother. I'm sure there is a solution to your dilemma." Of course, I didn't dare mention that as president of the ladies' auxiliary she often complains about how much work is involved in organizing the annual events.

At precisely nine o'clock, my grandmother kissed me on the cheek. I left her and Uma hugging each other and walking into the apartment at the senior center where Uma resides.

Fifteen minutes later, I found a parking space at the hospital. The pathology department at University Hospital is located below ground in the heart of a maze of small offices. Because this is also a teaching facility, miles of corridors branch out in all directions, connecting the non-medical departments charged with the actual running of the facility. There is a steady flow of pedestrian traffic today, people in hospital uniforms wearing identifying neck lanyards, all scurrying around to meet hectic schedules.

I entered an elevator and punched the button to the basement. The doors opened and I stepped out, standing for a moment to get my bearings. You might expect a place where cadavers are kept and autopsies performed to be ominous. The pathology department is pleasant, spacious, well lighted, and cheerfully decorated with coastal and mountain scenic artwork on the royal blue and gray walls. At least fifty to sixty lab technicians worked there to accommodate the blood, bone, and tissue specimens sent down from above.

I stepped to a desk. The receptionist greeted me. "May I help you?"

"Yes, I'm Dr. Tullah Holliday. Dr. Delaney is expecting me."

She glanced down at a list, placed a checkmark by my name, and handed me a visitor's badge, one of those peel-and-stick types to place on my shirt. "Of course." She pointed over her shoulder. "Down this aisle to the first left, then left again. Her office is the second door."

I didn't tell the woman wearing bright red-rimmed bifocals and chomping on gum that I had spent many hours down here working as Dr. Delaney's lab assistant before deciding that I was more suited for veterinarian medicine. After nine months of cutting open John and Jane Does, sifting through their intestines, and never getting the smell of ammonia out of my nose, I decided that a career in pathology wasn't for me. I've always enjoyed the sunshine and fresh air much more than spending my days underground like a lab rat.

I knocked on the door, then entered.

"Tullah!" Dr. Delaney pushed out of her chair and held out her hands to grasp mine. "So good to see you. How's your dad, still sheriff?"

"Yes, ma'am." I sighed. "He loves his job."

She smiled. "Don't we all. I'm looking forward to lunch and catching up with your life."

I had never really known Claire Delaney's age. I hadn't seen her in over three years. Her hair style hadn't changed. It was short, thick and curly, a lot whiter than I remembered. Her hands were the warm tones of a caramel-colored crayon. Age had given her face a softly crumpled look, like a freshly laundered cotton sheet that needed ironing. She wore a white coat over surgical blues.

After a brief hug, she looked me up and down. Her laughter still lilted. "The same Tullah. Jeans, flannel shirt, cowboy boots." She handed me a white coat and a pair of surgical booties, gloves, and scrub cap. "Your Mr. Rakestraw has gone through the required cooling period. Are you ready for show time?"

All business as usual. "Yes, ma'am, lead the way."

As we walked to the morgue, she asked, "Tell me why you are interested in this particular subject."

I explained about finding Alma's body and how her death had been ruled unintentional with no autopsy performed due to her known heart condition, and just a few days afterward I'd found Forest's body. "It seems odd that both victims presented with the same symptoms beforehand—nausea, chest pains, stomach cramps, and shortness of breath. Rakestraw was age thirty-three and considered the picture of health." I also described the wild glassy-eyed look and how their mouths were shaped at time of death, and the sweet scent I'd detected.

"Uh-huh." She bobbed her head up and down. "Are you telling me you suspect poisoning?"

"That's why I'm here. My dad doesn't agree. I'm doing this on the sly. That way if natural causes are determined, then only you and I know I was here. If we find evidence that points to a crime, then I'll have to face Dad's wrath, which he'll get over. You will keep my visit confidential." It wasn't a question, and I knew she understood.

She touched my arm, offering a smug smile. "Or I can simply email him the preliminary pathology results with a blind copy to you, and your little secret remains safe."

I laughed. "It works for me."

We entered the morgue. Dr. Delaney instructed the diener, aka morgue attendant, to ready cadaver Rakestraw number 9123352147. The attendant opened the refrigerated storage bin and slid out the slab, moving the body to a dissection table.

The air was scented with formaldehyde, that acrid perfume for the deceased. I had forgotten the normal temperature in a cold chamber is approximate thirty-six degrees Fahrenheit to slow decomposition. I resisted a shiver, glad that I'd worn a flannel shirt, and thankful for the lab coat.

Dr. Delaney pulled closer the mic suspended from the ceiling. "Mark the time as ten o'clock, Thursday morning, March twenty-fifth. Dr. Claire Delaney, Chief

Pathologist, with Dr. Tullah Holliday assisting, and Javon Williams, diener."

The diener removed the plastic covering. A once vibrant man who considered himself a rich and debonair playboy now reminded me of a statue molded from pasty white clay. When I was a child, it seemed mischief was my middle name. Grandmother often told me that people who play with fire will eventually get burned. Apparently, Forest had played with fire one time too many, or at least I hoped the autopsy results would prove my theory correct.

Dr. Delaney offered me a wink and a nod. "Go ahead. You do the honors and make the cut."

I picked up the scalpel, drew in a deep breath and blew it out as excitement surged through me. For a split second, I almost regretted leaving pathology.

Four hours later, we had extracted remaining food particles, gastric juices, and plucked microscopic particles that might be leaves of some sort, and closed the cadaver of what was once a handsome jock. We removed our gloves and booties, freshened ourselves, and walked outside. Compared to the frigid autopsy room, the temperature outdoors was pleasantly warm.

We enjoyed a short walk from the hospital to the Szechuan Kitchen, where I ordered the egg drop soup, egg roll, Mongolian beef, and a pot of jasmine tea. Dr. Delaney ordered her favorite, Szechuan chicken over refried rice.

The waiter asked if we'd like chopsticks. I've never quite mastered chopsticks and opted for a fork.

"Tell me, Tullah, do you enjoy working with animals more than with cadavers?"

"I have to admit it's kind of nice when the patients

can't bite, scratch, or kick. But, yes, I love what I do." To fluff her ego a bit, I added, "In a pinch, I might reconsider pathology. A teeny-weeny pinch."

To which she laughed.

"If I recall correctly, Dr. Delaney, it will take approximately twenty-four hours to get the preliminary results?"

"You remembered. Yes, that is correct. I'll email the results as soon as I'm finished with my analysis. I agree with you about the possibility of poison, especially since we extracted what appears to be some sort of leaf." She deftly lifted the chopsticks to her mouth and savored a piece of chicken. "Of course, it might take as long as six weeks to get the full autopsy results."

"I'm hoping there will be enough in the preliminary report to prompt my father to open a criminal investigation." I hesitated.

"What is it…what are you thinking?"

"That if Forest Rakestraw died from poison, we may have to either convince Alma Tackett's husband to give permission to exhume her body or get a court order."

Delaney wiped her mouth with a napkin. She lifted a cup of tea. "How long since the female subject was embalmed?"

I knew embalming interferes with most toxicology studies. "At least six days."

"Hmm, it's possible to extract some positive chemical analysis from the tissue. As you know, any time longer than a week and the embalming may confound the analysis."

"I understand. This is why I appreciate that you're

adding a priority status on Rakestraw."

The waiter cleared our plates and along with the bill gave each of us a fortune cookie. Dr. Delaney laughed when she read her fortune. "Be on the alert to recognize your prime at whatever time of your life it may occur." She munched on a piece of cookie. "I'm certain my prime has already passed. In fact, I've put in for my retirement and will leave at the end of the semester. Thirty-five years is enough."

This news shook me. "What are your plans?"

"Don't look so shocked, Tullah. One day you will reach my age and will look forward to a slower pace. As for my future, I've booked a world cruise." A smile crinkled the edges of her eyes. "One hundred days of bliss and new adventures. Afterward, I plan to write a forensics manual, and then—who knows." She made a little motion with her hands. "Go ahead. Open yours."

I read, "A golden egg of opportunity will fall into your lap. Wait for it." A sense of dread filled me. "What do you suppose it means?"

Delaney flashed a smile. "Don't look so serious, Tullah. A golden egg might mean you'll win the lottery and never have to work another day in your life."

After lunch and two pots of tea, we strolled back to the hospital. I didn't accompany her inside. Dr. Delaney again promised to get the reports to me stat. "If I can help in any way, you know how to contact me."

I gave her a brief hug and thanked her. I checked the time. If I hurried, I could make it to the veterinary medical supply store, load my supplies, and get to my cousin Uma's before five o'clock.

In Enigma, it's rare to pass more than one vehicle when making house calls. I hated driving in traffic where there are too many impatient drivers and all trying to get nowhere fast. I breathed a sigh of relief once I pulled through the senior living center's gated drive and stopped in front of Uma's small apartment. My mind was awhirl with possibilities concerning Alma's and Forest's deaths. I yearned to get home.

I rang the doorbell. Uma reminded me of an overly ripe prune, all dark and wrinkled but still sweet. She clasped my hand and drew it to her cheek. "Still tall, with eyes as blue as a mountain lake. You remind me of me when I was your age."

Giving her a dutiful peck on the cheek, I followed her inside. Grandmother stood in the tiny kitchen, a plate of cookies in her hand. The apartment, spit-and-shine clean, smelled of cinnamon and ginger. I felt ashamed of my earlier thoughts, because Grandmother and Uma had made my favorite cookie.

"Sit, Niece. It hurts my neck to stare up at you." Uma looked like a small child when she settled her wizened body in a yellow overstuffed chair. "Tanti tells me you are not married. You are not one of those funny people, are you?"

I thought, Oh, no, here we go with the twenty questions. I searched for a quick diversion. With my metabolism, I never worry about calories, and helped myself to a handful of ginger snaps. Grandmother chose to sit in a rocking chair, and I was left to sit on an ottoman. Between bites, I avoided Uma's question and asked, "Did the two of you catch up on each other's lives?"

Grandmother rocked quietly. Uma appeared to have dozed off. Both seemed to have forgotten about me. I glanced at my watch. "Grandmother?"

"Yes." She hesitated slightly. "Uma will soon celebrate her ninety-second year and thinks this coming winter will be her last. She has a wish and wants you to help her fulfill it."

Holi Moli. Chills prickled the hairs on my arms. If my cousin, twelfth removed or whatever, thinks I'm going to help her die— Whew! To my relief, Uma rallied from her reverie and said, "When I was a girl, many, many moons ago, I rode pinto horses. I wore my long hair loose, and it flowed in the wind, and even though the great wars were over, I pretended I was a warrior-ess riding into battle. Before I go to walk with my ancestors in the sky, I wish once more to ride a great pinto horse and feel the wind in my hair."

The hopefulness in Uma's eyes tugged at my heart. I cut a glance toward my grandmother, and suddenly there were seams that I'd never noticed lining her almond complexion. In her and the old relative, sitting in a chair that looked as if it were trying to swallow her, I saw my own future.

"I will make this possible, Uma. When would you like to do this adventure?"

A grin smoothed the wrinkles in her cheeks. "The sooner the better, my child."

"What about Saturday? I have a friend who owns a herd of gentle pintos. I'm certain she will pick a horse that is extra special for you to ride."

Uma struggled to get out of the chair. She clapped her hands together and giggled like a happy child. "Tanti, your granddaughter has a good heart. Now, help me out of this chair. Let us pack my suitcase."

While Grandmother helped her cousin pack, I dialed my friend, Natalie Fletcher, at Happy Hooves

Equestrian Center and explained the reason for my call, and asked if she could help an old woman's wish come true.

Natalie replied it was her pleasure. "We have mounting steps to make getting into the saddle much easier. Our horses are especially gentle and trustworthy."

"While I have you on the phone, Nat—" I explained about the foal and that she'd be ready to wean in about five weeks. "Her name is Blue Belle. She's part Gypsy Vanner and part Thoroughbred, and sweet natured. The owner doesn't want her and asked if I'd find her a good home. Naturally, I thought of you."

"I couldn't pay much for her. You know we work mostly on donations and grant monies."

"That's the best part. There's no fee. He owns a Thoroughbred brood mare farm, and his only desire is to find Blue Belle a loving home."

"Then by all means, we'll gladly take her. The children will love spoiling a foal, and having her will help build confidence in our autistic children. Thank you, Tullah."

"Great. See you Saturday."

I was feeling pretty full of myself by the time Grandmother and Uma announced they were ready to leave.

Uma was practically skin and bone. Helping her into the back seat of my truck was like lifting a cloud. Once on the road, she and Grandmother chattered like a couple of teenagers going on a grand adventure. Grandmother, who hasn't ridden in several years, stated that she, too, wanted to ride a pinto horse.

I was nearing Charlie's place when Uma yelled,

"The Whitehorse Saloon. Does a real warrior own that or is it a made-up name?"

Grandmother replied, "As pure as they come. Charlie Whitehorse is a longtime family friend. He and Henry fought in the war together."

Uma leaned between the front seats. "Good. Tullah, I have a sudden thirst for a beer. You know, at the senior center alcohol is forbidden, and so are French fries. Cholesterol, bah!"

No matter how anxious I was to get home to type notes while the autopsy information was still fresh in my mind, I refused to disappoint a ninety-two-year-old woman who'd once dreamed of being a warrior-ess. I slowed the truck and wheeled into a parking spot near the front door. "Beer and a large order of French fries all around. My treat."

As he usually does when he spots me, Charlie left the bar to greet us. I introduced him to Uma. He bowed and greeted her in Apache, "*Ya'ateh shichu.* Hello, Grandmother. It is my pleasure to meet you, Uma. Welcome to the Whitehorse Saloon."

He escorted us to a booth and took our order. As he turned away, Uma blurted, "What tribe are you from?" She looked him up and down. "I am full-blooded Cherokee."

I inwardly cringed. Maybe people in their nineties thought they were privileged to ask *none of your business* questions. Then again, I wanted to know the answer, too, since Charlie had always been tight-lipped about himself.

He didn't seem the least bit discomfited when he answered, "My father was Jicarilla Apache from New Mexico. He went on an adventure in Alaska and met my mother, who was Aleut."

He offered no further explanation. He simply said, "Draft or bottle?"

Uma grinned. "Draft, no head, and a cold glass."

Grandmother and I ordered the same.

He returned and set the icy mugs in front of us. Uma drew a healthy sip. She closed her eyes and murmured blissfully, "Ooo! My tastebuds are smiling."

Chapter Nine

I toted the bags while Grandmother helped Uma inside and to the bathroom. Before I left for home, Grandmother stood at the front door. She lowered her voice to a conspiratorial tone. "I almost forgot to tell you. I heard through the grapevine that Sam took out a life insurance policy on Forest in the amount of a million dollars."

Personally, I didn't find the news unusual. This is something most parents do. "Okay, thanks for sharing." I turned to leave.

She grabbed my shirt, nearly pulling the tail out of my jeans. "You don't understand. He took it out only six months ago. Don't you think that's a little odd? I mean, isn't a son expected to outlive his father?" She lifted her eyebrows as if to say, *Catch my drift?*

I quirked my mouth upward. "Grandmother, when I asked if you thought foul play was involved in Alma's death, you poo-poo'd it. Now, you're implying that…" I dropped my voice to a whisper. "That Sam might've killed his own son to collect on a life insurance policy?"

She leaned forward, also whispering, "Well…people do weird things. I'm just sayin'."

I kissed her on the cheek. "G'night. Saturday morning at nine."

She wrinkled her nose, leaned closer, and sniffed. "What is that odor?"

Uh-oh, busted. I averted my eyes, searching for an answer. "The only thing I smell is the dumpster. What day does the garbage truck come?"

"The truck picks up on Friday." Grandmother leaned closer. "Ammonia. You smell like when you used to work at the hospital."

Quick, think quick. "Um, I mentioned I was having lunch with Dr. Delaney, didn't I?"

"Of course, I must've forgotten. I never liked hospital smells, and don't worry. We'll be ready Saturday."

As much as I wanted to get home, I stopped by the office to check in with my dad, and filled him in about taking Grandmother and her cousin to the equestrian center. I asked him if he'd heard about the insurance policy.

"Nope, who told you?"

"You know Grandmother. She has a nose like a bloodhound when it comes to news."

"Yep, and you smell like a hospital. Where've you been?"

I lifted my arm and sniffed my flannel shirt. My nose failed me. "I had lunch with one of my former professors."

He narrowed his eyes and pierced me with one of his looks that always makes me squirm. I offered nothing further.

Dad reshuffled a stack of papers and plopped them in a wire filing basket. "I wouldn't put too much stock in it. Maybe it was a mutual agreement between father and son. Maybe Sam and Forest knew something about his health that's none of anyone's business."

"Yeah, but Dad, wouldn't that be fraud?"

He thought for a minute. "If Forest passed a physical and the policy was approved, then where's the fraud?"

"Sometimes you frustrate me." I headed out the door and over my shoulder added, "In a good way."

He called after me, "You ladies have a good time ridin' horses Saturday."

Joyce glanced up from the computer. "Better go next door to the drug store and stock up on Epsom salts. Tanti and her cousin are a long way from being spring chickens. Come Sunday morning, they'll be so sore they won't want to get out of bed."

"Yes, ma'am, good idea."

I made haste at the drug store. Once Mr. Jenks starts talking it's difficult to get away from him. "Say, Doc, dredging up dead bodies runs in your DNA, doesn't it?" He guffawed.

"Not funny, Mr. Jenks. None of us gets to choose our ancestors, do we?" I grabbed what I needed and paid. "Sorry to rush off. It's late, and I still have work to do."

Once outside, I decided to sneak in a little grocery shopping while I was in town. I hustled down the aisles, picking up essentials like peanut butter, strawberry jelly, bread, hot dogs, milk, and wine.

I checked in with Cindi. She assured me the day had gone well while she helped me unload the supplies and store them inside the medicine pantry. "Luanne Sterns picked up Gigi and the puppies. I told her I would gladly take both of them when they are weaned."

I handed Cindi a case of oral antibiotics for horses. "What did she say?"

"Nothing much, except to call and let her know

before I come get them."

"She's a bit eccentric, don't you think?"

Cindi shrugged. "If that's a nice way of saying she's weird, then yes, I agree."

I am thankful for daylight savings time. Almost eight o'clock and still enough light for me to muck out the stalls, feed the animals, and give River and Rascal some much-needed attention.

I told Cindi about my plans for Saturday and invited her to come along.

"Wow, I hope when I'm in my nineties I'll be spry enough to get out of a rocking chair, much less ride a horse. Thanks for the invite. I'd love to tag along." She beamed. "Anyhow, I plan to drive to the city and shop for curtains and throw pillows, a bedspread, cookware." She did a little dance. "I'm excited to decorate my new home." She tapped her cheek with a finger. "I'm thinking about a coastal theme. I've always loved the beach. Whatta you think?"

"If it makes you happy, then go for it." This seemed to make Cindi quite pleased.

"Oh, I almost forgot," I said. "Only Mother Nature knows how much longer the cold weather will hang around. I bought you a ceramic heater as a housewarming gift." We both laughed at the pun.

She followed me out to the truck. I handed her the box, then invited her over for a glass of wine, and was halfway relieved when she declined. I entered the house through the back door and went straight into the kitchen. I buttered a stack of saltine crackers and poured a glass of merlot. The dog and donkey followed me to the living room and got comfy on their favorite rug next to my recliner.

I munched on a cracker and washed it down with a healthy sip of wine while waiting for my laptop to boot up. Scrolling to the file labeled Enigma Deaths, I felt a sense of gratification as I read over my previous summaries before opening a new document.

Another sip of wine, and I typed notes regarding today's autopsy. My main concern was that I didn't forget details that might prove helpful to Dad in the event murder was involved. Once I had recalled what transpired in the autopsy room, I sat back and pondered what it all might mean—if anything at all.

The initial autopsy revealed no evidence of heart disease or heart defects. The lungs were clear. No brain swelling or hematomas, no leaking blood vessels or signs of drug abuse, which ruled out cerebral hemorrhage. There were polyps in the colon. Two presented positive for pre-carcinoma. However, this bit of information wasn't relative to the actual death.

Examining the stomach is my least favorite part because the stench is revolting. I started paying close attention when Dr. Delaney began pulling out food that was partially digested. Really. A partly digested baked potato, enough chunks to identify a jelly donut, a chocolate-covered donut, a glazed donut, and a French fry. The man certainly had a sweet tooth. There were also miniscule elements that resembled pink tissue paper. This was a puzzle.

Still, all of this proved inconclusive. Nothing pointed to murder. I finished off the last cracker and stared at the page on the screen. What did it all mean—anything? Or nothing? I wasn't sure what I felt—relief or disappointment. Relief that there wasn't a lunatic loose in Enigma, or disappointment that my instincts had let me down. If the toxicology report came back negative, at least I had the gratification of knowing my probing—though unofficial—was tactful and Dr. Delaney would keep my involvement confidential.

I opened the page I'd generated listing suspects and motives. Although I considered it inconsequential, in the column beneath Sam's name I added the million-dollar life insurance policy. I counted backward six months from March and typed in September as the possible date of purchase.

Taking a break from the depressing work of analyzing motives for possible murders, I opened my email. Correspondence could always be counted on to encourage abandonment of such thoughts in favor of catching up with friends, answering business questions, and paying bills.

Night had finally dropped its cloak over the countryside. Tomorrow's appointment book promised a busy schedule. It'd been a long day. I decided to pack it in.

I stood under a hot shower for a long time before toweling off, gargling with mouthwash, and pulling on my flannels, then piling into an unmade bed. An overactive brain kept me awake. I replayed the autopsy results, fretted over the possible outcome of the preliminary toxicology report, rehearsed the what-ifs of exhuming a body, the fallout from my dad if he discovered I attended the autopsy, how to keep my grandmother busy now that the newspaper was closing, and juggling all of it with my growing clientele.

Another thought plagued me. Why did a silly saying in a fortune cookie upset me? Anything golden had to be good. Right?

I pulled the covers tightly around me. My bones had begun to ache. It was a long time before I got warm.

Chapter Ten

In the morning, I felt whole again. I ate a big breakfast, washing down bacon, scrambled eggs topped with cheddar cheese, and a buttered biscuit with strawberry jam with a glass of apple juice and three cups of coffee.

The sky was a stark, cloudless blue, and the air crisp. Off in the distance, the land was a subdued overlay of pale lavender, the mountain ridges reminding me of crushed velvet, wrinkled dark gray along the face. There is something appealing about a vast open land as yet unconquered, miles and miles of grassland, and terrain without traffic lights, billboards, and tall buildings to mar its beauty. In my sleep, I'd heard a tree frog chirping its mating song and the forlorn answering cries. I wondered what it was like when Uma was a child riding bareback, wild and free. I remembered the wistful look on her face when she'd asked me to help her relive a lost part of her childhood.

My mind drifted to Alma and Forest. I wondered what thoughts went through their minds as they drew their last breaths. Did their lives rush before their eyes as I've often read happens? Did they experience nano-seconds of regret for not fulfilling adventures?

My mother's face flashed before me and faded just as fast. I remember the shape of her eyes, almond, and with a hint of mischief. She had a dimple in her right cheek that deepened when she smiled and her infectious laughter. She'd never see another sunrise...never capture life on a canvas, ever again. And for the rest of my life, I will miss her. I cannot speak more of my mother's death. The memory is still too raw. Another time. Another time.

I was angry with myself for allowing these meandering introspections to hover over me like a dark cloud. Where had they come from? Was it the autopsy and waiting for the report that marred the morning's beauty and threatened to spoil my day?

The crunching of gravel drew me from my reverie. Mrs. Frezoli struggled to exit her antique VW. Honestly, her behind reminded me of two basketballs rolling around in a gunny sack. She loved cannoli so much that she convinced Patty Sweet to add them to the menu at Sweet's 'n' Eats.

Mrs. Frezoli leaned into the back seat and extracted a cat crate. Her face was beet red from exertion, and she huffed trying to catch her breath as she walked toward me. "Yoohoo, Tul-lah."

A widow, Mrs. Frezoli was my sixth grade language arts teacher, now retired, and always pronounced my name with two syllables. She never addressed me as Dr. Holliday, which was somewhat annoying since I earned my title.

I noticed her hands were crisscrossed with rainbow-colored Band-Aids. "Mrs. F, what happened? Were you in an accident?"

Beads of sweat lined her brow. "Not exactly, dear. I swear Miss Scarlett has a sixth sense. She knows, the minute I dig out the crate, she's coming to visit you." The red in her face deepened. "Oh, dear me, I didn't mean to imply…" Her voice trailed off as I relieved her of the burden.

"No offense taken, Mrs. F."

"Oh, bless you. Anyhow, Miss Scarlett pitched a terrible hissy fit. She hid behind the pie safe, and you know, I can't get down on my knees. I can't begin to tell you how many treats it took to entice the naughty girl out from her hiding place." She held up both hands and waggled her fingers. "And this is the result."

Miss Scarlet was a twelve-year-old orange, overweight, fluffy, mix-breed with the temperament of a rabid lioness. We entered the office. "There's bottled iced tea and sodas in the refrigerator. Make yourself comfy while Cindi and I update Miss Scarlet's vaccinations."

"Oh, and Tul-lah, Miss Scarlett is favoring her right paw. She nips me every time I try to look at it."

I nodded. "We'll take good care of her."

I heard the refrigerator door slam. She called out, "Terrible about Alma, and you poor dear, how awful that you had to find her, well, dead. I hope it didn't give you nightmares." She prattled on, and I imagined her face growing even redder because I hadn't heard her draw a breath. "Of course, you being a doctor and all, but still, I suppose finding a dead animal isn't nearly as traumatic as finding a dead person." She did a little gasp. "Oh, dear, you must think I'm positively cold-hearted."

"Not at all, Mrs. F. Just so you know, we're administering a mild sedative to calm Miss Scarlett. There are a couple of new spring home décor magazines on the table if you'd like to look at them. Relax and enjoy a beverage. We'll be about forty-five minutes."

"Oh, take your time, dear. I'm in no hurry."

Cindi administered a mild sedative wrapped in a treat to insure that neither of us suffered bites or scratches. As soon as the feline appeared calm, I opened the crate door and lifted Miss Scarlett out. I placed her on the scale, and shook my head. "We tell Mrs. F every time to put the cat on a diet."

Cindi recorded the weight. She administered the distemper cocktail while I moistened hair on the right paw with alcohol. "Ah, here's the problem." I reached for a pair of tweezers and latched onto a thorn embedded in the paw. After removing the long spike, I cleansed the pad with warm water and a little soap before administering antiseptic. I also trimmed the long hair between Miss Scarlett's toes.

"All done, Mrs. F." I carried the crate to the car. "Miss Scarlett will be a little groggy when she wakes up. She had a thorn in her paw. However, there is no infection." I suggested she keep an eye on it and call me if there was a problem. I'd given this talk before and knew I was wasting my breath. "Mrs. F, Miss Scarlett is twelve years old. She's sedentary and overweight..."

My former teacher rolled her eyes and sighed. "I know, dear. She and I both need to diet and exercise. I'll think about it tomorrow." She squeezed between the steering wheel and driver's seat and wiggled around trying to get comfortable.

"I don't mean to speak ill of the dead." She adjusted a pair of sunglasses on the bridge of her nose. "I did not like Alma Tackett. I didn't vote for her the first time and that lothario, Forest Rakestraw, I wouldn't vote for him either." She glanced around as if searching for eavesdroppers. "You know my back yard backs up to the alley that runs between my house and Father Sterns'. Humph. There was plenty of hanky-panky going on during the midnight hours. Oh, yes, his sister isn't as lily-white pure as she'd like people to think."

This tidbit startled me right down to the tips of my boots. "Really? You saw the, um, hanky-pankying?"

"Oh, yes. Sometimes I wake up in the wee hours and can't go back to sleep. I find sitting on the back porch helps me relax. Of course, I never turn on the light. Who wants to see an old fat lady in her nightie? Anyhow, that young man was playing both ends against the middle. It was only a matter of time before Alma and Luanne figured out he was a no-good, double-timing scamp." She chattered on. "My lands, what did he see in either of them—a woman old enough to be his mother, and a shriveled up old maid?"

She went on, "It's no wonder George and poor Wakefield spent most of their time at the farm. Of course, George does have a business to run. I'm telling you, the way Alma would yell at that poor boy, calling him an idiot and other terrible names, it's no wonder he stutters." She peered over the rim of her sunglasses. "It got so bad that one time poor Wakefield actually threatened to take a baseball bat to her."

I swallowed the gasp. "He actually threatened his mother?"

"Well, now, dear, my ol' ears don't hear as good as they did when I was teaching." She tapped the steering wheel. "Yes, I'm certain he said something like, 'If I had a bat I'd bash'—or maybe he said, 'mash'—'your head in.' "

Mrs. F was on a verbal avalanche. It was like the On button to her mouth had gotten stuck and she couldn't shut it off. "Oh, and something else—you know I'm on the election committee. Sam has filed to run for mayor. He said he felt as if it was his duty. Now, isn't that something?"

I was taken aback by this information. "Has anyone else filed besides Sam?"

"Not as of yesterday." The old bug roared to life. Mrs. Frezoli rolled down the window. She stuck out her flabby arm, waved and yelled, "Ta-tah."

For a moment, I stood watching the little yellow car rattle down the drive, while I tried to wrap my brain around all she had said. Did Wakefield murder his mother? I made a mental note to add him to my list of suspects.

Throughout the day a flow of service guys kept Cindi and me rather distracted. First it was the pest control, then the power company, the sewage company to hook into the septic tank, and the plumber to connect the trailer to the well, and the cable and internet guys.

We also had a steady stream of patients. Our most unusual for the day was to de-scent and neuter a little boy's newly acquired pet skunk. By the time we locked the office, I was ready to kick off my boots and imbibe a glass of wine. Cindi excused herself, saying she wanted to give the trailer a thorough cleaning before moving in. She declined my offer to help—it was her first home since officially being on her own, and she wanted to do it all herself. I truly didn't mind.

I walked down the barn's aisle, opened the stall doors, and led my horses to the corral and opened the gate to the pasture. It was almost as if the horses sensed their freedom from being cooped up all winter. I laughed when they bucked and squealed and tossed their heads like happy children being let out for recess. All three of them raced across the field, their tails hiked like flags, their hooves tearing up soggy clods of grass.

I had checked the email on my phone several times hoping Dr. Delaney had sent the autopsy results. From the time the autopsy was performed yesterday, I hoped to hear something by six o'clock this evening. I checked again. Nothing.

Questions hummed around in my head, but I was almost too tired to think. Of course, I reminded myself that today was Friday and I might not get the results until Monday. I think I was okay until Mrs. Frezoli mentioned the secret meetings, and Wakefield's alleged threat against his mother.

I filled the automatic feeders and waterer for River and Rascal, put a couple of chicken drumsticks and a sweet potato in the oven to bake, and went upstairs to grab an armful of dirty clothes to launder. After starting the washing machine, I poured a glass of wine and tossed together a handful of lettuce, diced tomatoes, green olives, and bleu cheese dressing to munch on until dinner.

The dog and donkey followed me to the living room and found their usual favorite place. I kicked off my boots, reclined, and opened my email. Disappointment greeted me. I spent time reading my notes, which I knew almost verbatim. Forty-five minutes later, the oven timer alerted me that my food was ready.

To help pass the time and to get my mind off the nonexistent email, I flipped on the television and watched several of my favorite do-it-yourself programs and the nightly news. I polished off my wine and carried my dishes to the kitchen and loaded them into the dishwasher. I called the animals to follow me upstairs. Once there, I stuffed wet clothes into the dryer and readied for bed. Have I mentioned that grocery shopping and housework are my two least favorite activities? However, eating and wearing clean underwear are two of life's little necessities.

I actually looked forward to the next day and spending it with my grandmother and Uma. My plan was to take pictures so Uma could remember her adventure.

I lay staring up at the ceiling, rehashing Mrs. Frezoli's surprising revelation. Should I share this information with my dad? Would he think it relevant? I had just reached that wonderful heavy stage of sleep where your nervous system turns to jelly and you feel as if your body has liquefied, molding you to the mattress, when the pink panther theme played on my laptop, notifying me that an email had arrived. I squinted at the clock and, sinking deeper between the folds of my quilt, I pulled the pillow over my head.

****

The morning was predawn gray when an enterprising rooster somewhere in the countryside began obnoxiously heralding the day. Try as I might, I couldn't block out the annoying cockadoodling. Visions of a steaming pot of chicken 'n' dumplings danced in my head.

As much as I wanted to sneak in a few more winks of sleep, there was no denying a braying donkey and a seventy-pound dog licking the sole of my foot—their way of telling me it was time to begin the day.

I rolled to a sitting position, stretched, and yawned. I remembered the email alert from last night and grabbed my phone.

Disappointment, again.

The email wasn't from Dr. Delaney. It was from my grandmother and read, *Didn't want to call you in case you were asleep. Meet us at Sweet's 'n' Eats. I'm treating us to Patty's blueberry pancakes. Nine sharp.* She signed with a smiley face emoji.

Grandmother and Uma remind me of wizened little girls dressed in blue jeans, plaid flannel shirts, and western boots, their long hair plaited in braids that draped over their shoulders. Uma stood the moment she spotted me walk through the door to flag me to the table. All through breakfast and between bites of pancakes and bacon, she chattered away like an excited magpie.

Grandmother trained her eyes on me, taking a long look. It reminded me of how Mama used to look at me. Maybe she was recalling her own memories of long ago. I reached over and wrapped my hand over hers.

I didn't like it when my own memories chased after me. "We should probably go. It's about a twenty-minute drive." I pulled out my credit card.

Grandmother flashed me a devious smile. "I paid before you got here." She pushed back her chair. "C'mon, Uma, we have horses to ride."

I'm certain the caffeine from two cups of black coffee amped up Uma's energy. I wondered if I should ask Natalie if she provided safety belts to keep riders from toppling out of the saddle.

On the drive to the stables, I said, "Did you know

Sam filed to run for mayor?"

Grandmother's eyebrows shot up. "Who told you that?"

"Mrs. Frezoli. She said he filed and paid the fee on Thursday."

"Hmm, first he takes out a million-dollar life insurance policy on his son, and now he's running for mayor. Makes me wonder if something is going on that doesn't meet the eye."

"I don't think so, Grandmother. Don't let your newswoman imagination run away with you."

She shot me an evil eye.

I loved when she got her dander up. "Anyhow, I was thinking, since the newspaper is closing and you're worried about being at loose ends, maybe you should run for mayor."

This time she rolled her eyes. "You have got to be kidding. Nah-uh. I'll find another way to fill my time." She tapped a finger against her lips. "You know, Sam might win by default if no one else files."

My heart lurched when she said, "Do you know if Henry has received the autopsy results?" I had to remind myself that only Dr. Delaney and I knew about my attending the autopsy.

"If he has, it's a secret, because he hasn't said anything to me."

"Of course, it's just like a lawman to keep important details quiet, especially if foul play is involved."

I gave her a quizzical stare. "Why would you say that?"

"Because Henry said you wanted to attend the autopsy and got upset because he thinks the cause of death is due to normal health issues, and basically he told you to mind your business."

I wheeled through the arched entrance to the equestrian center and bypassed the Visitor's Only parking lot. Due to Uma's advanced age, Natalie had given me permission to park close to the barn.

"I still think he's wrong."

Before Grandmother had a chance to reply, Natalie walked out of the barn. She lifted her hand and waved. "Hello. It's a beautiful day for a ride."

I introduced her to Uma and Grandmother. "We're all excited."

Uma said, "Yes, where is the pony you have picked for me?"

Natalie motioned for us to follow her. "We'll start you ladies in the exercise corral and see how you do before we begin our trail ride."

Standing in the shade were two brown-and-white pintos, a sorrel with a blonde mane and tail, and a buckskin. "Miss Uma, this is Patches. He's as sweet-natured as they come. Miss Tanti, you'll ride Sunshine. She's as sunny as her name. And Tullah, sometimes Rebel lives up to his name. We don't use him or Old Boss with our clients."

I nodded my understanding and hoped with all my heart that Uma didn't pull any unexpected tricks, like gouging Patches in the flanks. I didn't wish to see a ninety-year-old woman sailing over the pinto's head because she caused him to buck.

Natalie led Patches to the mounting steps. I steadied Uma until she climbed into the saddle. I held the reins while Natalie led Sunshine over for Grandmother to mount. I stepped back and clicked away with my phone camera. A surge of pride bubbled inside me. My grandmother and cousin sat like experienced riders, as if the memory of moving with the motion of the animal had never left them. Two complete circles around the corral and Uma declared she was ready for the wide open spaces.

I toed my boot into the stirrup and swung into the saddle. The long-legged sorrel horse hunched. I thought, *Oh, no, you don't.* I gave a strong yank on the reins and jerked his head up. A horse with its head up can't buck.

Natalie grinned as she hauled into the buckskin's saddle. "I guess you showed him who's boss. He'll be okay for the rest of the ride."

One of the ranch hands opened the gate, and we played follow the leader. Natalie led, with me bringing up the rear. The pace started slow to allow the two older women to get the feel of the saddle. About ten minutes in, we cantered and then went to a nice easy lope. Neither Grandmother nor Uma showed any sign of slipping sideways.

We rode through a canopy of oaks. Working long hours and with the harsh winter, I'd forgotten how much I missed the freedom of being on horseback, enjoying countryside filled with a symphony of bird trills and air that smelled fresh and clean.

Natalie held up her hand and motioned us to halt. She placed a finger to her lips, then pointed to a herd of deer. I clicked more pictures, hoping to capture the wonderment on Grandmother's and Uma's faces.

On any spring day, storms can rise up without warning. A peal of thunder rumbled in the distance. Natalie said, "We'd better head back."

A ripple of unease filtered through me. I was uncertain if Grandmother and Uma could keep the pace if we had to gallop back to the barn.

Uma laughed aloud. She spread her arms wide and lifted her head to the sky. "The mighty warriors are beating their drums. They say it is a good day to ride like the wind."

Thunder pealed again, this time closer and with a streak of lightning fingering the sky. Rebel shied, and I brought him under control. The two older horses also showed their jitters.

Natalie expressed her concern about racing to safety.

I reassured her. "We'll ride in at a lope. Lead the way, and don't worry, those two women were riding long before you and I were born. I'll accept full responsibility for both of them, and the horses, if any injuries occur."

My phone vibrated. As much as I wanted to see who was calling, I resisted. With the rain beginning to sprinkle us, it wasn't the time to be concerned about a phone call. We nudged the horses into a slow gallop. The rain came faster. I blinked to clear the water from my eyelashes.

Grandmother yelled, "Don't worry about us. If these old horses don't drop dead under us, we can run 'em in."

Natalie motioned her hand forward—giving her okay. We all hunkered in the saddles and let the horses set their gait as we raced toward shelter.

My phone vibrated again...and again. I hoped it was Dad or Dr. Delaney and not an emergency that required my services.

Chapter Eleven

We were drenched to the skin by the time we reached the stable. Beset with shivers. Grandmother and Uma didn't complain. Natalie provided towels for us to dry off as best we could. She said, "My crew will take care of the horses. Go home and get into dry clothes."

Uma bubbled. "Thank you for a wonderful day! This old woman will sleep tonight and forever with happy memories of feeling a horse beneath me again, and the rain and wind lashing my hair." Her face drifted from buoyant to sad. I imagined she was thinking of the coming winter and her dire prediction.

We hustled to the truck. I lifted Uma into the back seat and then helped Grandmother, whose legs seemed a bit wobbly. I shouted to Natalie, "Please let me know if the horses need tending." I guessed the pintos' ages at between fifteen and eighteen. They were too old to run the distance we had come. Knowing Natalie and how much she loved her animals, I'm certain all four horses were rubbed dry and blanketed, and probably given an extra ration of oats.

She waved and disappeared in the barn's dark interior.

Inside the truck I turned on the heat to help dry us out and to avoid getting the chills. I also removed the phone from my back pocket and set it in the cradle.

"I'm sorry, Grandmother, but stopping at Charlie's is out of the question unless the rain stops."

She replied, "I can phone a to-go order. I'm certain Charlie won't mind running the food out to us."

I nodded, and commanded the Bluetooth to phone Charlie. Uma said, "How did you do that? No hands. Is it magic?"

Grandmother and I exchanged smiles. She explained the magic of a hands-free phone device. When Charlie answered, she placed the order for hamburgers, fries, and bottled beer, and said we'd be there in ten minutes. When she disconnected, she said, "You have two missed calls and an email."

Suspecting and hoping the email was from Dr. Delaney and the calls from Dad, I said with a smile, "I'll check them later."

"What if the calls are important or it's an emergency?"

For my grandmother's sake I tried not to look disgruntled. "At this precise moment, there is nothing more important than getting you and Uma home. The calls can wait."

Thankfully, The Whitehorse Saloon came into view just then. The windshield wipers worked overtime until I reached the saloon's front door. I directed the phone to call Charlie.

Charlie asked, "Are you here?"

"We are. You should consider installing a drive-thru window."

"It is a worthy suggestion, little sister. Food's ready. Be out in a minute."

The door opened and Charlie appeared beneath a large green-and-white golf umbrella. I rolled down the window and grabbed the bags he held. He grinned. "Too bad the rain spoiled your day."

Grandmother and Uma answered over each other, declaring the foul weather made the ride even better. They told him the names of the horses they rode and happily exclaimed about spotting the herd of deer.

Charlie told Uma he enjoyed meeting her and wished her a safe journey as she continued to walk through life.

"Charlie Whitehorse," she said, "you are one fine warrior. If I were a young woman, I would chase you until I caught you, and we would dance under the marriage blanket."

Charlie laughed and winked at her.

I thanked him for always being a good friend before I backed out of the parking spot. "Uma, there is an umbrella on the floorboard. Pass it up here, please."

At the apartment I declined the offer to come in. I first protected Grandmother with the umbrella so she could unlock the door. I said, "What time do you want to leave for Lexington tomorrow?"

She answered, "If it's raining, I'll call the senior center and let them know Uma is staying another night. If the weather is clear, I'll drive us."

"Grandmother, you don't usually enjoy driving such a distance alone."

"I'm not. Vera Mayhew is riding with me. She's vice president of the ladies' auxiliary, and we have ideas to discuss about this year's festival."

I cautioned her to be careful and call me when she arrived home.

I assisted Uma into the apartment. She motioned for me to bend down and planted a kiss on my cheek with a weepy goodbye.

****

By the time my house loomed into view, I felt stiff and eager to strip out of my damp clothes. A sudden feeling of exhaustion swept over me. River and Rascal sat on the back doorstep, as eager to get inside the house as I. A glimpse toward the barn let me know Cindi wasn't at home.

I set my sack of food inside the microwave to keep a sneaky dog from enjoying my lunch. My desire at the moment was a hot shower. The headache creeping up the back of my neck was what happens when I haven't eaten in a while, but the shower eased the throbbing in my head faster than eating would. Wrapped in my bathrobe and toting my laptop, I padded downstairs, grabbed my phone off the counter and the bag of food from the microwave, and plopped in my recliner. The hamburger took precedence over the missed phone calls.

Replete with food, and sugar from a large cola, and with my energy restored, I checked my phone. Both missed calls were from Dad. I listened to his voice message. *Tullah, I received the preliminary autopsy report on Forest. I think you'll be interested in it. Give me a call.*

The second voice message said—*I forgot you're with your grandmother and cousin today. Give me a call when you get home.*

The message from Dr. Delaney shot a dose of adrenalin through me. I double-checked the email. She had sent it as a blind copy. Dad was none the wiser that I also knew the autopsy findings.

I opened the attachment and read through the

postmortem report, mentally summing up a lot of technical details. Dr. Delaney reported no carbon granules deposited in the bronchial passages or lungs, in the blood, or in other tissues. She added that additional lab tests revealed no alcohol, chloroform, or drugs in the system. Toxicology presented high levels of gastrointestinal bleeding and aspiration of vomit and a contagion. Chemical analysis of blood and viscera obtained postmortem confirmed the presence of colchicine. Colchicine poisoning is potentially life-threatening because of its high toxicity and unavailability of specific antidotal treatment. Cause of death: multiple metabolic and cardiac complications. Conclusion: The decedent, a thirty-three-year-old male, died from colchicine poisoning. The manner of death was classified as homicide.

In the body of the email, Dr. Delaney added a personal message—*Tullah, elevated microscopic magnification and extensive toxicology testing reveal the pink tissue-like substances we extracted from cadaver Rakestraw are undigested particles of flower petals. We know certain floras are highly toxic to both humans and animals. Due to your particular interest in this decedent and the extenuating circumstances, I placed a rush on the identification of this specific plant, which identifies as Autumn Crocus, also known as Meadow Saffron or Naked Lady, and is highly toxic and simulates cardiac arrest. You were correct in your suspicions the decedent did not die from natural causes. Always trust your instincts.*

Dr. Delaney went on to thank me again for lunch, with an invitation to visit anytime. She promised to send me an invitation to her retirement party at a to-be-determined date in June.

A distinct wave of relief washed over me. For a moment, I harbored the fleeting hope that Beverly Rakestraw had killed her husband. I also concluded it was time to convince my father that Alma Tackett's death was not a heart attack, or at least not one brought on by natural circumstance. I wondered if Autumn Crocus smelled sweet like honey and made a mental note to add this question, and its answer, to my list of information.

The phone rang just as I decided to return Dad's call.

"Hi, Dad."

"Punkin, just calling to find out if the rain ruined the horse riding?"

Hmm, he was beating around the bush. "Almost. I wish you could've seen Grandmother and Uma. They were awesome. Like they were born to the saddle. It's a day I will never forget."

"Glad to hear it. Did you take pictures?"

"Yes, I did. But, Dad, you didn't call to chit-chat. What's up?"

He cleared his throat. "I, ah, got the preliminary autopsy report this morning."

I willed myself to sound surprised. "Oh, and…?"

"You know I'm not the kind of man who likes to admit he's wrong."

There was a lengthy pause.

"Are you there, Dad?"

"Yeah, the long and short of it is that Forest's death was caused by some kind of poison with a name I can't pronounce."

I resisted the urge to squeal like a silly girl. "Sooo,

I was right. We're looking at homicide."

"Yeah. Now we have to prove it."

"You just said *we*. Does this mean I get to help?"

"I didn't mean as in you and me, more like Deputy Goodbody and me."

"Ah, Dad, you're such a killjoy."

He laughed, and then the timbre of his voice deepened. That was never a good sign. When I was growing up and Dad had caught me at some mischief, he'd sit me down, look me square in the eye, and in a low, resonant tone that made me squirm, he'd ask me if I had done whatever it was it was I had done. This was one of those moments.

"Tullah—"

This really wasn't good. He'd called me Tullah instead of Punkin. "Yes, sir?"

"You've never lied to me."

Oh, snap. The hairs on my arms prickled. "I might've stretched the truth, but never intentionally lied."

"Is there something you want to tell me about the autopsy report?" He hastened on, saying, "And before you answer, I'm asking for the same reason I asked when I smelled ammonia on you after you'd returned from Lexington."

I was so busted. "Okay, I admit I visited Dr. Delaney and, well, I assisted in the autopsy, and it wasn't ammonia, it was formaldehyde you smelled. Listen, Dad, um, I have some theories, if you'd like to hear them."

Silence. I knew I'd royally ticked him.

A long, aggravated sigh filtered through the phone. "You'll only pester me to death if I don't listen."

I did a victory arm-pump. "How about coming for lunch tomorrow? I'll make your favorite—chicken 'n' dumplings and lemon meringue pie."

"Can't turn that down. I thought you were driving Tanti and Uma to Lexington tomorrow."

"She's got it covered." I explained about Vera Mayhew accompanying Grandmother. "Dad, there's something else you should know."

"Out with it."

"Dr. Delaney sent me a copy of the report. She also added some extra information she might not have shared with you."

His voice was tight when he responded. "Like what?"

"If you don't mind, I think it'll be easier to explain it over lunch tomorrow."

We parted with a mutual goodnight. I felt relieved when the call ended. Opening my laptop, I printed copies of my Enigma Deaths notes, including the email from Dr. Delaney. Dad never likes it when I interfere with an investigation, but in the end, he always gets over his initial irritation with me.

I figured I was entitled to a little celebration and did a slight jig as I strolled to the kitchen to pour a glass of merlot.

At dark-thirty, a horn beeped. River and Rascal set up a fuss. I looked out the window and breathed a sigh of relief. Cindi had parked as close as possible to the trailer. I made a note to purchase a new roll-out canopy to help keep her dry during inclement weather. Her arms and hands were laden with packages. It appeared her shopping trip was successful. In a few minutes, the windows in the travel trailer glowed with light. She deserved to be alone, decorating to her heart's content.

I sauntered to the bookshelf and searched through the new mystery books I had ordered and not yet read. I debated between Agatha Christie and Ellery Queen, and ended up selecting Sherlock Holmes. Inviting the animals to follow me, I climbed the stairs and read in bed while enjoying my glass of wine.

Before turning out the light, I scrolled to the photo gallery on my phone. Each shot of Grandmother and Uma brought a smile. I texted several pictures to Grandmother with the promise I would print and mail copies to Uma.

She texted back.

—*Uma says, best day ever. I agree.*—

I planned to rise early enough in the morning to bake two pies—one for Dad to take home—and to make enough chicken 'n' dumplings for leftovers to divide between the two of us. After a time, my eyelids drooped. I yawned and closed the book. I suppose most single women my age dream of hunky men and erotic vacations. Unlike most women, I mentally sort and examine clues while dreaming of solving murders. I know what you're probably thinking, except there's nothing wrong with my libido and every so often it does need scratching, but the when and with whom is no one's business.

Chapter Twelve

I opened the front and back doors to let some fresh air in, and I'd put on the coffeepot. It wasn't quite noon yet. I had about an hour before Dad was due to arrive and busied myself cleaning the kitchen and setting the table. I poured a mug of coffee and walked to the front porch to enjoy the pleasant spring day. The month of April, with Easter, was right around the corner.

As I swung back and forth in the porch swing, theories flittered inside my head about who in our quaint town might be a killer. I promised myself to stay out of Dad's way. He was the sheriff and knew more about catching criminals than I did. Well, maybe I'd try to keep my nose out of his investigation.

At the sound of his 4Runner, River and Rascal launched off the porch like two torpedoes and raced down the drive.

He parked in his customary spot under a large oak tree. Dressed in his usual attire—faded jeans, long-sleeved denim shirt with his sheriff's badge pinned to the pocket, and scuffed cowboy boots—he stepped from the vehicle and greeted me with his natural dimpled grin. Dad looked more like a horse wrangler than a sheriff. We hugged, and I asked if he wanted to eat first or discuss the postmortem first.

"Eat. I'm starved. It's been a long time since I've had chicken 'n' dumplings."

I almost blurted out it was Mom's recipe but caught myself. Some days, four years seems a lifetime since she died, and other times it feels like yesterday. He opened the screen door, and I followed him to the kitchen. I asked, "Iced tea, coffee, or beer?"

He slapped his hands together and grinned. "Tea. I'm on duty. I'll save the coffee for the pie, and I hope that second one is for me to take home."

We filled our plates, savoring the delectable rich broth and fluffy dumplings. A pained expression crossed his face before he hid it behind a mask of impassivity. I reached over and touched his arm. He nodded, cleared his throat, and plopped a dumpling into his mouth.

While we enjoyed lunch, I filled him in about the Happy Hooves Equestrian Center and their mission of providing therapeutic treatment for children and adults with various disabilities. I showed him pictures of Grandmother and Uma on the pintos, and also related that Denver March had donated the Gypsy Vanner filly to the center.

We managed to get through the main meal without bringing up the autopsy. Somehow lemon meringue pie and gastric fluids didn't seem to go together.

However, Dad waved his fork in the air. "Tell me more about colchicine poisoning. Just exactly what is it?"

The frown on his face made me ask, "You're not still mad at me for attending the autopsy?"

He cut himself another piece of pie and slid it onto his plate. "Nope, got over all that last night. Now, you were saying—"

Ordinary people might barf up their innards while

discussing the extraction of partially digested food and bile stench. Not us. I explained about the microscopic pink particles Dr. Delaney and I initially thought were tissue paper. "Neither of us could think of a reason why Forest would eat paper or how paper got into his system." I excused myself to get the email and read the message with the extra details Dr. Delaney had included.

Dad finished off his pie and washed it down with a slug of coffee. "Let me get this straight. Forest ate a pink flower, a poisonous flower, and it caused heart failure, and he died."

I put my fork down. "That pretty much sums it up. Here's the thing, Dad. Don't you think it coincidental that Alma died from a heart attack, too, and only a little over a week later, so did Forest?"

"It's been in the back of my mind from the beginning." He stared off as if in deep thought. "Without an autopsy, and with Doc Ritter signing the death certificate, my hands were tied. Here's a question for you, Punkin…I'm having a hard time wrapping my head around how Forest ingested the flower."

I explained, "From the contents of his stomach, we surmised he'd eaten three different kinds of donuts. Dr. Delaney and I plucked particles out of all the donuts. Somebody really wanted to make sure he got a full dose of poison."

"It 'pears that way. What kind of flower are we talking about?"

"Autumn Crocus, also known as Meadow Saffron and Naked Lady."

"Is that a flower common to Kentucky?"

"As far as I know, it's fairly common in most

states. I don't remember seeing crocuses growing here, and certainly not wild, because they're just as deadly to animals. In fact, none of the necropsies I've performed involved any known variety of this particular flower."

Dad scrunched his forehead together. "I'm thinking we need to exhume Alma's body."

I don't know why, but I was shocked in an excited way. If you recall, Enigma is virtually crime free, and I was actually getting to help solve a major homicide? My first real murder!

"There's something you need to know, Dad. Exhumation is a great idea. There's just one problem."

A scowl warped his features. "I don't want to hear it, Tullah, but go ahead."

"Embalming interferes with most toxicology reports."

He made a sound of disgust. "You're saying exhuming the body is a waste of time?"

"Nuh-uh, not at all. I'm saying the longer she's in the ground the less likely it will be to get conclusive chemical analyses that will point to homicide. George and Wakefield were mighty anxious to be done with the funeral, though, and I'm not sure they'll give permission to dig her up."

Dad tapped a finger on the table. "Make me a copy of what Dr. Delaney sent you. After I leave here, I'll pay Mike Duval a visit. I'm certain once he reads the report he'll give me the necessary paperwork to make it happen."

Judge Michael Duval, Charlie, and my dad are fishing buddies. Their friendship spans over twenty years or longer. The judge, tough on crime, is a reasonable and fair-minded man. As Dad likes to say,

"He'll git 'er done."

He pushed back his chair. "I hate to eat and run, Punkin. You understand."

"I do." I plucked at his sleeve. "Before you go, will you take about five minutes to look at a file I've created? It's important." Directing him to the living room, I didn't want to give him the physical documents. I had it in my mind we'd sit together and discuss the list of suspects and their possible motives. I booted up my laptop and opened the file.

Dad whistled. "How 'bout I come by tomorrow after five. Tiny can hold down the office while I'm here. By that time or before, I'll know where Mike stands on issuing an exhumation order."

He grabbed the pie-taker handle, and I followed him to the door. He said, "Don't cook. I'll go by Charlie's and bring whatever he's prepared for the day."

He stood at the door for a minute. The expression on his face said he had something else on his mind and didn't know if he should tell me or not.

"Okay, Dad, what is it?"

"Earl Redfern is a guest in my cell for the next few days."

"What'd he do this time?"

"Same as always—drunk and disorderly at the Lucky Horseshoe."

"I'm glad Charlie banned Earl from The Whitehorse."

"Here's the thing, Punkin, I want you and Cindi to keep your doors locked at all times." He nodded toward dog and donkey. "And keep them in the house at night. Earl knows Cindi is living out here with you."

I didn't like feeling as if Earl Redfern was holding me captive by long distance. "I've already told her he isn't welcome and what I'd do if she takes him in."

"All the same, I worry about you girls. Keep your weapons loaded, and call me on my special number if he shows up. I'm not saying he will. If he does, don't be nice. All the years of drug and alcohol use has done more than pickle his brain."

"You have my word, Dad. We'll be careful." I gave him a hug and waved when he pulled away.

Back in the kitchen, I cut a slice of pie and carried it to the trailer and knocked on the door. "Hey, Tullah, come in." Cindi held the door wide.

Grinning, I handed her the plate. "I was afraid Dad was going to eat the entire pie. I managed to save you a piece."

I glanced around. "Holi Moli, Cinci, this place is beautiful. You've really captured the beach theme."

A grin widened her face. "Take a seat and close your eyes."

I did as she instructed. One minute I'm hearing the gentle ebb and flow of waves against a beach and seagull mewls, and the next it sounds like a storm crashing against the shore, and then back to the soft relaxing lapping waves. I said, "What a great way to de-stress after a long busy day."

She handed me a small white bag. I lifted my eyebrows. "What's this?"

"Open it." She held her hands together in excitement. "It's not much. You deserve more for being so kind to me."

I reached in and removed a CD of Native American flute music. Tears welled in my eyes, and I swallowed the lump that had risen in my throat. "It will give me many hours of enjoyment. Thank you."

I didn't have the heart to tell Cindi the bad news about her father. I sometimes wonder why good children, young or adult, get stuck with rotten parents.

I walked to the bedroom and back. "You've managed to turn this tin can into an inviting retreat. It makes me think I should consider doing some redecorating." Yet in my soul I knew I'd never remove my mother's paintings from the walls or the small touches she'd added here and there, like the ceramic vases and crocheted doilies with Native American designs she'd created. To do so would be like erasing her from my heart.

"I think your house is perfect the way it is," Cindi said, much to my relief.

I waved the CD in the air. "You've given me the perfect Christmas gift idea for my grandmother. It's really difficult to buy for someone of her age."

Cindi seemed pleased and told me the name of the store where she had purchased it. "Of course, you can always save yourself a trip and order it online."

I assured her that ordering online was the better option. We discussed tomorrow's lineup of appointments, which promised a busy day. As I excused myself and headed to the barn to do some chores, she thanked me for the pie.

I set aside thoughts of Alma and Forest and strolled to the barn. It seemed a shame to waste a pleasant day sitting indoors. I saddled Gandalf, a black-and-white pinto. He was my mother's horse. Maybe that's why he was my favorite. We both needed the exercise, and I had an urge to commune with nature. I tend to be a solitary person. Aloneness doesn't bother me the way it seems to affect some people. Maybe it's my ancestral DNA.

The outside security light shone by the time I returned to the barn. Three hours in the saddle and stiffness had settled in my body. I took extra care currying Gandalf and rubbing down his legs with liniment. Like people, horses get stiff after a long workout, too. Moon and Banjo ambled into the barn and entered their individual stalls. I gave each one a little attention and promised to ride them soon.

I looked forward to a hot leisurely soak in the tub with a chilled glass of scuppernong wine and listening to the CD Cindi had given me. On the way to the house, my phone trilled. I opened the text from Dad.

—*Court order for exhumation approved. Mike notified the funeral director. GT not happy. Bringing Tanti tomorrow.*—

I felt my face brighten. This was good news. I wondered if George Tackett was unhappy because of religious reasons or if he was guilty of murder.

I answered.

—*I'll contact Dr. Delaney Mon. A.M. Okay w/ U if I attend?*—

He responded with a thumbs-up emoji and,

—*go 4 it*—

Continuing toward the house. I deliberated stopping by to tell Cindi about her father and to make sure she locked the doors. Not tonight. Earl was still locked safely in Dad's jail. I decided to invite her for dinner tomorrow and let him relay his concerns. It would be more official coming from a lawman.

I sent another text to Dad.

—inviting Cindi to eat w/ us. U tell her about Earl—

"Hey, Tullah, you're just standing there staring at your phone. Is anything wrong?"

I waved off her concern. "Text from Dad. He and Grandmother are bringing food from Charlie's tomorrow, and you're invited to share."

"That's really nice. Thanks."

Yeah, I thought, we'll fill your belly and then tell you what a rotten a-hole your father is and bid you not-so-sweet dreams. What a rotten thing to do to a friend. "Have a good night."

A few minutes later, I lowered into a tub of hot water filled with salts to soak away potential sore muscles from two days of horseback riding. Taking a healthy sip of wine, I scooted down until the water touched my chin, and closed my eyes. I let my mind go blank and allowed melodic flute music to soothe me.

Chapter Thirteen

My morning started off with a frantic phone call from Talmadge Crandall. His English Mastiff had been bitten by a rattlesnake. It's spring, the weather is warming up, critters are venturing out of their burrows, and snakes are crawling.

Crandall demanded I drive out to his farm. Yes, that's right. He spoke to me like he was a drill sergeant and I was a lowly private.

"Where was he bitten?" I asked.

"On the hind leg."

"Are you certain it's a rattler, Mr. Crandall?"

He snapped. "I killed it. Of course I'm sure."

I apologized for upsetting him. "It's better if you bring your dog to my hospital where I have the proper equipment to treat him, and bring the snake, too."

I had to hold the phone away from my ear to keep him from bursting my eardrum. "You're going to stand around with your thumb up your ass and let Marlo die. I'll sue you, Tullah Holliday. I'll ruin your reputation. You'll never practice anywhere when I get through with you. What kind of vet refuses to make house calls?"

You can't imagine the words that begged to spew out of my mouth. I sucked in a calming breath. "Stop shouting, Mr. Crandall. Your dog needs treatment in a sterile environment. You can stand there wasting time making threats, or you can put the dog in your vehicle and get him here asap, or you can call Dr. Cooper. The choice is yours."

Anger shook me from head to toe when I disconnected the call. The look on Cindi's face expressed my own sentiments. She said, "Can you believe that guy? What is it with rich people anyway?"

"Beats me." I opened the mini-fridge and grabbed a cola to treat my quivering system to a healthy shot of sugar. "He'll call back. He knows it's two hours to Dr. Cooper's versus twenty minutes to here, so this is the better choice. Get the surgery ready."

"You're sure he'll call back?"

I nodded and grinned, held up my fingers and counted, "One...two...three..." The phone rang. "Holliday Veterinarian Clinic, how may I help you?"

Crandall didn't sound as brash when he said, "We're on our way."

Cindi tsked. "Amazing, Tullah. You are my heroine."

Adult male English Mastiffs weigh approximately two hundred pounds. It would be a struggle to get Marlo out of Crandall's vehicle and into the treatment room. For such occasions, I have a gurney. The dog's weight was a plus. With the bite being on the hind leg, it would take a while for the poison to work through his system.

Cindi and I were ready by the time Crandall screeched his truck to a halt in front of my office. We met him with the wheeled stretcher. Thankfully, Crandall had the good sense to place the dog on a blanket, which made pulling him from the bed of the truck to the stretcher easier.

"Mr. Crandall, do you know if the rattler hung on

when it struck or if it scratched the area on Marlo's leg?"

"How the hell should I know? I heard Marlo yelp and then saw the snake coiled. I grabbed a hoe and chopped off its head. Then called you."

I didn't bother to explain as I called over my shoulder, "Help yourself to the coffee. This may take a while."

Cindi administered a mild sedative to calm the dog while I checked the puncture marks on the hindquarter where the fangs had entered. The area had begun to swell.

I said, "It appears the puncture is superficial. Thankfully, it's not a full strike."

Cindi replied, "That means not as much poison, right?"

"Exactly. Still deadly, nonetheless."

Two hours later, after emergency treatment that consisted of an intravenous fluid support, antibiotics, antihistamines, pain management, and antivenin, Marlo was resting well and would live to chase more rabbits.

I left Cindi to clean up while I spoke to Mr. Crandall. His cheeks tinted slightly as I looked him straight in the eyes and addressed him firmly. "We've moved Marlo to our intensive care chamber and will monitor him throughout the night. We'll also keep him here until we're positive he's out of the danger zone. However, he's one lucky dog."

Crandall rocked back and forth on his heels, apparently caught off guard by my next comment. "Dr. Cooper is an excellent veterinarian. In the future, I suggest you take your business to him. I will not allow you or anyone else to threaten or intimidate me into making decisions that do not benefit my patients."

He huffed, "Now see here, Tullah—"

I seriously worked to keep the sarcasm out of my voice. "It's Dr. Holliday, Mr. Crandall. I'll send you the bill after Marlo is released. Now if you'll excuse me, I'm expecting another patient in a few minutes." He looked flabbergasted when I walked to the office door and opened it. The verbal castigation I expected didn't happen. Crandall walked outside without saying a word. Needless to say, I heaved a sigh of relief.

Today proved to be one of those days. We had to shuffle a few appointments when I received a call from an owner that his mare was having difficulty foaling. He was certain the foal was breech. To our surprise, the mare birthed twins, and I was pleased that the spindly-legged babies were up and nursing by the time I left to return to the office.

When five o'clock rolled around, I was ready for a hot shower and clothes that didn't reek of afterbirth and manure. Cindi and I closed up the office, both of us dragging from a nonstop day. "I sure do appreciate the invite to supper, Tullah. I'm starved and too tired to even open a can of soup."

I knew the feeling. "Dad said to expect him around six. That'll give us enough time to clean up and catch our breath. See you in about an hour."

Punctual as always, Dad and Grandmother arrived with River and Rascal as the exuberant welcoming committee, although I suspected River was more interested in the mouthwatering aroma of barbeque coming from the large sacks in Dad's hands than in being patted on the head.

Cindi called hello from the kitchen screen door and

joined the party. I had already set the table. Dad pulled out a couple six-packs of beer and opened bottles all round while we women opened Charlie's signature to-go boxes to reveal honey barbeque, garlic, and parmesan cheese chicken wings, along with potato salad, fried mushrooms, and onion rings.

Seated around the kitchen table, we filled our plates. There's nothing more comforting than good company and yummy food. I was excited to share an idea with Grandmother, and hoped she'd buy into it.

Between chews, I said, "Grandmother, since the newspaper is closing and you're not interested in running for mayor, I have an idea that might interest you."

I selected another chicken wing. Her eyebrows shot up. I said, "Don't give me that look. You might like this. Why not start your own electronic newspaper? Most people read on their electronic devices, so give them a tri-weekly newsletter they can read on their cellphones or computers. You could call it Tanti's Grapevine, or Enigma Online, or some other name. Maybe you can convince a few of the local business owners to purchase ads to offset your cost for internet usage or purchasing special graphics to make the newsletter appealing. It'd be free to the readers, and subscription might be slow at first, but I'm sure over time you'd gather a vast readership. Okay, that's it in a nutshell."

Cindi said, "Oh, Mrs. Crow, it's a brilliant idea."

Dad saluted me with his beer bottle. "We've got one smart cookie, Tanti. A worthy idea you should consider."

Grandmother's face crinkled into a smile as she

lifted her own bottle. "I'm all in. How do I get started?"

The conversation drifted from hashing out different names for Tanti's e-newsletter to the birth of the twin foals, and finishing with Talmadge Crandall's huff and bluster over his dog.

I plopped another fried mushroom into my mouth. "Rude and obnoxious is the only way I can describe Crandall. Honestly, I hope he does take his business to Dr. Cooper."

Dad scowled. He didn't answer immediately. "If I wasn't the sheriff, I'd take him out behind the woodshed and teach him a lesson in politeness."

When Cindi declared it was getting late and she should go, Dad asked her to stay for a few more minutes. A *should I be worried* look covered her face as she eased back into the chair. Dad explained about her father being locked up. "Here's the thing, Cindi. I have to release Earl tomorrow. He knows you're out here, and sooner or later he's gonna show up. He doesn't have a job, and it's my understanding he's sleeping in his truck. He'll want money. My main concern isn't if you decide to give it to him, but for the safety of you girls."

The color drained from Cindi's face. I reached over and clasped her hand. She said, "Sheriff, I'd never bring harm to Tullah. I'll gather my things and leave tonight."

"You will not," I blurted. "We're friends. Friends stick by each other."

Her voice whispered, "Okay." She shifted her focus to Dad. "He's mentally unstable, Sheriff. You saw what he did to my mama before she finally packed up and left. Isn't there a way for you to keep Earl locked up, or sent away as a habitual offender, or even put in a mental hospital? I'm scared...really scared."

I watched Dad's adam's apple working up and down. He'd find a way to put Earl Redfern out of commission. It might hedge a little too close to the unlawful precipice, but it'd still be within the law. He ran his finger around the lip of the bottle, his eyes shifting from me to Cindi. He was speaking to both of us. "The best way for me to keep you safe is for you to keep your doors locked at all times, even when you're at work. At night, whatever you do, don't answer unless it's me, Deputy Goodbody, or Tanti. If Earl does succeed in breaking in, shoot him, or bash him in the head with a baseball bat. It's better he's dead than you. In the meantime, Cindi, I'll do everything within my power to legally put Earl away for more than a couple of days or months. You have my word on that."

Cindi's lips curved into a doubtful smile. She thanked Dad for the dinner, and before saying goodnight, offered to help Grandmother with technical training and setting up the electronic newsletter if she decided to give it a go. Since Earl had not yet been released, Cindi politely declined Dad's offer to escort her to the trailer.

As soon as she left, we briefly discussed how we felt about Cindi's situation. Dad and I filled Grandmother in about the autopsy results. He was then ready to filter through my list of suspects. I retrieved my laptop and opened the file.

"By the way," Dad said, "we're exhuming the casket day after tomorrow. After presenting Wilcox, the funeral director, with the court order, he was more than cooperative about arranging excavation equipment. He's also personally delivering the casket to Lexington.

I've notified Dr. Delaney." He looked at Tanti. "She verified what Tullah said about getting iffy results from Alma's corpse due to the embalming fluids."

It always felt good when Dad complimented me. "We have a small window of opportunity to prove Alma's death is also a homicide. By the way, I have a full appointment schedule for the rest of the week. As much as I'd like, I can't attend the autopsy. Dr. Delaney is the best forensic pathologist there is. If there's any evidence remaining, she'll find it. Also, since there's no telling what Earl might do, there's no way I'd leave Cindi here alone to run the clinic."

Tanti pushed back her chair. "Shame on me for forgetting. We left a box in the truck."

Dad and I were discussing the list of alleged suspects when she returned holding a white box. I recognized Patty Sweet's signature label and cringed.

Tanti's eyes glittered with happy expectation as she opened the package. "Red velvet donuts with cream cheese icing."

Somehow the thought of eating a donut didn't appeal to me. I shifted my glance to Dad. He remained silent. Grandmother bit into the red confection. "What? Why are you looking at me like that?"

"Um, Grandmother, don't get upset, I know you and Patty have known each other your entire lives…" I dreaded telling her what was on my mind.

She brushed a crumb from the side of her mouth. "Out with it. What am I not supposed to get upset over?"

"We have to add Patty to the suspect list. The postmortem showed ground-up pieces of Autumn Crocus leaves inside several partially digested donuts in

Forest's system. That's why we're exhuming Alma's body to see if she was also poisoned. Sort of death-by-donut."

Dad added, "If so, we have a double homicide."

I waited for the explosion of temper. To prove her point, Grandmother swallowed the bite and stuffed the remainder of the donut into her mouth. I forced myself not to laugh at her chipmunk cheeks while she struggled not to choke. I pushed the unfinished bottle of beer toward her, which caused her to grimace when she washed down the remains of the dessert.

She slammed the bottle to the table. Oh, here it comes. Dad and I readied ourselves. She spoke through gritted teeth. "I don't give a rat's patootie if a flower was the cause of death to two very deserving people. Patty Sweet did not...let me repeat...*did not* murder anyone. First and foremost, Alma was Patty's best customer. Tell me why she would kill the hand that kept her cash register full? As for Forest, I have no explanation."

She drew a breath and continued, "How did the flower petals get in the batter? All the ladies who work for Patty have been with her since she opened the shop. They're not exactly the apple dumpling gang. In our circle, we poke fun about our dead libidos. None of us would have any reason to kill Forest or Alma."

Dad narrowed his eyes. "Simmer down, Tanti. All we're doing here is speculating. From your years as a crime reporter, you know the law has to look at every potential suspect. It's nothing personal against Patty."

"I know, Henry. Of course, you're right." Grandmother waved an age-spotted hand. "Patty is a grandmother. She's done so much for this community.

142

She and I are the same age. What possible motive would she have for committing murder?"

My grandmother suddenly looked tired. She had fallen into a glum silence. Maybe inviting her to sit in on this discussion wasn't a good idea.

"If it'll make you feel any better, Talmadge Crandall, Beverly Rakestraw, Evelyn March and Denver, even Mr. Tackett and Wakefield made this list, too," I told her.

I went on to relate what Mrs. Frezoli told me about overhearing Wakefield threaten to take a bat to his mother. "That's probably the reason he stutters. With his history of a nervous breakdown, do you suppose his mother pushed him over the edge? If he did kill her, can't he plead insanity?"

Dad said, "If he did, yes, a judge will consider Wakefield's mental state."

Grandmother rubbed her temples. "Poor George. I never understood why he stayed with Alma. He had to know he was the secret laughingstock of the town." She continued, "Everyone you named had better reasons than Patty."

I did a recap of possible motives for each person on the list. "At the rally, Crandall threatened to wring Alma's neck."

Dad reiterated, "He was upset over Alma's lustful stallion. We have to consider that Talmadge was blowing off steam. The question is what beef did he have with Forest?"

"I can answer that." Tanti brightened. "Bambi Crandall is barely out of her twenties. Talmadge is in his sixties. It's not what's inside Talmadge's pants that keeps her satisfied, but more likely her healthy monthly allowance. Sources say he caught Bambi and Forest doing the ol' bump and grind. It's my understanding Talmadge threatened to geld Forest, which probably put the fear of God in him."

"How come I didn't know about that?" Dad wanted to know.

Tanti shrugged. "Apparently no charges were pressed."

We discussed the remaining names on the list and were about to call it a night when Grandmother snapped her fingers. "Councilwoman Sue West had a personal grudge against Alma. Sue's husband and Alma had a thing going. She threatened to divorce her husband and then got in Alma's face and made some serious threats."

Dad asked, "Is this gossip or fact?"

Grandmother gazed wistfully at the box of donuts. "Maybe a little bit of both. Alma's secretary told someone who told someone else. You know how it goes."

Dad and I both agreed. He asked Grandmother the date of the last print edition of the newspaper. When she replied Easter Sunday, he said, "In this Friday's edition, I want you to print a story stating the pathology report for Forest came back homicide and the reason for exhuming Alma's body is suspected homicide. Don't print anything about cause of death. Whoever the murderer is, I want that person to think we know more than we do."

"Dad, when will Forest's body be released?"

"The funeral director is bringing it back with him when he returns from delivering Alma's corpse. I've already notified Sam and Beverly so they can prepare a

144

memorial service."

Grandmother sighed when she tossed the remaining three donuts into the trash. "If I were a betting person, I'd put my money on Beverly Rakestraw, and she had good cause. Apparently, Forest couldn't seem to keep his pants zipped. Still, infidelity is never a justifiable reason for murder."

I handed Dad copies of the file. He cautioned me to stay alert, and I promised. I wrapped my arms around Grandmother and whispered, "I'm sorry for making you angry."

She kissed me on the cheek. "It's the situation that made me angry. Not you." She hesitated. "I'd almost forgotten. There's another name to add."

Dad and I each gave Grandmother an incredulous look. Together we said, "Who?"

Dad quirked his mouth to one side. "Is this more gossip?"

"Not exactly." Grandmother's voice was hushed as if the walls were listening. "I went to church to do my weekly confession, and before I went inside the confessional, I heard someone sobbing. It was Luanne. I must have caught her at a really bad time, because you know what a sourpuss she always is." Grandmother heaved a dejected sigh. "I asked if I could be of comfort, and that's when she told me about her and Forest."

I nearly choked. "Luanne Sterns...the priest's sister...that Luanne?"

Grandmother nodded. "Luanne said that in a weak moment she allowed Forest to visit her, and on more than one occasion, and sometimes they'd have a secret rendezvous at a secret location."

"Grandmother, she isn't even remotely attractive. What would entice Forest to sleep with her?"

"Only he knows that, and he's dead. Anyhow, apparently Forest said all the right things about loving her and them having a future together, and made a bunch of false promises, all to get inside her bloomers, and then he laughed at her, called her ugly, and said he bedded her because she was always mooning over him and he felt sorry for her. She needed to confess her sins but couldn't, at least not to her brother. So, in her moment of desperation, I became the substitute." Tanti glanced around. "Here's the thing, after spilling her beans, Luanne got bull-stompin' mad, and the things she threatened to do to Forest—well, let's just say they were pretty drastic. Of course, I didn't take any of it seriously. She was a woman scorned and blowing off steam."

Dad blew out a whistle. "Might as well add Sue West and Luanne Sterns to the list, Tullah." He pinched the bridge of his nose. "I didn't realize Enigma had become such a den of iniquity."

Chapter Fourteen

The *Gazette*'s Friday morning front page headlines elicited a whistle when I read aloud, "Rakestraw Death Ruled a Homicide."

"Wow," Cindi exclaimed, an avid look of interest on her face. "That's certainly an attention-getter." She filled our mugs with freshly brewed coffee and settled in the swivel office chair. "We have time before our first appointment. Read it out loud."

I blew on the steaming liquid and drew a careful sip before setting my mug on the desk. I leaned back in my chair and read, "The Lexington Director of Pathology's office has officially ruled Forest Rakestraw's death a homicide. Rakestraw's body was found in a horse stall at his Make My Day Horse Farm. As foul play was not suspected, the initial cause of death was attributed to a heart attack. However, postmortem results proved otherwise.

"Six days prior, on March 15th, Dr. Paul Ritter declared cardiac arrest as the official cause of Mayor Alma Tackett's death. At the request of the mayor's immediate next of kin, no autopsy was performed. Due to the close proximity of the two deaths, Sheriff Henry Holliday states that in his opinion there is a suspected link in Rakestraw's and Tackett's demises. To support his theory, Sheriff Holliday obtained a court order to exhume the remains of Mayor Tackett. Exhumation will begin Saturday. The Wilcox funeral director will deliver the remains to the pathology laboratory in Lexington immediately following. The exact cause of Rakestraw's death is being withheld until Tackett's postmortem report is released. Rakestraw's wife and father invite friends and family to attend a viewing at the Wilcox Funeral Home, Tuesday from 10:00 a.m. to 11:00 a.m. Graveside services will be held at 12:30 p.m. at the Cedar Hill Cemetery. A catered luncheon will follow at the home of Mrs. Beverly Rakestraw."

I lowered the newspaper. "Tuesday, we'll put a note on the office door stating we're closed to attend a funeral."

"Are we closing for the entire day?"

I gave Cindi's question some thought. "I suppose we could open around three."

Cindi rose from the chair. "Our first appointment just arrived. How about I open at three and you stay after the funeral and do a little eavesdropping?"

I looked out the window to see a truck pulling in and almost agreed to accept her offer. "Being here alone probably isn't a good idea. We promised my dad we'd be careful. We'll close for the entire day. Our clients will understand. "

"We'll have patients until five o'clock, so I'll be okay. Tullah, I hate being on constant alert. Heck, Earl might never show up. It's not fair that he has us looking over our shoulders and jumping at shadows."

"I totally agree. Earl is practically holding us prisoner, and I don't like the feeling. Still, as Grandmother always says, 'It's better to err on the side of caution.' He'll mess up again, and when he does my dad will nail him. No if, ands, or buts. We're closing.

You can ride in with me."

Cindi offered a dejected sigh. She stood and greeted our client and patient. "G'morning."

It seemed every person who walked through the office door had comments and questions about the news article.

We were between patient visits. Cindi took advantage of the break to wolf down a sandwich while I cleaned cages. She shouted, "Tullah, you're not going to believe this."

I dumped my rubber gloves in the disposal can and rushed to the office. "Believe what?"

"Look." She pointed to a property-for-sale notice in the *Gazette*'s classified ads.

My jaw dropped when I read the notice. "They're selling the Freckled Fanny Farm for over a million dollars?"

"Tullah, it's only been a little over a week since Mayor Tackett died. Don't you think putting the horse farm up for sale this soon is a little suspicious?"

I grabbed a cola and my peanut butter-and-banana sandwich from the fridge. Between sips and chews, I said, "It certainly does. Then again, it takes a lot of money to run a horse farm. Maybe Alma lived beyond their financial means and they need the money." I thought for a moment. "On second thought, if I were in Mr. Tackett's and Wakefield's shoes, I might want to escape from a town that had always silently pitied me."

Cindi wadded her napkin and tossed it and the empty bottle in the trash. "I suppose you're right." She brightened. "Did you see your grandmother's editorial?" She folded back the paper and handed it to me.

By the time I finished reading, my face hurt from grinning. Grandmother's editorial addressed the newspaper's closing. She had thanked the subscribers for their years of loyalty and business owners for their support. She had also explained the advantages of reading and advertising online and invited readers to subscribe to the *Enigma Bulletin* and listed the email link. I lifted my phone from my back pocket and typed in the link address. "I hope I'm Grandmother's first subscriber."

Cindi did likewise. "She is an inspiration."

By the time we closed the office, I felt like I had developed lockjaw from answering questions about the newspaper article. After closing and while Cindi cleaned and straightened the office, I tended my animals and mucked out stalls. We left the barn at the same time, and I walked with her as far as the trailer. "Lock the doors."

The sound of a car drew our attention to the driveway. I sighed. "This must be an emergency and whoever it is didn't have time to call. We'd better head back to the barn."

As soon as the silver coupe came into view, I said, "Isn't that Wakefield's car?"

She shaded her eyes against the evening sun. "I believe so. Maybe his Jack Russell is sick."

I laughed. "Or maybe he wants the dog neutered. Remember how upset Luanne Sterns was over Gigi's pregnancy?"

"Look, he's pulling in front of your house." She touched my arm. "I don't think you should let him in."

Sure enough, Wakefield stepped out of the car. He seemed to hesitate, and then he spotted me and waved as if beckoning me toward the house. "Cindi, I have a strange feeling. It may be nothing, but there's no reason for him to visit me."

"Maybe you should call your dad."

I smiled. "Don't be an alarmist. If push comes to shove, I can handle Wakefield. You just make sure you lock your doors. See you tomorrow."

"Okay, I'm giving you fifteen minutes and then I'm coming to check on you."

I trudged to the front of the house. "Hi, Wakefield, what brings you out here?"

"I-I n-need to t-talk to you." Between stutters he managed to say it was important.

"It's a nice evening. Do you mind if we sit on the porch?" I indicated one of the rocking chairs, prayed he'd accept the invitation, and was thankful when he sat.

"Make yourself comfortable. I'll bring us a beer, or would ice tea suit you better?"

"B-beer w-would be n-nice."

I was glad he said beer, and hoped a little alcohol would help stem his stuttering. In the kitchen, I created a cheese-and-cracker plate, and added a handful of grapes. I used my toe to open the screen door and set the plate on a table. Wakefield accepted the bottle, and to my surprised chugged down half the beer in a long gulp. He expelled what might have been a sigh of relief.

"Wakefield," I said, "I know you can't help stuttering, but I need to understand what it is you have on your mind. If you feel yourself getting upset, just stop, take a deep breath and blow it out slowly." Otherwise, I feared we'd be here all night with me trying to decipher his words.

He nodded and lifted the newspaper that lay on his lap. Uh-oh, I thought. Maybe this isn't going to be so good.

"T-tullah, p-eople—"

I held up my hand. "Close your eyes. Inhale deeply and exhale slowly."

He obeyed, and began again. He thumped the article about Forest and his mother. "Tullah, people are gonna think I k-killed my mother because they think I'm…" He pointed to his head and circled his finger to indicate crazy. "They call me W-wacky T-tacky."

As much as I wanted to give him a touch of reassurance, I didn't. "It's wrong of people to make such assumptions." I wanted to ask if he had killed his mother, but resisted.

In one long swallow, he finished off the beer and set the bottle on the table. He inhaled and exhaled. "She was nasty to George and mean to me. I don't know why she d-didn't like me. I hated her, too. Sometimes, I hated her so much that I wanted to bash her head in. But I'm too much of a c-coward."

He rocked back and forth as if trying to calm himself. I waited.

He reached around to his back pocket. I tensed until my spine hurt, and sighed with relief when he removed a yellowed envelope. He held it forward. "O-open it."

It was addressed to Alma Lewinger. Doubt and curiosity warred with each other as I unfolded the document. At first, I quickly scanned, then went back and slowly read. This was Wakefield's birth certificate. I lifted my eyes. His face was scrunched into a painful frown. I continued to read. "You were born in

Wakefield, Kentucky at Wakefield Memorial Hospital."

He barked a scurrilous laugh. "Yeah, ain't it a hoot. I'm named after a town. Keep on reading for the *big* surprise."

Mother was listed as Alma Ann Lewinger. I skimmed past day and time of birth, expecting to read George Tackett as the father. Holi Moli! Was I ever wrong. I almost choked. This couldn't be right. My fingers moved across the raised seal. I was holding the official birth certificate—not a copy.

Wakefield said, "Yeah, I had the same reaction. S-she didn't even have the decency to name me after my real f-father."

"Does George know?"

Wakefield nodded. "Since before I was born."

"How long have you known?"

"R-right after the f-funeral. I was cleaning out her closets and going through her p-papers. I found it in a locked b-box. I asked George. I always wondered why he n-never let me call him D-dad. I asked if h-he killed her. I thought maybe he did and that's why he didn't want an autopsy done. He told me the whole story. S-she told him up front that James March was my f-father, and that he was married. She said her father would disown her and cut off all the money if he found out she was having an illegitimate child. George comes from a middle-class family. He didn't know why she picked him but figured what the heck, he was marrying into money. Only he didn't know his life would become a living hell."

"Why didn't he divorce her?"

"M-money, what else." Tears welled in Wakefield's eyes and just as quickly he brushed them away. "C-could I have another b-beer?"

A plethora of emotions filled me as I went inside to the kitchen. Why had Wakefield brought this to me? I mean, it's not like we're friends, because he's several years older in chronological years—maybe not in maturity. I opened a beer and a cola and returned to the porch.

"Wakefield, why did you bring this to me?"

He fortified himself with a long swallow. "M-maybe Mrs. M-march murdered my m-mother. W-will you go with me to see her?" He seemed nervous, which increased the stuttering. I barely understood when he said he was afraid of what she or Denver might do to him if he showed up.

"Did you ask George to go with you?"

Wakefield nodded. He spread his hands wide. He inhaled and blew out slowly. "H-he said now that she's dead he's only concerned about selling the farm and living his own l-life."

"What about you? Is he splitting the money with you?" And then I said, "Did Alma leave a will?"

He nodded but couldn't seem to get the details out. I felt sorry and told him as long as he inherited something, the rest was none of my business. I leaned forward in the rocker and studied Wakefield's face. There really wasn't a reason why I should have noticed a resemblance between the two men. The kids had tormented Wakefield to the point that Alma had enrolled him in boarding school, and Denver was seven years older than me. But now I could see it—Denver March and Wakefield Tackett were definitely brothers.

"Wakefield," I said, "if you suspect Mrs. March or Denver of killing your mother, then neither of us should put ourselves in harm's way. I suggest we tell my dad about this. He'll go with us. What do you say?"

"When?"

I did mental calculations. The exhumation would take place the next day. Forest's memorial and the funeral would be Monday. "What about Sunday?"

For a moment he looked like an animal caught in a trap. "S-sure."

"Do you mind if I make a copy of the birth certificate?"

He stared at me long and hard. With an acquiescing tilt of his chin, he stood. "You are very smart, Tullah. I hated my mother but I also loved her. She didn't deserve to be murdered, if she was."

I used my phone to snap a picture of the certificate, which I carried with me to my office while I printed a copy. I assured Wakefield that if his mother was the victim of a homicide, my dad would use all his skills to find the murderer and bring that person to justice, and I would let him know if my dad was available to accompany us to the March farm on Sunday.

I hoped Wakefield hadn't noticed that I kept the original copy with the raised seal and placed the copy in the envelope. I could always plead innocence if he discovered the difference. My rationale was that in his current mental state he might change his mind about contacting Evelyn and Denver March. And the Marches could always say a copy of the birth certificate was a fake.

Anxious to contact my dad, I patiently waited until Wakefield drove out of sight. I punched in the numbers on Dad's non-emergency line. He answered in a jovial voice. "Hello, Punkin, what's on your mind?"

Unable to contain my excitement, I blurted, "Dad, Wakefield Tackett and Denver March are half-brothers."

"Whoa...whoa, we must have a bad connection. I thought I heard you say—"

"You did." I went on to explain in detail about the surprise visit and the birth certificate. "This makes my blood boil. After the way he's been treated all these years, it's a wonder Wakefield's not loonier than he is. And if Alma's death is ruled a homicide, Wakefield is afraid he'll be blamed, and—get this—he suspects the *Marches* as prime candidates and plans to confront them. I convinced him to let you handle this. Dad, he's more agitated than usual, and I'm afraid of what he might do. I know you're busy with the exhumation crew tomorrow morning, but what about after they've finished?"

Dad blew out a long whistle. "You're talking a mile a minute. Slow down. I'm having trouble wrapping my head about this news. I knew James March, even played golf with him on occasion. For all practical purposes, he was an ordinary guy, devoted to his family."

I harrumphed. "It appears looks were deceiving."

Dad agreed. He said, "Saturday's out. The crew is scheduled to arrive at the crack of dawn."

"Why so early?"

"To avoid curiosity seekers. Once the casket is brought up and loaded into the ambulance, Mr. Wilcox will leave immediately to deliver the remains to the pathology lab in Lexington. Another reason for the early hour is the weather report states a storm is blowing in with predicted hail by midmorning, to last into late afternoon. I think Wakefield is smart enough to stay indoors until Sunday."

"I agree. He's living at the rental house in town until he's finished cleaning out the closets and packing up his mother's belongings. That's how he found the birth certificate. In his present state of mind, it's probably better if I'm with you when you pick him up. I'll drive to town. We can meet Grandmother for breakfast."

"Sounds fine, Punkin. I don't need to caution you to keep this under your hat until after we meet with Evelyn and Denver."

"Mum's the word." Another thought occurred to me. "Dad, did you see the real estate ad in this morning's paper listing the Freckled Fanny Farm for sale?"

He muttered. "Haven't had time."

The telltale squeak of his office chair reached my ear, and I imagined him leaning back and propping his boots on top of his desk. "You really should fix that."

He drawled, "Along with a half-dozen other repairs needing attention. I'll get around to them, eventually. See you Sunday."

I dashed up the stairs and took a brief shower. The weather had warmed enough that I pulled on a pair of shorty pajamas. Back in the kitchen, I heated the leftover chicken wings, boiled two ears of corn on the cob, slathered them in butter, grabbed a cola, and got comfy in my recliner. I switched on the local news and was surprised to see my dad being interviewed about Forest's death and the exhumation of Alma's remains. My heart swelled with pride. Not only was my dad movie-star handsome, he was the epitome of professionalism and exceptionally good at his job.

Before retiring for the night, I opened the file on my laptop and added the birth certificate information to my list, cross-referencing it to Denver and his mother. I lay in bed, staring at the ceiling, recalling Denver's revelation about his father not being present at his birth. Could it be possible that Denver or his mother—or both—had conspired to bump off Alma? If so, for what reason? Revenge? No, that wasn't logical. Why wait thirty years to seek retribution? Or maybe she simply died of a heart attack.

Chapter Fifteen

Saturday morning arrived dark and overcast. I knocked on Cindi's door to ask if she'd heard the weather report. She assured me she wasn't afraid. I said, "It might sound like a war zone, with hail pounding this metal trailer."

She pointed to a pair of earbuds. "I plan to drown out the noise with music, a new romance novel, a bag of potato chips, and ginger ale. Don't worry. I'll be fine."

I waved goodbye and sprinted to the barn to secure my horses in their stalls. I found a couple pieces of plywood and hammered them in place to protect the office windows. I wondered how the excavation went. Glancing at my watch, I calculated that Mr. Wilcox should be on his way to Lexington by that time, and said a little prayer for his safety.

Storm clouds rolled in. River and Rascal raced me back to the house. I had barely made it inside when hail the size of chicken eggs began to fall. My nervous pets tried to seek comfort in my lap, which isn't large enough for either a mini-donkey or a large dog, let alone both.

Twenty minutes of a constant barrage of ice balls seemed like an eternity. I switched on the news and got weather updates predicting damaging winds and possible tornadoes. Don't get me wrong—I'm not easily frightened. It was when the power went out that an itchy chill prickled my scalp. If there was ever a perfect time for Earl Redfern to show up, it would be now.

I groped my way to the hall closet. Wanting to save the battery on my phone, I briefly used the flashlight to spot a plastic bag filled with an assortment of candles, extra batteries, and two battery-powered lanterns. I secured the front and back doors, grabbed a handful of snacks, beckoned the animals to follow me, and sought refuge in my bedroom.

I set a lantern on the night stand and opened the drawer. I checked the clip of my Sig Sauer and slipped the revolver under my pillow. Concerned about the wind and Cindi's safety, I phoned her. "You okay?"

"Yes, the trailer is tied down tight. It's not even swaying. I have a lantern, extra batteries, and the doors are locked." She hesitated. "Do you think Earl will show up on a day like this?"

I had no idea what her errant father might do, and tried to set her at ease. "Earl may be crazy, but I don't think even he's stupid enough to brave this storm. If you'd feel safer, bundle up and come to the house. I'll wait for you at the kitchen door."

"In this raging wind, I'm not sure I can make it to the house. I'll hang tight here."

We disconnected, and I grabbed *Murder in the Mist*, the latest mystery novel on my night stand. I plumped the pillows and tried to relax against the headboard. Thunder vibrated the house, and the wind howled like a wounded animal. The sound was eerily disconcerting.

My phone rang. It was my grandmother asking if I

was okay. I was glad she called. I talked to her long enough to calm my nerves and was careful not to mention Wakefield's birth certificate or the creepy feeling I had about Earl. We discussed Dad's television interview. She mentioned that she had risen early to take pictures of the exhumation to use as soon as the pathology lab released its report. It was true there was a murderer living among us in Enigma.

Although I had the misfortune of finding both bodies, the murders had nothing to do with me. As far as the murderer was concerned, I knew nothing, and there was no reason to believe he or she was after me.

But the feeling of being observed refused to leave. I rose from the bed and peered through the venetian blind slats. The swaying trees reminded me of poofy-headed bodies doing a macabre dance.

Finally, after telling myself I was being ridiculous, I carried the lantern downstairs and rummaged in the pantry for a bag of chips, grabbed a cola, holed up in my bedroom, and opened the book.

Reading about a lunatic killing a woman in coastal Maine didn't relax me. The time passed, somehow. I wondered if Dad and Deputy Goodbody had evenings where they felt as if shadows were watching them.

Finishing the last chapter and setting the book aside, I was able to sleep in fits and starts.

****

I awoke to a rainy Sunday morning. My first priority was to check on my horses. Dressed for town and wearing a raincoat and boots, I sloshed through the mud. Cindi opened the trailer door and asked if I needed help. I waved her off, telling her I was headed to town, then continued to the barn. The horses were skittish after last night's storm and eager to leave their stalls. I left the boards on the office windows.

When I arrived at the sheriff's office, Dad asked how I'd fared the night. After my mother's death, I was often besieged with nightmares. I almost told him I'd sat up expecting the bogey man. But I didn't want him thinking of me as a fearful, trembly little girl. Instead I suggested we not keep Grandmother waiting. After a sparse supper, I looked forward to a stack of blueberry pancakes and several cups of her special coffee. When I say special, it's because she brews it in an old-fashioned, blue-speckled coffeepot and then drops a fresh eggshell into the coffee. According to Grandmother, the eggshell removes the acidic taste and creates a mellow flavor.

I asked if she'd heard from Uma, and suggested we drive to Lexington to spend Easter with her. Grandmother agreed as she filled my plate. We discussed going to Forest's wake and funeral.

She asked, "How long will it take to get the pathology report?"

Between chews, I said, "Dr. Delaney knows the importance of the case. Hopefully, less than a week."

As I helped her load the dishwasher, she said, "By the way, what are the two of you up to?"

Dad intervened. "Tullah and I haven't had any father-daughter time in a while." He grabbed his hat and motioned toward the door. "We're going for a ride in the country. Might even look over a couple of horses to add to her collection."

I'm not completely sure he convinced Grandmother of our total innocence. Sundays are usually her crossword puzzle days, so thankfully she didn't invite herself to go along.

On the drive to the rental house I said, "Dad, if a person tells another person something in confidence, but that person thinks it might be relevant to a possible murder case, should said person break their promise and reveal the secret to the sheriff?"

Dad gave me one of his looks. I half expected a rebuff. "Tullah, you are just like your mother and grandmother. You talk half way round your tongue and get nowhere when it'd be just as easy to say exactly what you mean."

He tapped the steering wheel. "In a simple word—yes." He pulled into the rental house's driveway. "Whatever it is on your mind will need to wait."

I hadn't expected to see Wakefield sitting on the step waiting for us. Actually, I'd anticipated he might chicken out.

I opened the door and waved him to the front passenger side while I climbed into the back seat. Conversation was sparse.

Wakefield turned sideways so he could face Dad and also look at me. He spoke matter-of-factly. "How do I go about changing my n-name?"

Dad glanced at me in the rearview mirror. I wondered if we were on the same track with our thinking. Did Wakefield kill his mother, and was he trying to throw us off track by accusing the Marches before he changed his name and disappeared?

Dad said, "Go to the clerk of the court's office, pick up the change-of-name forms, and pay the filing fee. Judge Duval will review the forms and grant the name change."

"Why do you want to change your name?" I asked.

He twisted more to frown at me. "G-george isn't my father, and how would you like people calling you W-wacky T-t-tacky?"

"Hmm, I see your point. Have you decided on a new name?"

"In the B-bible, David slew the g-giant. I want a s-strong name." Without stuttering he said, "James David March."

I said quietly, "James after your father."

"Yes."

I thought about Alma and wondered if she had died at the hands of someone she trusted. Her husband or her son?

We had deliberately not notified the Marches of our visit. Sometimes the element of surprise gets the most honest reactions. As we pulled onto the March property, I glanced around. I'm always thrilled at the sight of horses grazing in a green pasture. This morning was no exception. It was a relief, too, to see Denver's truck and Mrs. March's town car parked under the carport with a horse weathervane on top of the cupola. I have to admit, my heart was still racing a mile a minute, though.

We followed Dad up the manicured walk to the wide veranda with its craftsman-style columns wrapped with tumbled stone. He stepped forward and buzzed the doorbell several times. Mrs. March eventually opened the door. She was a woman in her middle fifties, slender, remarkably well groomed, and dressed in white slacks and a lavender silk blouse.

"Sheriff Holliday, to what do I owe the—" Her voice trailed off when she spotted Wakefield. "Why is *he* here?"

From somewhere in the house, Denver called, "Who is it, Mother?"

Dad spoke succinctly, "I'm here on official business, Mrs. March. May we come in?"

She raised her voice to answer her son. "It's Sheriff Holliday, and he's brought…" It was as if she searched for the correct words. "He's brought his daughter and Wakefield Tackett." She ground out his name.

She held the door wide and invited us inside. We followed her to a screened-in sitting porch. A ceiling fan oscillated, making a pleasant breeze. She motioned for us to sit. Plump cushions with horse patterns filled wicker chairs.

Denver hustled to the porch. He stood for a moment before pulling a chair next to where his mother sat. "Is there a problem, Sheriff?"

I glanced from him to Wakefield. The two men could definitely pass for brothers except that Wakefield had blond hair and Denver's hair was a light brown. Both combed their hair to the left side. Both had brown eyes. Both had a cleft chin and heavy jowls. How could Mrs. March not see the strong resemblance?

Dad sat straight, his face serious, and said, "Denver, Mrs. March, our visit is both personal and business. Wakefield requested we accompany him here today because he has uncovered an important document that may interest you."

Denver said, "I don't see how a document of his concerns Mother and me. We have no dealings with the Tacketts."

He was lying, of course. Had he forgotten the burdensome secret he had shared with me? Deep in thought, I almost missed Dad saying, "Wakefield, why don't you explain to Mrs. March what you found."

Wakefield cleared his throat. He began but couldn't get the words out. He gave an exasperated growl. "T-tullah, p-please." His eyes pleaded with me.

I removed the envelope from my purse. "Wakefield found this when he was going through his mother's personal belongings." I leaned forward and handed it to Mrs. March. "I believe you will find the contents—interesting."

She removed the certificate and unfolded it. At first she appeared mystified, and then much to our surprise she ripped the page in half and tossed it at Wakefield. Her breasts heaved, and rage filled her voice. "Even in death that…that witch continues to bedevil me." She pointed a finger at my father and screamed, "Get this illegitimate mongrel out of my house and off my property."

Denver bent forward in his chair, picked up the torn document and placed the two pieces together. His eyes widened in disbelief as he read. I was glad the original certificate was safe inside another envelope tucked inside my purse. He shook his head as he stared, incredulous, at Wakefield. "If this birth certificate is genuine, then my father was your father, and we were born on the same day."

Mrs. March screeched, "I always suspected the reason he wasn't at the hospital with me was because he was with *her*." She seemed to rally her emotions. "I don't know why you brought this to me, but hear me loud and clear. I owe you nothing, and from me you will get nothing. Your wicked mother stole everything from me and my son."

Accusation rode heavy on Denver's voice. "I

always wondered why Father missed almost all of my birthdays. Maybe it's because he was with you and your mother."

The pain in Wakefield's face was unbearable. Tears leaked from his eyes. He tried to speak. I laid my hand on his arm and said, "Take your time. Inhale, then exhale."

He did. "At l-least you got his name. W-when he visited me at school, I only knew him as Uncle James. A-all those years I thought h-he was my m-mother's brother." He paused as if calming himself, debating whether to say it or not. He looked at me and I nodded. His voice rasped, "D-did you kill my mother?"

Before any of us could react, Mrs. March stood and slapped Wakefield so hard it sounded like a gunshot. Dad sprang to his feet and grabbed her wrist before she could attack again. He led her back to her chair and ordered her to sit down. "It's a reasonable question, Mrs. March. Answer it."

Denver rose from his seat and placed his arm around her shoulders. "Mother?"

She heaved a sigh. Rage still shone in her eyes. "I hated...hated...*hated* Alma Tackett. I'm glad she's dead and may she rot in hell. First she stole my husband, and as if that wasn't enough, he was with her when the car crashed. After his death, she had the audacity to move to Enigma and buy the farm next to ours." Anger caused her to gasp for breath. "She purchased that ugly Gypsy Vanner stallion and allowed it—do you hear me?—*allowed* it to get out. Denver constantly had to catch the animal to keep it away from our mares." She cut a mean eye toward me. "And Tullah, you know what happened to my favorite mare.

Even more reason for me to detest Alma."

She clasped her trembling hands together in an effort to calm herself. "I was in Lexington on a buying trip when Alma died. I can't tell you how many times I dreamed of killing her, but she died of a heart attack, so why are you asking me this question? Why don't you ask wacky-tacky if he killed her?"

I wondered if Evelyn March was telling the truth. I raised my eyebrows slightly, and Denver lowered his eyes, flushing red. I had to force myself to stay seated. I gripped my hands together, willing them to be still. "Mrs. March, you cannot blame Wakefield for the problems in your marriage. He didn't ask to be the product of infidelity. In more ways than one, he has suffered the most. He's always known George wasn't his father. He's had to live with the knowledge that he is illegitimate, and then he was shipped off to boarding school." I said softly, "Denver, your mother says Alma took everything from you. She didn't take away the most precious gift of all—your mother's nurturing love. That's one hundred percent more than Wakefield has ever known."

Thunder rumbled in the distance. Clouds bunched together, and a light mist grayed the yard and the pastures. Maybe it was the low barometric pressure, or maybe it was the intense tension that brought on my headache. I massaged my temples and longed for an ice-cold cola.

Denver spread the two torn pieces of paper together on a coffee table. He drew a deep breath. It looked as if he were trying to conjure a smile. "I'm sorry, Wakefield…"

Evelyn March shrilled. "No, you will not

apologize—"

Denver sharply admonished, "Be quiet, Mother." He seemed very sad as he looked at Wakefield. "This piece of paper doesn't prove anything. Your mother seemed to delight in finding ways to torment my mother. Who's to say Alma didn't simply name my dad as the father? The person filling out the birth certificate wouldn't know any different."

I patted my purse. "I anticipated your reactions would be just as you've demonstrated. The original with the raised seal is in here, where it will safely remain. I printed that copy from my copy machine."

Denver nodded as he smoothed the two torn pieces. "So what? I stand by what I just said." He turned to my dad. "Sheriff, I will attest that my mother was in Lexington the day Alma died. You can also check with the buyers she visited." He stood and approached Wakefield and held out his hand. Wakefield also stood. He accepted Denver's olive branch. Denver said, "What happened to us isn't fair. I don't know how to make it right, but I'd like to get to know you, if you're willing."

"No, Denver. I forbid it! I will not have him in my house."

A miserable smile covered Denver's face. "In many ways, my life and Wakefield's have paralleled. Yes, Mother, you loved me, but you've done everything in your power to keep me weak, to keep me tied to you, and you've never stopped reminding me that this is your house, your horses, your farm. I appreciate that you've worked hard to become a success. It's almost like you were constantly trying to prove to Alma that you were better than she…and, like you've hated me because I remind you of my—perhaps our—father." He pointed to Wakefield. "I'm sorry for you, Mother."

Although a wealth of pain hid behind his words, I silently applauded Denver for acting like a man and standing up for himself.

To my surprise, Wakefield said, with barely a stutter, "When the Freckled Fanny Farm sells and I get my share of the profit, I plan to buy a travel trailer and visit every state. Mrs. March, you won't ever need to worry about seeing me again. I want nothing from you or Denver, except t-to say that James Denver March is listed on the b-birth certificate as my father. I deserve to have part of his name. So I'm p-petitioning the court to change my name to James David March."

It was as if Evelyn March had silently signaled it was time for us to leave. She said, "And I'm telling you that I don't give a tinker's damn what is printed on that…that certificate. Wakefield Tackett, you are not related to *my* son, and you have no right to *his* father's name."

Dad appeared on the verge of standing. Wakefield slouched deeper into his chair. He shook his head slightly. His eyes met mine as if pleading. Pleading for what? I had no idea…to prove that he and Denver shared the same father? This entire situation was clearly out of my league. I had to think of *something*. Ideas clanged around inside my head until I inadvertently blurted, "DNA."

All attention shifted toward me. Mrs. March's eyes narrowed to a victorious smirk. "You are clearly grasping at straws, Tullah. My husband died fifteen years ago. His DNA died with him."

"Oh, but you're wrong, Mrs. March. DNA testing has advanced over the years until it's now possible to carry out a paternity test using samples from family members that have genes common to those of the alleged father. Such DNA relationship testing can now legally be used to determine paternity, and is carried out on suspected siblings. The results of these tests can be used to determine whether or not Denver and Wakefield share a common father."

"T-tullah, you are a g-genius."

I swear, Mrs. March actually growled. She curled her hands into fists. "You are *not* suggesting that Denver submit to a DNA test, are you? No, I won't hear of it."

"Mother, I'm over thirty years old and can clearly decide for myself." Denver shoved his hands into his pockets, rocking back on his heels. "Tullah, where does one go for such a test?"

"I'm fairly certain Dr. Gannon or one of the doctors at the hospital can accommodate you. Explain to him you would like to rush the results."

He gave his mother an apologetic shrug. "I play golf with Richard Gannon. I'll phone him and set up an appointment for tomorrow morning. Wakefield, meet me at his office. Eight sharp. The sooner we get this nonsense cleared up, the sooner we can get on with our lives."

Evelyn March lifted her chin in such a haughty manner that I wanted to pay her back for the slap she'd laid across Wakefield's face. She stood as if to leave the porch. My dad blocked her way.

"Mrs. March, until I receive the results of Alma Tackett's toxicology report, I strongly advise that you not leave Enigma, for any reason." Dad added, "The same goes for you, Denver."

Denver escorted us out to the veranda where we had entered. The resentment Mrs. March harbored toward Wakefield was never going to go away. I was glad he planned to leave Enigma, because I feared ramifications would progress if he stayed. At present, negative feelings ran deep between both men. I hoped that before Wakefield left town he and Denver might meet and have lunch, and end any future unpleasantness. I also wondered if Denver and his mother planned to attend Forest's memorial and funeral.

The drive to Wakefield's rental house was in silence. Dad parked in the driveway, allowing the engine to idle. Wakefield's fingers combed through his hair. "I don't know what I expected, certainly not such venomous anger." His shoulders lifted on the sigh. "I suppose Mrs. March has a right to hate me."

He opened the car door and stepped out. Before he turned away, I said, "Do you still think she killed your mother?"

"P-part of me thinks so, and p-part of me isn't as sure as I was an hour ago." He leaned down to look at me. "T-tullah, do you think Denver looks like me?"

Holi Moli, how was I supposed to answer that? "They say everyone has a twin. What I think doesn't matter. How do you feel about the DNA test?"

A play of emotions crossed his face. "I have mixed feelings. My mother was a lot of things, including a liar. She missed her calling. She should have been an actress, with the way she was able to fool people into thinking she was…honest."

I stepped from the back seat to join my dad in the front. "I don't imagine Mrs. March will ever change the way she feels about you. Sometimes living with hate becomes a means of coping with disappointment. But if the test does prove you are brothers, it might give you peace of mind, and maybe Denver, too."

Wakefield was one of those people who have naturally sad eyes that remind you of a basset hound. I slid in beside Dad. Wakefield shut the 4Runner's door. "You're a good person, Tullah."

Dad cautioned Wakefield not to leave Enigma.

"Sure, I understand. A-and, from now on, please don't call me W-wakefield. I'm James." He scooched down to look at my dad. "Thanks for the advice, Sheriff Holliday. I'll fill out the name change forms tomorrow."

I waved at Wakefield as we backed out of the driveway.

Dad said, "He's right. You are one of the rare ones, Punkin. I'm proud of you."

As he wheeled into a parking space in front of the Whitehorse Saloon, he added, "C'mon, I'll buy you a hamburger."

Before we went inside, I asked, "Do you think Mrs. March is guilty?"

"Raw emotions aren't necessarily an indicator of guilt. Let's just say I'm considering her and Denver as persons of interest."

Chapter Sixteen

March had been a monotonous succession of foggy mornings, misty afternoons, and chilly nights. Unlike the frigid, snowy weather for Alma's funeral, on Monday pale remnants of sunlight shone through the clouds, tinting the community with gray-blue light. The temperature by midday was in the mid-sixties.

Cindi stayed home, nursing a sore throat, and decided to forego the service. She promised to keep the doors to the trailer locked and to call my dad if Earl showed up. The Cedar Hill Cemetery sat outside the city limits, situated in pastoral surroundings. I drove through the arched gate and parked behind a line of vehicles.

I was certain the memorial would be done with a touch of class and perhaps a lot of garishness, even though it had come to my attention that Sam and Beverly had butted heads because she had ordered Forest's casket closed. In the end, Sam won the argument.

The heels of my boots sank into the soggy ground as I made my way across the green toward my grandmother. I touched her arm, and she leaned to whisper that Dad had been delayed and Deputy Goodbody would lead the procession to the Rakestraw farm.

"Did you drive?"

"No, I rode over with Tiny, knowing you'd drive me home after the reception."

"Not very traditional, is it?"

She tsked. "Nothing about the Rakestraws is traditional."

"Have you spotted Janie and her husband?"

A mischievous smile glinted in Grandmother's eyes. "I heard Sam was spittin' mad because you called Janie. I also heard that she and Sam are keeping their distance."

"Is there nothing you don't know, Grandmother?"

Her smile flicked into an impish grin. "Well, I am a newswoman, after all."

We inched our way forward. I'm not a fan of funerals. Two in less than two weeks was enough to last me a lifetime. I didn't like the way the flesh looked after the stillness of life had left it. No longer the rakishly handsome playboy, Forest looked pasty and artificial. Janie approached. Her husband gripped her elbow. She whispered, "Goodbye, Forest. I love you," and turned away quickly. Her face was blotchy from weeping. Janie and I are the same age and graduated high school together. We moved in different social circles, so it wasn't as if we were best friends. Somehow I instinctively knew that, after the funeral, she and her physician husband would return to Texas, never to be part of her father's life. As Janie approached her chair, she gently touched my arm and said, "Thank you for contacting me, Tullah. I shall forever be grateful for this moment."

"Is there any hope of reconciliation between you and your father?"

Janie dabbed at a tear. "Probably not. My husband

is a loving father, devoted husband, and an excellent surgeon. We have two beautiful children." She gave a heavy sigh. "It's too bad Sam Rakestraw will never know his grandchildren."

"You've done all you could, Janie," I said. "It's Sam's loss."

Doctor Hari Nadisu cupped his wife's elbow. "Unfortunately, Dr. Holliday, there are no winners here." He offered a contrite smile before guiding Janie to her seat.

As soon as the last person passed by the casket, the minister cleared his throat and asked the attendees to be seated. The church service was mercifully short. Beverly had selected music more fitting for a festive celebration and a variety of non-Biblical quotes. Several people were invited to give eulogies. Some offered quips, some funny, some seemed in poor taste. I wasn't close to Forest. I'm not sure I really liked him. Even so, there were moments when I felt my face heat up and my eyes blur with tears. It was more than his loss. It was all death, every loss, human or animal—and my mother. I missed her with an aching intensity as I sat there staring at the neat rows of headstones stretched out in all directions.

A breeze rustled the treetops and flirted with the canvas tent flaps. We sat dutifully while the minister conducted the final rites. Forest's casket was a massive affair of glossy walnut and brass like an oversized blanket too large to fit a small space. A garland of red roses in the shape of a colossal horseshoe with a gold banner stating—In Loving Memory—stood next to the casket.

Off to one side, I spotted the freshly dug mound of

dirt and the gaping hole that waited patiently to re-welcome its occupant once the autopsy on Alma's cadaver was complete.

The minister, in his black robes, gave Beverly a solemn look, which she seemed to ignore as she rose to move toward the limousine. Sam, in a show of good manners, lingered long enough to shake a few hands and accept a few condolences.

Disgust laced Grandmother's voice. "Did you see the *Vote Sam for Mayor* button on his lapel? Campaigning at his son's funeral—shame on him."

The limo driver stood next to the vehicle's open door. There was a delay while some people hurried to their cars parked along the road. Others milled around as if they had no particular purpose. At a signal, the driver of the limousine slid behind the steering wheel and slammed the door shut. I escorted Grandmother across the lawn to my truck as the limo driver pulled in behind Deputy Goodbody's patrol car.

The funeral cortege seemed to stretch for over a mile, cruising through the town with people standing on the sidewalks gawking as if a parade was taking place. We wound down the long driveway to the Make My Day farm. At a fork in the lane, the procession turned left, away from the stables and corrals. Solemn-faced men dressed in dark suits stood ready to oversee the parking.

Inside the house, we were directed to sign the guest book, then led to a dimly lit room where the family was receiving guests. Somber individuals stood about in small clusters, chatting quietly.

"Mrs. Crow, Tullah, it's kind of you to come." Beverly was totally composed, calm, gracious, and attending to every detail of Forest's memorial. Clad in a black dress that accentuated her breasts and barely covered the essentials between there and the hemline, it seemed to me she was operating on a different plane—and not that of a grieving widow.

My eyes drifted from Beverly's face to Luanne Sterns. Luanne stared at me, unemotional. Behind her, I thought I saw Councilwoman Sue West, but I couldn't be sure. I shifted around, hoping to make eye contact, but the face was gone.

"Ms. Sterns, how are the puppies?"

She gave a nervous tug to her navy blazer. "Cute. I'm counting the days until they're weaned and your assistant can come and get them."

Her brown eyes showed no signs of weeping. She wore a smartly cut blue suit with a crisp white blouse. Her face did look a bit more thin and pinched than when I'd last seen her. I said, "Cindi has already named them—Ozzy and Pogo."

An awkward moment passed as if she didn't know how to respond. She maintained her glacial aloofness until I lowered my voice. "If Alma weren't already dead, I would have pointed to Alma as the possible murderess. Who do you think killed Forest?"

Luanne's eyebrows shot up. She hissed, "That woman was a *viper.* Too bad she died of a heart attack. And I'm sure I don't know who killed Forest."

"Are you completely certain? I heard a tiny bit of gossip that you and he were—friends."

Streaks of red fingered up her neck, and she clutched her throat. "I hope you're not implying that I—"

At the most inopportune time, Grandmother patted

my arm. "If you don't mind, I'll catch a ride home with Patty. We have things to discuss."

I cast a warning look. "Grandmother—"

"Don't worry. My lips are sealed."

Deep down, I was happy. Don't get me wrong, I adore my grandmother and would give my life to keep her from harm. Having the extra time to observe the emotions of Forest's former paramours and a few enemies was an opportunity not to be missed.

By the time Grandmother left to join her friend, Luanne Sterns had escaped to the other side of the room. She wore a mask of impassivity. I had apparently touched a raw nerve. She would definitely remain on my list of suspects.

The mourners, comforted by good wine and lavish hors d'oeuvres, seemed to lighten in mood. I wondered what it was that caused people to shrug off death so quickly. There must have been a hundred people crowding the living room and spilling out onto the brick patio and pool area. It all seemed okay. I recognized nearly everyone, and I wondered how many of those I didn't recognize had known Forest and come to pay their respects or simply came to enjoy the free food and liquor.

I snagged a glass of wine and inched my way toward Grandmother and Patty Sweet. Then, remembering Patty was on the list of suspects, I changed my direction. Evelyn and Denver entered. Denver wore his perpetual glum expression. Mrs. March spotted me, rolled her eyes, and directed Denver away from where I stood.

I was hungry and needed to replenish my wine glass. I filled my plate with grilled shrimp, mushrooms stuffed with crab meat, tuna topped with red pepper mousse, satay beef skewers, cream cheese-filled strawberries, raspberry cannoli bites, and foods and pastries that I never knew existed. And, on a sterling silver three-tiered serving stand was an array of Patty Sweet's festively iced miniature donuts. One thing for certain, Forest's repast was a foodie's delight.

Servers rearranged the offerings of food and consolidated hors d' oeuvres so the platters didn't look empty or half-eaten. It had never crossed my mind that being rich took so much work.

I picked up a fresh glass of wine and chose a seat close enough to the others that I wouldn't seem rude, but far enough away that I wouldn't have to engage in conversation with anyone. What could we possibly discuss—how many stallions I'd gelded? Thinking of the word *gelded* reminded me of the conversation regarding Talmadge Crandall's threat when he had caught Forest and Bambi together. I searched the room. Surely, Talmadge wouldn't make an appearance.

I tried to keep a look of interest on my face while I sat there mentally reviewing my list of suspects. Mrs. Frezoli loaded two plates of treats, then threaded her way to an empty chair. She wasn't on my suspect list. I had filed her under "witness."

Engrossed in thought, I jumped when a voice stammered, "T-tullah."

Mentally, I dusted myself off. "I'm surprised to see you here, Wakefield—or should I say, James?"

He wore a wide grin. "We did it, Tullah. Denver and I took the DNA test. We should get the results on Friday."

"Are you excited?"

"I'm a mishmash of emotions. I also filed the papers with Judge Duval. He looked at the birth certificate and said to bring him the DNA report. Either way, he agreed to okay my name change."

I noticed Denver had downed a glass of champagne and picked up another. He headed our way. He held the flute up as if to salute. "I guess Waa...uh...James told you the news. Mother is hopping mad. She's threatened to cut me out of her will."

"Holi Moli. Unbelievable."

Denver shrugged. "I'm not worried. She'll get over it." He smiled at Wakefield. "I found a picture of Dad when he was our age. Honestly, Tullah, if James and I aren't brothers, then it's a fluke of nature, because we both look just like him."

So much for keeping Denver and Wakefield as murder suspects. However, Evelyn March was still a strong contender. "What are your plans? I mean, it's not like your mother will welcome Wakefield—uh, sorry, James with open arms."

Denver drained his glass. "Regardless of the test results, I'm throwing in with James. It's time to cut the apron strings and live life on my own terms. At least for a couple of years. I've thought this through. Leroy Banks is our brood mare barn manager. Mother can promote him to farm manager. We also have a couple of long-term guys capable of taking over his job."

I spotted Sue West again. This time her eyes were red-rimmed and her cheeks mottled, with makeup smeared as if she'd been crying. Her husband wore a grim frown. I made a mental note for later. Not wanting to appear distracted, I wished Denver and James good luck. "Keep me posted about the test results. I hope

Friday brings you healing news."

A flurry of loud profanity interrupted the festivity. Beverly shrilled, "Only a slut without a shred of decency would have the audacity to show her face."

Bambi Crandall's curvaceous figure flattered the long, black, silk dress that clung to her like a second skin. The woman reeked of sexuality. An obvious hush fell over the room. In a husky voice, Bambi cooed, "Why, Mrs. Rakestraw, dah-ling, I merely came to pay my respects to the *dearly* departed."

Before anyone could react, Beverly flung the contents of her champagne glass in her archrival's face. The Waterford crystal flute shattered against the porcelain tile floor. Apparently hearing the commotion while waiting outside on the veranda, Talmadge Crandall bulled through the crowd. His nose collided with the business end of Sam's fist. Blood spurted like an exploding ketchup bottle. The words volleying back and forth between the two couples were enough to make a crew of sailors blush.

Hmm, I thought, perhaps Grandmother called it correctly. Maybe Beverly did feed her husband poisoned donuts.

Tiny and Joe Belker plowed forward. Tiny pulled the men apart while Joe suffered a couple of claw marks to the face trying to separate Bambi and Beverly. Tiny bellowed, "Break it up before I haul all of you off to jail."

He pointed to a far corner of the room. "Joe, seat Mr. and Mrs. Crandall over there."

The frown Tiny wore would have put the fear of God in even the worst criminals. He commanded, "Don't even think about moving until I say so. Joe, make sure they don't leave." He then barked at Sam and Beverly to sit down.

I saw Sam move as though to touch Beverly's arm. She didn't turn her head, but radiated a rage so limitless that he withdrew his hand, intimidated by the force of it. This piqued my interest. What else was going on behind the scenes of the Rakestraw household? Whatever it was, Sam seemed to sense he wasn't part of this new scheme. I kept eating because I didn't know what else to do.

Janie wore a quizzical frown as she rushed to my side, her husband in tow. "What's going on, Tullah?"

I wasn't exactly enthusiastic about answering her question. As Dad always says, be honest even when the truth hurts. I finished off my wine. "Since you asked, Talmadge Crandall caught Bambi and your brother...rolling in the hay. Talmadge threatened to end Forest's romping days by gelding him."

Janie's eyes widened. She clamped a hand over her mouth. "That's disgusting." She cut her eyes toward where Bambi Crandall sat. "She's his wife? Why, she must be at least forty years younger than him. Doesn't he have a daughter about her age?"

I wanted to remind her there was a ten-year difference between the ages of her brother and his wife, but I bit my tongue and simply shrugged. I wondered if I should add Bambi to my list of suspects. What if she had tried to dump Forest and he wouldn't get lost? That begged the question of how this tied in to Alma's death.

Someone had turned down the lilting music, which seemed to signal that the party was over. The house became mantled in that dull quiet that follows too much noise. Soon after, almost at a gesture, people started getting into the goodbye behavior mode. Tiny allowed Beverly and Sam to stand by the archway that led from the living room to the sweeping porch, being hugged, having their hands pressed in sympathy. Everyone said the same thing. "Such a tragedy. He died far too young. You know we love you. Be sure to let us know if you need anything."

I followed the line of well-wishers, and said, "You must be exhausted. Try to get some rest."

Beverly smiled wearily. "Forest was often like an irresponsible child. We had our differences. Even so, he didn't deserve to be murdered."

I gave her hand a reassuring squeeze. "Don't worry. My dad is good at his job. He'll find out who did this." I couldn't help myself. "Do you have any idea how his death connects to Alma's?"

She withdrew her hand and gave me a look that would turn the Sahara Desert to ice. "Thank you for coming, Tullah."

Outside, I caught sight of Angela Teasdale standing at the edge of the parking area. I was surprised to see her toss a cigarette butt to the ground and grind it with the toe of her shoe. I didn't know Angela very well. She was relatively new to Enigma. With all the people inside, I must have missed her. Conveniently, my truck was parked next to her sedan.

"Miss Teasdale?"

Her manner ever so slightly guarded, she greeted, "Dr. Holliday, hi."

"Quite a turnout, wouldn't you say?"

Angela Teasdale's eyes were puffy and red. She removed a tissue from her skirt pocket and blew her nose. "Forest had an ego as big as two football fields. If he were alive, he'd be disappointed that more people didn't attend."

Did I detect a note of bitterness? Had she been crying? I recalled the covert smiles she had shared with Forest the night I'd discovered Alma dead in the bathroom stall.

Angela sneezed and sneezed again. She waved a tissue in the air. "Allergies. If you'll excuse me."

The heady scent of gardenias, mingled with the lemony aroma of magnolias, permeated the air. My own nose itched. Angela turned back. "I'd like to arrange for you to give a presentation to my junior 4-H members about equine care, to help get them ready for this year's festival."

"Sure. Call me with more details." I reached in my purse and handed her a business card. "I'll need to arrange my day at the clinic to coincide with the date and time you select."

She thanked me, opened the door to her car, and climbed inside. I did the same with my truck. I waited for her to back out, and when she didn't immediately leave, I glanced over in time to see her lay her forehead against the steering wheel, her shoulders lifting up and down as if she were sobbing. It appeared that Angela suffered from hay fever with a large dose of grief mixed in.

What is it about storms that send people scurrying like ants? Angela at last backed out and drove down the long drive leading to the main road. The sky darkened and thunder pealed, sending guests to their vehicles. The same men in dark suits that had earlier directed the parking now appeared with umbrellas to escort people to the cars. I was glad to see Grandmother and Patty being given that courtesy. I decided to wait until Patty drove past me so I could follow her and Grandmother to town. Large drops of rain splattered the ground, and I wanted to make sure these two dear women arrived home safely.

Chapter Seventeen

I followed closely until Patty drove through the only traffic signal in town. I flashed my lights, and she beeped her horn to indicate she'd seen me. I debated about stopping by Dad's office and decided getting drenched wasn't an option. Instead, I did a U-turn and headed home.

My phone bonged to indicate I'd received a text. Grandmother had sent a heart and thumbs-up emoji, which made me smile.

The wipers worked overtime to swoosh sheeting rain off the windshield. Normally, I enjoy the rain, especially this time of the year when it washes away all the green allergens and replenishes the earth. I'm not sure what it is about lightning and thunder that unsettles me. I cringed when bolts of white splintered close enough to cause my eyes to squint. I leaned forward to peer through the deluge. It was dark as pitch and not quite four o'clock. Surely tomorrow would bring clear skies and sunshine.

Needless to say, I was happy to park under my carport. I glanced toward the trailer to see the lights on, and felt a surge of sympathy that Cindi was weathering the storm alone. To keep from getting wet from the slashing rain, I scooted to the passenger side, opened the door, and dashed up the steps. Whining and braying greeted me. I unlocked the door and stooped to hug my dog and donkey. I had left the doggie door up for them to go in and out as needed, but now I closed it and locked the kitchen door. River and Rascal followed me upstairs and stayed close. The storm also made them nervous.

Usually, I'm a bundle of energy. Maybe it was the events during and after the funeral, or driving home in a storm, or a combination of all of it that left me feeling drained. The air had chilled. I changed into a pair of flannel pajamas and then padded downstairs to heat a can of tomato soup and brew a cup of hot tea.

I was typing notes of today's observations when my phone chimed. "Hi, Dad, you missed all the action at the Rakestraws' today."

"Yeah, Tiny filled me in."

"Did Crandall press charges against Sam for punching him in the nose?"

Dad chuckled. "No. Tiny convinced all parties concerned that emotions were running high. He gave Sam and Beverly the choice of apologizing or hauling them in on assault and battery charges. Tiny said the apologies came with great reluctance. So everyone is sleeping in their own bed tonight instead of in my jail."

I brought him up to date on my observations and finished by saying, "Judge Duval signed the papers so Wakefield is now officially James David March. He and Denver are excited to get the DNA results on Friday. Dad, I truly hope they're not disappointed."

"I hear you, Punkin. Listen, the toxicology report on Alma came in a few minutes ago. I've emailed you a copy."

"Okay, don't keep me in suspense."

"Same as with Forest."

"Autumn Crocus."

"Yep."

"Holi Moli, Dad. That's a double homicide." I hesitated. "Do you think Patty Sweet did this?"

I envisioned Dad scratching his head, a scowl on his face. "I can't say one way or the other. I'll hold off on releasing this information until I visit Patty to ask a few questions."

"Please not at your office, Dad. You know how tongues wag in this town. How about at Grandmother's apartment? She'll want to be there, and so will I. Patty will need moral support. Besides, guilty or not, a thing like this could ruin Patty's business."

"I'll keep it as low-key as possible, Punkin. Today is Tuesday. Wednesday and Thursday are out. Call your grandmother and have her invite us for lunch Friday."

"She'll want an explanation. What should I tell her?"

"The truth." It was as simple as that—short and to the point.

"I hate this, Dad. Patty lives up to her name. She's sweet and kind, and this is really going to upset Grandmother even more. We have to figure out who did this."

"You know I love you, Punkin, and I respect your intelligence, but there is no *we*. A murderer is on the loose and living among us. Don't make me worry about you. Mind your business and let me do my job."

I understood his concern. Ever since my mother's murder, he had become overly protective of me. The little girl in me wanted to cross my fingers and hide my hands behind my back so he wouldn't see that I was making a false promise. "I hear you loud and clear."

"Good. Are your doors locked?"

"Yes, sir, and River and Rascal are in the house. Stop being such a worry wart."

I could hear the smile in his voice. "You're my little girl. It's my job to worry."

We disconnected. I opened my email and while sipping my soup read the toxicology report.

A thunderous boom vibrated the house. The lights flickered off and on, and then the power went off. I really needed to invest in a generator. I peeked out the window toward the trailer. Cindi was also sitting in the dark. I punched in her number.

"Hey, Tullah. Some storm."

"We may be in the dark for a while."

"As long as I've got my phone, a flashlight, and a bathroom..." She laughed. "And a book and snacks, I'm good. How was the funeral?"

I filled her in and added a detailed description of the altercation between the Rackstraws and the Crandalls.

Cindi coughed and cleared the hoarseness from her throat. "I wish I'd been there."

"Call me if you need me. Are your doors locked?"

"Will do, and, yep, I'm locked in and safe."

Before going upstairs, I double-checked the doors. I also locked down the doggie door. In the bedroom, I used my phone flashlight to guide me to the bed, and switched on the battery-powered lantern. Like Cindi, I had a good book. By the time I'd finished the last chapter of *The Hound of the Baskervilles*, my eyes had begun to droop.

I was out by the time my head hit the pillow. I'm not exactly sure how long I'd slept when River's low throaty growl woke me. Rascal stood next to him, emitting his own warning, which sounds like a cross between a bray and a suppressed sneeze.

Lightning flashed, outlining that dratted tree branch scratching across the bedroom window. I reminded myself to trim the limbs. "Hush, River. It's just the wind."

I reached down and patted their heads, then shifted to a comfortable position. Just as I was drifting to netherland, thunder reverberated. River bumped my arm with his wet nose. I ran my hand over his neck and felt the raised hackles. "It's just the thunder. Nothing to be afraid of."

River's growl deepened, and Rascal planted his tiny front hooves on the edge of the bed. I shushed them and strained to listen. I drew in a deep cautious breath, and patted the bed, allowing the animals to join me, which is generally forbidden. My Lab is well trained. I ordered him to lie down. Rascal is a grand mimic and did the same.

That's when I heard the tinkling of breaking glass. I grabbed my phone. It was a little after three—Dad would be asleep. I punched in his emergency number. It rang, and rang, and I was frantically whispering, "Pick up...pick up!"

His voice croaked, groggy from being rudely awakened, "Punkin?"

My heart hammering, I spoke softly, "Dad, there's somebody in the house. They must've broken the window on the kitchen door to get in."

"Where are you?"

"In the bedroom."

"I'll be there in ten. Shoot if you have to."

The third step from the top of the stairs squeaked. "He's coming up the stairs."

"Keep the line open, Tullah. I'm on my way."

I laid the phone on the night stand and reached to open the drawer. I'm an excellent markswoman, but the only thing I've shot at is paper targets at the firing range. I'm a healer, not a killer. Before I could react, the bedroom door crashed against the wall. I shouted the attack command to River. The dog lunged from the bed. All seventy pounds of him landed square against a tall dark figure's chest.

A man screamed, "What the h—"

I scrambled from the bed and in the process tripped over the donkey. I fell hard enough to knock myself breathless. I heard Dad yelling, "Tullah, talk to me…"

Ferocious growls mingled with cursing, and rolling thumps, a painful yelp, and silence. Whoever had broken into my house had tumbled down the stairs and had hurt my dog in the process. A sickening weight settled in my stomach as I bounded down the stairs. Moonlight spilled into the foyer. Even so it was almost impossible to spot my loyal black dog. The man stood, and the intensity of his glare chilled me to my bones. He was tall, in his fifties, with thinning hair, thin-faced, with a five o'clock shadow that reminded me of cactus spikes. His clothes hung on his skinny frame and looked as if he'd purchased them from a thrift store. He radiated the smell of stale whiskey and unwashed body.

Rascal made sorrowful chuffing sounds and went to lie beside his buddy.

"You!" I screamed. "My dad is on his way."

He stepped toward me. I glanced at the front door, since he was between me and the kitchen. "What do you want?"

His tongue was thick. He teetered, and when he spoke his fetid breath nearly bowled me over. "Where's my daughter?"

"She's not here."

"Liar. She works for you. Lives with you. I need money. Get me money, now!"

He reached around his back. Was he going for a gun, a knife? I lowered my head and charged at him with all my strength. I equaled him in height, but this man outweighed me by thirty pounds. I head-butted him in the chest. He cursed, his arms flew up, and he doubled over. I reeled backward from the impact, staggered, and landed hard on my buttocks. He fell right on top of me.

I fought to get him off. He slapped me across the face. I bucked, and pushed, and heaved, but he was too heavy. Pain splintered my jaw from the force of a balled fist. He was spewing profanity, and the glimpse I caught of his face was terrifying. I was more frightened than I had ever been. He was tearing at any part of me that he could get hold of. I reached forward and raked at his eyes, leaving claw marks on his cheeks. He grabbed a fistful of my hair and banged my head against the wooden floor. Pain exploded in my brain, and for a second the world went dark.

A loud braying broke through my fogginess. My tiny teacup donkey had come to my defense and was biting the leg of my attacker. With the strength of a madman, my assailant flung the little animal against the wall. He lifted on his knees to get a good swing at my face. I seized the opportunity to kick upward with my knee. The blow brought a pained whiteness to his face.

This only enraged him more. He grabbed my hair again, and in a split second I managed to latch on to his arm. I bit through his shirt sleeve. He yowled and banged my head against the floor again. I had another moment of darkness, and then with what little energy I had left, I grabbed his ear and twisted with all my might. He straddled me, both of his hands wrapped around my neck. My hand lost its grip on his ear and fell to the floor.

And then there was a sound, dull and nauseating. The weight on top of me went limp. There was an oddly peaceful moment. Then I became aware of voices. Voices I could trust.

I gasped for air when someone dragged the body off me.

"Deputy Goodbody, read this piece of scum his rights. Then get him out of my sight before I'm tempted to do him bodily harm."

"Gladly, Sheriff. Earl Redfern, you have the right to remain silent..."

My throat hurt when I tried to speak. "Dad, he hurt River."

"Shh. Lie still while I call for an ambulance." Footsteps retreated, then returned.

Cindi's tearful voice cut through my haze. "Tullah, thank God you're okay. I'm so sorry. If I hadn't been living here, this wouldn't have happened." She sat on the floor, gripping my hand and crying in deep, gulping sobs.

I tried to focus but achieved only a blur. "Not your fault. What about River?"

She spoke through sobs. "Don't worry. I'll take care of him."

Everything was fuzzy and vague when Dad knelt next to me. "Bubba's on his way."

"Did I hurt Earl?" My lips hurt. In fact, now that the adrenalin was fading, I realized my entire body hurt.

"You managed to hold your own." Dad smoothed hair back from my forehead. "You're a tough woman, Punkin. I'm proud of you."

I felt more than I saw him look at Cindi. "Earl will go away a long time for this."

****

The room was cold. A nurse brought a heated blanket to warm me. I didn't remember arriving at the hospital, and barely remembered Bubba and Dad lifting me onto the gurney, or the ambulance ride. I opened my eyes and blinked to clear my vision.

"Grandmother?"

She leaned over and kissed me. Tears brimmed in her eyes. "I don't ever want to receive another call in the middle of the night telling me my granddaughter had the stuffin's beat out of her. It brought back awful memories of when we received the call about your mother."

My throat hurt. I managed to rasp, "I didn't mean to worry you, Grandmother."

"I'm not scolding. Just upset, and thankful."

"Am I hurt bad?"

She sat in the chair next to my bed and reached through the bedside rail to clutch my hand. "For the beating you took, it could have been worse. You have a mild concussion where Earl banged your head against the floor. Thankfully, that monster didn't crush your larynx. You'll have a sore throat for a while. Both of your eyes are black. You have bruises from head to toe.

He split your lips, and your whole face is swollen."

My left wrist felt heavy and restricted when I tried to lift it. Grandmother said, "We're not sure if Earl hurt your wrist or if you fractured it when you fell down the stairs."

I muttered. "I don't remember."

There was a knock at the door. Dad entered. He bent to kiss me on the forehead. "How's my girl?"

It hurt to smile. "In pain. What about Earl?"

"He'll go away for a long time. We've charged him with breaking and entering, assault and battery, and attempted murder."

I enunciated with some difficulty, "I feel badly for Cindi."

"I believe she's relieved. At least she doesn't need to feel afraid anymore."

"How much time do you think he'll get?"

"Judge Duval is certain Earl is looking at no less than fifty years. I'm recommending with no parole."

Another knock. Cindi walked in carrying a gift bag. After the initial chitty-chatty greeting, and reassurance that I didn't hold her responsible for her dad's actions, she said, "I brought your favorites— marshmallow chicks, the yellow ones, marshmallow circus peanuts, a six-pack of cola, and sour-cream-and-onion potato chips—in case the hospital food doesn't suit you."

I giggled, which was quite uncomfortable. "River?"

"I x-rayed him. Nothing's broken, but he's limping a little from a bruised shoulder."

I thanked her for looking after him and for keeping the clinic running. I knew she was perfectly capable of handling minor cases; and we had a standing policy that Dr. Cooper would handle any emergencies.

"Dad, will Earl be able to make bail until his trial takes place?"

"Considering his past record, Earl is considered a flight risk and a danger to the public. No bail will be set. In fact, he spent the night in a room down the hall. He suffered a dislocated shoulder in the fall. He was so hopped up on alcohol and speed that he didn't feel the pain." Dad's shoulders shook with laughter. "He needed several stitches where Rascal bit through his pants leg. Now Earl is threatening to sue because he thinks he might have rabies."

He bent to kiss me. "I've got to get back to the office." Shaking his head, he added, "An attack donkey. That's one for the books."

"Dad, I'm really in pain."

Concern radiated in his eyes. He buzzed the nurse's station.

A plump, silver-haired nurse entered. She offered a warm smile as she inserted a needle into the IV. "You'll feel better in a few minutes."

I barely remember Cindi saying goodbye. After she left, I got drowsier and more comfortable, and coasted off to sleep.

Chapter Eighteen

A ripple of pleasure shimmied through me as Dad parked the 4Runner in front of my house. River and Rascal sat on the porch, all wiggly with happy quivers when they greeted me. Cindi sprinted across the yard. She grabbed out of my hands the hospital bag that held my personals, while Dad helped me up the steps. Every inch of my body felt as if I'd been stomped by a crazed bull.

"I replaced the back door, Punkin, with one that has double-paned safety glass and blinds between the glass. As a double precaution, I added a slide bolt lock at the top. I also installed a deadbolt on the front door, and motion sensor lights for you and Cindi as well as at the barn."

He escorted me to my recliner. "You're the best, Dad, but really, this incident with Earl was a once-in-a-lifetime thing. There's no need for all this precaution."

He quirked a serious smile. "Regardless of what *you* think, it makes me feel better."

Cindi set the bag on the sofa. "I know Earl will go away for a long time. Still, there's a part of me that doesn't trust he'll not finagle his way out. Having all the extra security makes me feel better, too. Thank you, Sheriff Holliday."

He patted Cindi on the shoulder, then bent to kiss my forehead. "Your grandmother is bringing supper.

I'll check on you later."

At the sound of a truck, Dad glanced out the window. "It's parking at the clinic."

Cindi peered over his shoulder. "Oh, yes, that's our four o'clock. German shepherd needs toenails trimmed, and a flea treatment. Catch ya later, Tullah."

I was dozing when River emitted a series of happy woofs. After Dad and Cindi had left, I managed to force my stiff body out of my chair to open the front door. In spite of his precautions, I hated being inside a closed-up house. Knowing Grandmother was on her way, I'd left the screened door unlatched.

"Yoohoo, Tullah."

"Door's open, Grandmother."

"Look who I brought with me."

Patty Sweet grimaced. "Tullah, your face…oh, my goodness." She held two of her signature boxes labeled *Sweet's 'n' Eats.* She must have read the expression on my face and sent me a soppy smile. "I promise there's no poison in these donuts, and they're all your favorites: glazed, chocolate-covered, crème-filled, lemon curd, and raspberry jelly-filled topped with powdered sugar."

Patty responded to the look I cut my Grandmother. "It's okay, Tullah. Henry has already taken my statement. He promised that no one would know about the donuts until he's able to make an arrest. Even so…" The pinched look on Patty's face deepened. "Once word gets out that Alma and Forest died from poisoned donuts, I'll be ruined. Anyhow, there's enough for the three of us, with extras for you to enjoy later. I've also brought a box for Cindi. Bless her heart, she must be terribly upset about Earl."

Grandmother huffed. "More like relieved than upset. Tullah, has she mentioned anything about contacting her mother?"

"No, ma'am, and I'm not going to ask. Cindi is grappling with an array of emotions. She's thankful Earl is going to prison. At the same time, she feels guilty because she's relieved that he's out of her life, and is embarrassed because she's had to contend with the looks from people when she goes into town. She's as much a victim as her father. Whatever she decides about her mother is between her and her conscience."

Patty sighed. "I can empathize with Cindi." She followed Grandmother to the kitchen and set the boxes on the table.

Grandmother called over her shoulder, holding up two bags, "Pulled pork sandwiches, spicy sweet potato fries, and cole slaw. Charlie sends hugs and said if you need him he's only a phone call away. I hesitate to tell you what he said he'd like to do to Earl." She added, "Call Cindi and tell her to come eat."

I groaned as I reached down and grabbed the lever to lower the recliner. Grandmother scolded, "Stay right where you are. Patty and I will fill the plates and join you."

Patty Sweet is a short, plump woman with twinkling blue eyes, short, wavy, black hair streaked with silver, and a perpetually friendly smile. She is a talented baker, respected by everyone, and lives up to her last name. In reality, I honestly don't believe she's capable of committing murder.

I accepted the plate Patty handed me as Grandmother set a tall glass of cola on the table next to my chair. I downed a muscle relaxer with a swallow of soft drink. Patty and Grandmother sat across from me.

I couldn't resist asking, "Patty, how do you suppose poison got in the donut batter?"

"I've asked myself that same question dozens of times." She picked up a sweet potato fry, looked at it with distaste and dropped it on her plate. In fact, she set the entire plate aside and folded her hands onto her lap.

I further questioned, "Do you have any new employees that maybe had a grudge against Mayor Tackett or Forest?"

Patty wiped a tear. "All my ladies have been with me for years. The only time I hire anyone new is during the summer and Christmas vacation, and those are limited to high school students so my girls can take vacations. Not since Christmas has anyone new been in the kitchen." She spread her hands wide. "All of which naturally points the finger at me."

Cindi opened the screen door and walked in. She smiled a greeting and accepted a plate, which she dug into without hesitation. I asked her about the day, and she gave me a brief synopsis of each patient. Nothing serious or worrisome.

I was hungrier than I thought and polished off my meal. "Patty, I'll take a glazed donut and a chocolate-covered crème-filled one."

She offered a sad smile. "Oh, Tullah, you're thoughtful, but you don't have to. I can take them back to the bakery."

Cindi piped up. "There's donuts? I'll have one or maybe three."

We laughed.

Cindi gathered our plates and headed for the kitchen and returned with a box.

I licked chocolate from the tips of my fingers, and then polished off a glazed donut. "Tell us about the last time Alma ordered donuts. Who delivered them to her office?"

Patty was thoughtful, as if remembering back two weeks ago. "Alma had a standing order for every Monday morning. Three dozen glazed donuts for the staff and a separate order of a half-dozen chocolate covered for herself. Usually, I deliver the donuts." She tapped a finger against her cheek. "As I recall, Sue West and her husband had breakfast at the café that morning. Just as I rounded the counter, Sue said she could deliver the donuts since she had to attend the meeting and was headed that way."

Grandmother's face was hopeful. "Maybe Councilwoman West switched Alma's box of donuts with some she'd made. It's no secret she didn't like Alma."

I willed the muscle relaxer to hurry up and do its thing. "It's a viable theory. Did you relay this to my dad?"

"Honestly, no. He didn't ask, and I didn't think of it until just now because I was completely rattled when he asked me to come to his office to give a statement."

Patty had everything to lose and nothing to gain by lying. "For what it's worth, Patty, I believe you. There's one thing wrong with our theory about Sue West."

Three puzzled faces glared at me.

"How does her delivering tainted donuts to the mayor tie in with Forest Rakestraw's death?"

Patty blinked back the moisture tipping her eyelashes. Grandmother placed an arm around her friend's shoulders. "Don't worry, Patty. My Tullah is more than a veterinarian. She has a talent for solving mysteries. And Henry is as good a sheriff as they come. You don't need to worry about a thing."

Too choked up to speak, Patty merely nodded and dabbed her eyes with a napkin.

"Since Patty knows about the donuts, I'm assuming Dad shared the results of the mayor's toxicology report."

Grandmother nodded. "I'll keep my news article precisely uninformative."

"That's an oxymoron, Grandmother."

The dimple in her cheek deepened with her grin. "Exactly."

Patty made a zipping motion across her lips. "Don't worry, Tullah. My lips are sealed. The bakery and café is all I have, and the ladies who work for me depend on the income."

The muscle relaxer kicked in and, hard as I tried to remain alert, my eyes kept closing. I could barely remember saying goodbye to Grandmother and Patty. Cindi stayed long enough to help me upstairs and to lock up the house. It was a really good thing the next day was Saturday.

****

Now that my apprehension about Patty's donuts had disappeared, I berated myself for over-indulging. Here it was Sunday morning and my sweet tooth was begging for a chocolate-covered crème-filled taste of heaven to accompany my mug of coffee and the Sunday paper.

Instead, I settled for two toasted waffles slathered in butter and maple syrup, with slices of crisp bacon. I carried my plate to the front porch to enjoy breakfast and reading the paper to the accompaniment of bird chirps and the creaking of my rocking chair. I gingerly sipped the hot coffee because my swollen, split lips were still tender.

A picture of Alma Tackett was featured on the *Gazette*'s front page with the headline *Who Murdered the Mayor?*

True to her word, Grandmother left out any mention of Autumn Crocus and donuts, simply stating the toxicology report specified homicide and that the murderer had used the same type poison, which both victims had ingested. The article also stated that Sheriff Henry Holliday was following up on strong leads and had created a list of suspects.

Below the article was another bold headline which elicited a groan when I read *Local Veterinarian Victim of Home Invasion* with a picture of me. Thankfully, she didn't take a photo of me lying in the hospital bed. The piece detailed the beating, the injury of my dog, and that my donkey had bitten Earl, which required stitches, and the court date set for the trial. She had also posted a reminder that Easter Sunday would be the last printed edition of the *Gazette* and, again, invited people to subscribe to the new electronic edition of the *Enigma Bulletin.*

Lulled by the cool temperatures and nature's music, I dozed until River growled and sounded throaty warning woofs. I blinked to clear my vision. A fancy, sleek RV had parked in my yard. I grabbed River's collar to keep him from lunging off the porch.

The RV door opened. Denver and Wakefield emerged, wearing happy smiles. I assured River they were friends and ordered him to stay. "Hello." I waved them forward. "Holi Moli, that's some rig."

Wakefield said, "We're doing a test drive to see if this is our new home away from home. Natalie Fletcher purchased the farm."

I beckoned the two men to sit, and offered them iced tea, which they declined. "Natalie is closing the Happy Hooves Equestrian Center?"

Wakefield sank into one of the chairs. "She's expanding, and keeping the name the same with a minor tweak. Where the first center is for adults and children with mental and physical disabilities, the new HHEC is specifically to treat military veterans suffering from post-traumatic stress disorder. She believes working with horses will help these men and women heal spiritually, physically, and emotionally."

We rocked in silence for a moment. Denver offered a sly smile. "The main purpose of our visit is to tell you that the DNA test came back 99.9 percent positive that James and I share the same genes."

"Yep, we are definitely brothers," Wakefield replied.

I was having a difficult time remembering that Wakefield was now James. I looked at Denver and clapped my hands. "How does your mother feel about the news?"

He shrugged and sighed. "She cried a lot. She may never come to terms with the fact that James and I are brothers. Maybe someday she'll be happy for us."

I glanced toward the RV. "When are you leaving?"

Their smiles faded. Wakefield, er, that is, James said, "Unfortunately, Denver and I are both suspects in my mother's death and possibly Forest's. We've given our statements to Sheriff Holliday. We had planned to leave as soon as the closing on the farm takes place in thirty days, but your dad cautioned us not to leave the county until after the hearing, and possibly the trial."

"Did Dad give you dates?"

"Thirty days for the hearing. As for the trial, he said the date depends on when the judge could get it on his calendar." As if he'd forgotten, Wakefield held the potted plant forward. "This and the bottle of wine," he nodded toward Denver, "is for you. It's a very small gesture of thanks for encouraging us to get DNA tested."

He set the plant on the small round table next to my chair. "The 4-H Club had tables set up in front of the grocery store. They were selling all kinds of goodies. We asked what kind of plant it is, but the little girls didn't know, and the sponsor wasn't around. The wine is from my mother's personal collection. I hope you'll like it."

To calm the thumping of my heart, I cleared my throat and asked, "After the trial is over, how long do you plan to travel?"

Denver steepled his fingers and leaned forward. "Since neither of us is guilty, and I can vouch for my mother's whereabouts, I believe we'll be cleared after the hearing. To answer your questions, James and I think it'll take a year to visit every state, and then we plan to travel to Europe and perhaps take an African safari." He was thoughtful for a minute. "I hope to meet someone special and fall in love, and have children."

"Will you return to Enigma?" I wanted to know.

Both men shook their heads. Wakefield said, "I want the same things as Denver. We've both agreed that neither of us are horse people although we've been around them our entire lives. Denver is interested in film and photography. I plan to write my first mystery novel, and perhaps turn it into a screen play." He rubbed the palms of his hands together. "We've lived under our mothers' thumbs until now. This trip is more like a journey of discovery. Once we figure out who we are, we'll go from there. Maybe we'll return to Kentucky, maybe not."

I stood when they stood. "It sounds like you're on the right track. You have my email. I hope you'll keep in touch."

We hugged, and I knew in my heart this was the last time I'd ever hear from either of them again. I remained on the porch until they drove out of the yard. Then I scooped up the plant and the bottle of wine. I knew exactly what the plant with the pale lilac petals was—Autumn Crocus. And I knew Angela Teasdale had mentioned being the 4-H sponsor. I cautioned myself not to assume she was the murderer. From my years as a 4-Her, I knew parents are expected to donate items to help raise funds for the kids to attend summer camp. Anyone could have donated this plant.

I stuck the bottle of wine in a cabinet and placed the flower on the windowsill above the kitchen sink, well away from where Rascal or River could reach it. Excitement vibrated through my body. When I tried to dance a little jig, my sore muscles reminded me that I was still recuperating from my tumble down the stairs and the beating from Earl Redfern.

As soon as I returned home from the hospital, I'd begun applying ice packs to bring down the swelling in my face and to reduce the bad appearance of my blacked eyes. Realistically, I knew it would take up to two weeks before my face returned to normal. I spoke to the image in the mirror. "There's no way you can go out in public looking like you were on the receiving end of a baseball bat." My image said, "Patience, Tullah. Remember, good things come to those who wait."

I answered myself, "Yeah, that's the problem, I don't want to wait. The hearing is in thirty days. I need to solve this mystery before the hearing."

"Hey, Tullah, do you have company? Who're you talking to?" Cindi's voice caused me to jump.

"No one. Just having a one-sided conversation with myself." I motioned for her to come in. I pointed to the plant. "Know what that is?"

"Nuh-uh."

"Autumn Crocus."

Her eyes widened. "No way. I saw Denver and Wakefield. Did they bring it?" She clamped her hand over her mouth and spoke through her fingers. "Oh, wow, are they the killers?"

I recounted my visit with them and why they had brought the plant and bottle of wine. "Those guys didn't even know what kind of plant it is, and I didn't tell them. Keep this between us. I have a plan."

"Tullah, your plans scare me. You should tell your dad."

"I will in due time. I need a favor from you."

Skepticism rolled over her face. "I'm afraid to ask. Does it include danger?"

"Not unless you consider being licked by hazardous puppies." I explained, "Make a house call to Luanne Sterns with the excuse that you're there to do a routine check on Gigi to make sure she's healing properly, to see if the puppies are getting enough milk, and to see if there are any noticeable birth defects or abnormalities. Ask to take Gigi to the back yard to watch her energy level, and while you're observing mama and her little cuties, see if you spot any crocuses. If you do, then pretend you're filming the puppies and take pictures of the flowers."

At her hesitation, I pointed to my face. "I can't go looking like a zombie from a scary movie."

She huffed. "Okay. When do you want me to do this?"

"Tomorrow morning."

She moved toward the back door. I caught her arm. "You can do this, Cindi. You're a natural."

"Yeah, and you owe me a glass of wine from that expensive-looking bottle." The door slammed behind her.

I filled an ice pack to apply to my face.

Charlie Whitehorse made one of his rare visits. He brought a large box filled with a variety of precooked food—chili, beef stew, barbequed beef and pork. Between him and Grandmother, I had meals to last for several months. I'm not complaining. I enjoy cooking, just not for one person. Zapping something in the microwave is more my style.

I sat at the table while he heated hamburger patties and fashioned a double cheeseburger with his special sauce, and crisped the fries in the oven. I was hungry, and my stomach let the world know it.

The brace on my wrist was cumbersome. Still, I was able to carry out most of my work at the clinic. Thankfully it was my left wrist. To make the burger more manageable, he'd sliced the bun into quarters. I opened two beers and placed a bottle in front of his plate.

He spoke between chews. "You should've seen your dad after he locked up Earl. I've never seen Henry as spittin' mad as he was that night. I think it was the badge that kept him from rippin' Earl's arms out of the sockets and stuffing 'em down his throat."

Charlie pointed a thumb at his broad chest. "Me, I wanted to go down to the jail and inflict a little tribal knife work on the SOB. Pardon my language."

I wiped my mouth. "You and Dad are my heroes. I guess you read the article about the mayor's death being ruled a homicide. Who do you think did it?"

He propped on his elbows and leaned forward. "If Rakestraw wasn't dead, I'd bet my money on him as the killer."

"I don't understand."

Charlie polished off the last bite of his burger with the beer. "Being in the bar business, I see and hear things that most people want to keep hidden in the closet. That is until they've had too much to drink. Then their tongues wag. In Forest's case, he couldn't get shuck of Alma. He said she was like a blood-suckin' leech. In fact, I happen to know that it wasn't only women who pursued Forest. He alluded to the fact that Alma threatened to tell Beverly and Sam about his secret if he didn't continue keeping her satisfied, and I believe she meant with blackmail money."

I nearly dropped the bottle I was holding. "She was blackmailing him? Maybe you'd better explain."

"Simple. Forest wasn't particular who he rolled in the hay with."

"You mean he liked both men and women?"

Charlie tsked and winked. "He was a real sick-o, if you ask me."

"Have you told my dad?"

"Yep, but until Forest filed an official complaint there wasn't anything Henry could do. All it amounted to was the confessions of a drunk slobberin' in his beer." Charlie glanced at the clock. He gathered up the paper plates. "I hate to eat and run. It's about time for Flora's shift to begin. The bar gets pretty busy after six o'clock."

He bent and kissed my cheek. "You need anythin'…" He put his hand to his ear to signal call him. The door slammed as he let himself out.

For a minute I sat trying to digest all the information Charlie had laid on me. This certainly put a new light on my list of suspects.

Chapter Nineteen

The past few days had been a nightmare. I was thankful for the muscle relaxers to help get me through the day. Even so, bad dreams and sleepless nights left me exhausted. I glanced at the large wall clock in my office, and it showed just after noon. I was beginning to worry about Cindi and was in the process of sending her a text when her little blue truck pulled up.

She strolled in trying not to look gleeful.

"Wel-l-l?" I drawled. "Don't keep me in suspense."

Her delightful squeal caused the hackles to stand up on River's neck and set up a maelstrom of barking from the dogs in the back.

"Oh, Tullah, I felt like I was on a secret mission."

"The afternoon appointments are clear. Take your time, and don't leave out any details."

She reached into the fridge and grabbed a bottle of water. After satisfying her thirst, she sat in the chair across from the desk and folded her legs Indian style. "First of all, Luanne Sterns is as stern as her name. Honestly, if her brother hadn't been home, I don't think she would have let me in." She rolled her eyes. "He has a pleasant smile and is a lot friendlier than his sister."

She lifted the water bottle to her mouth again. Her eyes widened. She leaned forward. "Tullah, the living room was filled with cardboard boxes."

"Really? Did you ask why?"

"Patience, I'm coming to that, but first, I did just like you said about examining Gigi and the puppies. Oh, Tullah, Pogo and Ozzy are so cute, and very healthy. I can't wait to bring them home."

I made a *hurry and get to the point* motion with my hands. She cleared her throat and offered an impish grin. "The walls were bare, no pictures, and all kinds of stuff was piled on the sofa and dining table. Both Luanne and her brother looked...harried. He wasn't wearing his usual black robe and white collar. In fact, he looked like a regular person dressed in blue jeans and a red T-shirt. I actually think he's younger than his sister."

A frown creased her forehead. "I glanced around and asked if they were moving. My question must have lit Luanne's fuse, because she flounced out of the living room and down the hall. The next thing I hear is a door slam loud enough to rattle the walls, and Luanne screaming like a banshee."

Cindi shivered like a chill had washed over her. She continued, "I asked Father Sterns if I'd said something wrong."

"Yeah, and what did he say?"

Her stomach growled, and she patted her stomach. "I wish I'd stopped for a burger."

"C'mon to the house. Charlie brought enough food to feed an army. I'll heat us up a bowl of chili." I locked the office and put up the Out to Lunch sign, with my cellphone number to call if it was an emergency.

River and Rascal trailed behind us as we strolled to the house. "Go ahead. We can talk as we walk."

"Father Sterns...Sterns sounds too harsh for a priest."

I would have glowered at her but the sun was directly in my face. "Cindi!"

"Okay. He apologized for his sister's behavior." She skipped forward to face me. "He said since Forest's death she had slipped into a deep depression, and her mood swings were getting worse. So I asked why that would cause them to move away."

I reached up to unlock the kitchen door. Inside, I pulled out the container I had thawing in the refrigerator and emptied it into a pot to heat. Cindi filled two glasses with ice, poured us each a cola, and set out the saltine crackers.

She continued, "Father Sterns seemed aggravated. I could tell by the tone of his voice. He said that some years ago, Luanne suffered a nervous collapse and spent time in a *facility,* and since he was her only living relative, her care fell to him."

"Did he say what had caused her nervous collapse?"

"Not at first. We sat quiet for a few minutes. When I got up to leave, it was almost as if he needed someone to confess to. He said that in Luanne's early years kids had bullied her. Later, in college, apparently to find a way to fit in, she became—promiscuous. That's the word he used. He kind of skirted around the details and ending by saying a couple of professors were involved and eventually they were fired and she was expelled. There was a lot of hoo-ha in the media. She was harassed and received a few death threats. Luanne couldn't handle the stress and downed a handful of pills, ended up in a psych ward, and then in a facility for the mentally infirm. When the doctors said she was better, he left the church in Ohio and moved here.

Except this isn't the first time he's had to move. He didn't say how many times, though."

"Holi Moli, doesn't he realize that resigning from the church and moving away points a strong finger of guilt toward his sister?" I filled our bowls. "Did you get pictures of the back yard?"

"No, I didn't, and that's just it. He didn't exactly resign. When the feud over Alma's dog started, Father Sterns said he knew trouble was brewing, again. He also knew about Luanne's involvement with Forest. That's when he contacted his superior and asked for a transfer. Ironically, his new appointment came the week before Alma's death. He explained that he had tendered his resignation a month ago, and was waiting for his replacement, who is due to arrive next week." A smile tilted her lips. "And you will never, in a million years, guess where he requested to be sent."

A conspiratorial gleam had entered Cindi's eyes. I savored a spoonful of chili. "I'll bite…where?"

"Cameroon, Africa. Can you believe it?" She looked across the yard as if studying the scenery. "Tullah, there was so much pain hidden behind his words."

I collected our bowls, rinsed them, and put them in the dishwasher. "C'mon, the weather's too nice to sit inside." We refilled our glasses and walked to the front porch. "I feel sorry for Father Sterns. I don't know him, but it must be a terrible burden, shouldering that type of responsibility, and then feeling like he has to give up a life of comfort to take care of a wack-o sister forever. Doesn't he realize that no matter where he goes, her problems will follow them? And, worse, leaving Enigma before Dad finds the murderer makes her look even guiltier, and makes him an accessory if she did commit the crimes."

We sat in silence for a few minutes. "I suppose we'll have to find another way to check out their back yard."

"No, we won't." She reached around and pulled her phone from her back pocket. "After leaving, I circled around to the back alley. At first I drove by slowly. Thank goodness, Mrs. Frezoli wasn't on her back porch. You know what a nosy body she is."

I nodded in agreement.

Cindi handed over her phone.

My eyes widened. Sitting against the outer wall of Alma's rental house was an oblong, rusted horse trough filled with a variety of flowers such as yellow daylilies, red tulips, and both lavender and white Autumn Crocus. "There were none in the Sterns' yard?"

"Nuh-uh. Except for vegetable plots, there was barely a blade of grass in their yard."

I worried my bottom lip, thinking. "This still doesn't clear Luanne, and repoints the fingers at George and Wakefield."

"What about Patty Sweet? The poison was found in her donuts, right?"

"That's the biggest conundrum of all." My mind raced with possibilities. "I need to get these pictures to Dad. Do you mind?" I opened the text window. She gave me a *go ahead* nod.

****

Toward four o'clock, Cindi yelled, "Tullah, telephone."

I walked toward the office and punched the button on the desk phone. "Doctor Holliday, may I help you?"

"This is Elizabeth Trowbridge. I'm the manager of the new Enigma County Extension Center."

"Hello, what can I do for you?"

"One of the horses we let the younger 4-H kids use to practice equine care on has developed a knot on his front leg above the hoof. We've tried to load him in a trailer. He's old and apparently in a lot of pain. We can't get him out of the stall. I'd appreciate it if you'd come take a look at him. He's not even standing on that leg."

"I'll be there in about a half hour." And I disconnected the call.

I touched my cheeks. "Does my face look scary?"

Cindi's liquid dark eyes took pity on me. "Everyone who reads the newspaper knows about the beating you took from Earl. The puffiness and bruising isn't as bad as it was three days ago. Tullah, you don't look scary. You look like a woman who put up a good fight and won. Now, collect your medical bag and go take care of your patient. I'll see you in the morning."

Cindi's declaration didn't reassure me as I trudged up the steps of the new extension building, and pushed through the double glass doors. My arrival was shortly before five. The minute I walked inside, the receptionist picked up the phone and spoke. She gave me a sympathetic smile. "Mrs. Trowbridge is on her way, Doc Holliday."

A woman of approximately fifty, wearing jeans and a purple plaid shirt, with reddish braids draped across her shoulders, strode forward from the hall doorway, assuming a pleasant position as she extended her hand forward. "Doctor Holliday, I'm Elizabeth Trowbridge. Please call me Liz."

I didn't miss the subtle gasp and the quick dip of her eyes when she looked at me. "Most people call me Doc."

"I'm sorry, I didn't mean to stare. I read about the home invasion. You are a lucky woman."

Slightly embarrassed by my bruised face, I thanked her and changed the subject. "I haven't had an opportunity to visit your new facility. What're the chances of a guided tour?"

I didn't know Liz Trowbridge. The smile seemed to brighten the freckles on her face. "The pleasure is mine."

I followed her into a long room equipped with sewing machine stations and long, metal-topped tables. She explained the facility was open to the public and classes were held for adults as well as the 4-H clubs. The next room was set up with six mini-kitchens, and more long tables. "This is our canning room. During vegetable season, we're available to help adults can everything from pickles to peas, okra, and a variety of jellies, whatever they bring in. Our junior 4-Hers enjoy learning how to make biscuits. In fact, this year we plan to sponsor a biscuit baking contest."

"If you need a judge, count me in."

She laughed. "Gladly, but I can't guarantee your taste buds or stomach will survive some of the creations."

As we passed along, I spotted a plate of donuts on the counter of one of the mini-kitchens. "It looks like Patty Sweet paid you a visit."

Liz Trowbridge expelled a hearty laugh. "I wish. We have a teacher and a couple of parent volunteers. They demonstrate a variety of pastry-making, including homemade pasta and pie crusts. Sadly, the donuts don't come close to Mrs. Sweet's creations." She motioned me to follow her. She pointed to an area across the wide reception area. "Behind those double doors is a conference room equipped with an overhead projector, white board—all the perks for meetings. We can seat up to fifty people."

I'm not usually drawn to most people the first time we meet. A part of me is stand-off-ish until I get to know the person. Liz Trowbridge had an aura about her that resonated with me. She was fair-complexioned and, like I said, had a face filled with freckles. There was honesty in her cerulean blue eyes. I matched her long stride. Animal smells greeted us as we left the main building to enter a long cement balcony that overlooked a large arena. To the right were rows of bleachers, and directly across was a series of livestock pens with gates that opened into the arena.

A wave of nostalgia rippled over me. "I think my days as a 4-Her and then an FFA student, plus my love of animals, were the reason I became a veterinarian. This reminds me of the good ol' days of showing my goats and calves and then horses."

"Did you participate in the local rodeos?"

"I did, and I always look forward to November. Normally, I'm the vet on call for the rodeo."

I followed her down the steps. We walked along the pens, where several students were tending their animals. Liz said, "Here we are. This is Buddy. He's an old guy. My guess is about twenty-five, but the little girls love him." She unlatched the metal gate and entered.

Buddy was a chestnut gelding with round gentle

brown eyes. Gray hairs covered his face. I stooped and ran my hand down his obviously painful leg and spotted a lump about the size of a walnut on his front pastern.

Liz squatted next to me. "Is it bad?"

"Just like a lot of aging seniors, Buddy has osteoarthritis and has developed ring-bone. The good news, it's high ring-bone as opposed to low."

Her face lost a bit of color. "Can it be cured?"

I met her concern. "There is no cure, but there is treatment which will give him comfort." I lifted all four of Buddy's hooves. His shoes were badly worn, which indicated it'd been a long time since he'd seen a farrier. "Who owns this horse?"

We stood. She shrugged. "Honestly, I don't know. I've only been here a few months, and he was already here. I'm not even sure there's a record on him. The administrator before me didn't keep...adequate records. Tell me what to do, and I'll make it happen."

"Buddy needs a new set of shoes. That will give him some comfort." I gave her the name of the farrier who tended horses around the county. "Clem is the best there is, and he won't charge you an arm and a leg, either. In the meantime, apply cold compresses about every four hours. I'm sure some of the little girls will be happy to give him the attention. Riding him is out of the question until he's properly shod."

Liz breathed what sounded like a sigh of relief. "I just hate to see any animal suffer." I followed her out of the stall. She said, "Usually we focus on soil and crops, along with animals. However, we've added a hothouse and are experimenting with houseplants. Would you like to see?"

I answered with a smile and followed her outside to

a long, plastic-covered greenhouse. Intoxicating scents greeted us. I regretted inhaling the exotic smells. Immediately, the inside of my nose itched, and I expelled a series of sneezes.

We walked among the elevated plant boxes with Liz proudly pointing out the names of plants that I never knew existed. Each row was labeled with the names of the students responsible for growing the flowers. "This year our students will sell their plants at the fair, which I understand is a huge event."

Before I could answer she stopped so unexpectedly I nearly collided with her. She frowned as she stretched forward to shift several pots aside. "I don't understand how these got here. There are two types of plants that are specifically forbidden because they are dangerous to the children, and I shudder to think what would happen if any of the animals got out and came in here."

She lifted out two pots. "Most plants have certain levels of toxicity, unlike crocus and oleander, which are deadly." Her face reddened and not from embarrassment.

My heart lurched. This was not good. "Who oversees the hothouse?"

She stammered, "Th-this has to be an accidental slip-up. Maybe the nursery from Louisville included them by mistake. Ms. Teasdale is super-conscientious."

Liz grabbed a plastic garbage bag. Before she dumped the plants inside, I asked, "Do you mind if I take a couple of pictures?" I searched for a reasonable excuse. "I'd like to print the photos and post them in my office with a warning for my clients to avoid purchasing these particular plants due to the danger involved."

"That is a smart idea, Dr. Holliday." She set the potted plants on the ground. "On second thought, I'll take these to my office. The next time Ms. Teasdale comes in, I'll show them to her with a caution to check all plants before assigning them to students. It's possible they were just pretty flowers to her."

My mind was whirling, and I was anxious to show the pictures to my dad. I thanked Liz for the guided tour. Before leaving, I handed her my card with a reminder to call me if Buddy or any of the other animals needed vet services.

I sprinted down the steps to my truck. The air had cooled and smelled of rain. A surprise greeted me when I opened the door. On the driver's seat was a white box labeled *Sweet's 'n' Eats*. My first inclination was appreciation of how thoughtful of whomever to leave me such a delicious gift. But the cautious side of me screamed—*Warning!*

I commanded the Bluetooth to call Dad. His secretary answered, "Sheriff's Office."

"Joyce, this is Tullah. Is my dad in?"

"Sure is. Hold and I'll connect you."

Joyce yelled, "Henry, Tullah is on line one."

He picked up immediately. "What's up, Punkin?"

I gave him a brief explanation about my visit to the extension center and finding the poison flowers and the box left on the seat of my truck.

"Did you open the box or touch it?"

"No, sir. I used my phone to push it across the seat. I'm hoping you'll find fingerprints on it that will lead us to who committed the murders." I slid inside and turned the ignition.

"Bring it to my office, and I'll dust it."

"I would, except I need my microscope to examine the pastries for crocus particles. Do you mind bringing Grandmother and Patty to my clinic? I want Patty to look at whatever is in the box. Hopefully, she'll know if the pastries are truly from her shop."

"Smart idea. Don't do anything until we get there."

I pulled to a halt in front of my clinic. "I won't." I retrieved a pair of disposable gloves from my medical bag and slipped them on before lifting the box. By now it was after six and Cindi had already closed the clinic.

I inserted the key and unlocked the door. Once inside, I relocked it—my experience with Earl left me a bit paranoid about being alone. Then I opened the box, to find six glazed donuts.

Chapter Twenty

Crunching gravel drew my attention to the door. I peered through the blinds and was glad to see Dad's 4Runner. He opened the passenger side to assist Grandmother and Patty to the ground. I held the office door open.

"Oh, dear." The moment she entered the office, Patty clutched her hands to her breast. "That's my box. I swear, Henry, I'm not the killer."

Grandmother placed an arm around Patty's waist. "No one is accusing you. Don't go working yourself into a dither."

Worry marred Patty's face. Feeling the need to set her at ease, I asked, "Is there any way you can tell if these donuts came from your shop?"

"I'll certainly try." She moved forward to lean over the open box. She offered a puzzled look. "No. No, no! None of my ladies created these."

Dad joined us to look at the six round circles. He asked, "How can you be sure, Patty?"

She reached forward. I cautioned, "Please, don't touch."

She jerked her hand back as if she'd been scalded. "First of all, these are perfectly round—like they were poured in a mold and possibly baked. My donuts are always a little irregularly shaped, and fried. Secondly, the glaze on my donuts is classic white, almost like icing, which gives the donuts a nice crunch that flakes when you bite into them. These have a syrupy glaze which slides off the donut and makes them super sticky. I'll bet my entire business that the insides of these donuts aren't light and fluffy like mine."

It's true, Patty's donuts are bites of sweet air that melt in your mouth, and the glaze sticks to your fingers so that you lick them clean. I opened my medical bag and withdrew a scalpel. "I'm about to perform my first donut surgery." My attempt at humor was lost. I sliced it in half, and then I sliced the remaining five in half. "You win, Patty. These are dense and cakey."

I opened my phone and scrolled to the pictures I'd taken of the flowers. "Liz Trowbridge said Angela Teasdale was in charge of the hothouse. She was as surprised as I to find these hidden among the other plants."

Dad regarded me with serious blue eyes. "Tullah, while you check the contents of the donuts for crocus, I'll dust the box for fingerprints."

I handed Grandmother the keys to my truck. "The red key is to the house. Make yourselves comfortable. We may be a while."

Grandmother cocked her eyebrows. "I'm a newswoman with an insatiable curiosity. Patty and I will make ourselves comfy right here. In fact, I'll brew a pot of coffee." She headed to the coffeepot.

Patty's lips curved downward. "I'm staying, too. My livelihood and reputation are at stake."

While Dad dusted the box for prints, I sliced down the middle of each donut. "Look, dried specks."

I selected several crumbs with visible dark flecks to place on a slide, laid it on the stage plate, and peering through the microscope's ocular lens, adjusted the focus.

"What do you see, Tullah?" Grandmother leaned over my shoulder, craning her neck.

"These dark flecks look like dried herbs. I can't be certain it's crocus, some other toxic plant, or maybe even rodent poop."

Patty removed a pen from a cup holder and used it to move the untouched slices around. She burped as if she were about to regurgitate, and using the pen tip, pointed. "Tullah, that looks like a worm. Oh, my stars in heaven. Who would want to do such a terrible thing to you?"

With precision, I sliced through the long edge of the donut and used a pair of tweezers to remove a stem with a tiny piece of purple petal. My veins felt like ice water had flushed through them. "We have our murder weapon. Good eye, Patty."

She blinked back tears. "Does this mean I'm no longer a suspect?"

I placed the evidence in a plastic bag. "None of us thought you were guilty. It's routine to consider all possibilities." I hugged her. "Plus, you've helped solve a mystery."

Patty accepted a cup of coffee from Grandmother. "I don't know how I feel about that. At the moment, I need to sit down, because I think my knees are too relieved to hold me up."

The long day was taking its toll. My face hurt and my fractured wrist ached. I longed for a hot shower and a glass of wine. Instead, I stretched the kinks out of my back. "You know, it's possible we've been looking at all the wrong people." I recounted seeing Angela at

Forest's memorial. "I thought she'd been crying even when she blamed the puffy red eyes on allergies. Then when she laid her head on the steering wheel, I believed she was crying. Still, memorials are sad. Now, thinking back on it, she must have been really upset and didn't want to show it in front of all the guests. Also, Dad, remember at the debate how she flirted with Forest?"

"I guess I didn't notice." Dad straightened. "I've got prints. Whoever handled this box left their calling card. I'll put a rush on these, and hope to have the owner's name by tomorrow morning—if the person is in the system."

A thought occurred to me. "Teachers are required to be fingerprinted. If those belong to Angela Teasdale, she'll be in the system."

He nodded toward the plastic bag containing the dissected donuts. He secured the pastry carton and the slides. "I could bring her in for questioning tonight." He shifted his stance. "Still, without positive proof, I wouldn't want to harm her reputation and possibly cause the school board to fire her."

I rubbed my throbbing temples. "I know you don't like me butting into your business, but seeing as how she tried to kill me, do you mind if I ride with you tomorrow when you pick her up?"

Dad patted the top of my head. I'm a grown woman who still likes the comforting feeling of her daddy's touch. "*Alleged.* We don't know for certain it was her. Until all the facts are in, it'd be a mistake to jump to conclusions. If the prints are hers, I don't want to give some hot-shot defense attorney any reason to yell bias." He faced me. "It'll be much wiser for Tiny to accompany me."

My shoulders slumped, more with fatigue than disappointment. However, Dad misread my posture. His blue eyes glimmered with a slight smile. "I'll let you know when we've picked her up. It's not against the rules for you to listen in while I interrogate Angela—as long as you keep quiet."

Grandmother piped up. "Our girl is all done in from going back to work too soon after getting out of the hospital. C'mon, Patty, I'm sure we can scare up something in her kitchen for supper."

I accidently bumped my swollen lip with the brace on my wrist, causing it to bleed. Dad's eyes clouded with concern. He grabbed a napkin and handed it to me. I applied pressure to my lip and mumbled, "Charlie brought beef stew, and other stuff. It's in the freezer. Right now, I could use a glass of wine."

In the kitchen, Dad checked in with Deputy Goodbody. While Grandmother and Patty prepared a makeshift meal, we all relaxed with a glass of wine. Well, cola for Dad since he was still on duty.

"How does this sound for a front page article?" Grandmother asked. "Two vicious murders have been committed in Enigma, and that impacts everyone who lives here—"

Patty spooned beef stew on top of individual bowls of rice. "I just wish it was over," she said. "Alma's and Forest's murders have the entire town on edge. At least that's what I hear from my customers."

I silently agreed. Knowing a murderer was wandering around Enigma had created a pervasive tension among the community, including me. To get through each day, I forced that thought from my consciousness. Becoming a target myself made me even more uneasy.

Much to my delight, Grandmother set a platter of fried pickles in front of us, with a homemade dipping sauce. Leave it to her to prepare one of my favorite comfort foods. I dug into the dish in front of me.

The sun had set, and chirping rain frogs filled the evening. After a cup of Grandmother's special coffee, I was unsuccessful at suppressing a yawn. Dad glanced at his watch and declared he needed to get back to the office.

I said, "Two wonderful cooks, good food, and great company. I'm lucky to have all of you."

With the table cleared and hugs passed around, I stood on the back steps as Dad escorted the ladies across the yard to where he'd parked his 4Runner. My cellphone rang, and I removed it from my back pocket. The screen said Caller Unknown. I cautiously answered, "Hello?"

"Doc Holliday," a female voice managed between sobs.

I bounded down the steps, and just as Dad was pulling forward, I frantically waved to get his attention. He slammed on the brakes and sprang from the vehicle. I pointed to the phone, and then put a finger to my lips to signal him to be quiet. I put the phone on speaker.

"Who is this?" I asked.

"It's me—Angela Teasdale. You gave me your card, remember?"

"I remember. What's wrong, Angela?"

"You have to come to my house. Please." The rest of her words were drowned in tears.

"Angela, try to get hold of yourself. I don't know where you live. Maybe it'd be better if you came to my office."

"No, I can't. I'm afraid to leave my house."

"What's happened?"

"I believe Patty Sweet is trying to kill me."

I gasped at this statement. "You need to explain."

"There's a note inside a white box filled with donuts that says, 'You know why you must die.' I called the sheriff's office and was told he was at your office."

Dad motioned for the phone. I handed it to him. "Ms. Teasdale, this is Sheriff Holliday. Give me your address."

"No, I'll only give it to Tullah. She has to come with you."

He raised his eyebrows and shook his head. "She'll be with me."

I climbed into the vehicle and quickly explained the phone call to Grandmother and Patty. Dad radioed his deputy with instructions to meet him at the rear high school parking lot. He spoke as he raced down the driveway to the main road. His voice was gruff and all business. "Tanti, Deputy Goodbody will take you and Patty home. No arguments."

Patty leaned forward and gripped the back of my seat. "Let me guess. The donuts were in one of my signature boxes?"

Dad growled. "Yes, ma'am. I'm afraid so."

"Henry, you have to catch this lunatic."

"You have my word, Patty. That's a promise."

I hung on as the 4Runner slewed onto the highway. Dad reached forward and flipped on the siren. He gunned the engine. I clung to my seatbelt as he barreled down the highway. I asked, "Where does Angela live?"

Keeping his eyes on the road, he said, "Across the railroad tracks from the school." Without shifting his glance, he continued, "Tullah, when we get there, stay behind me. For all I know, this might be a set-up."

I sizzled with curiosity. At the same time, a knot twisted in my stomach. "Don't worry. I'm not about to play the hero."

At the edge of town, Dad silenced the siren. He pulled into the parking lot next to Deputy Goodbody's patrol car and left the engine running.

Tiny reminded me of a giant standing there silhouetted by the security lights. He said, "Henry, you need me for back-up after I take the ladies home?"

"I'll radio in if I need you. Follow me to the house and wait for me to give me an all-clear signal." Dad poked his head inside the open door to the back seat. I heard him warn Grandmother and Patty, "Make sure you lock your doors tonight. If it's not too late when I finish here, I'll check on you."

He got back in the car and dimmed the front lights as we bounced across the railroad track. He drove slowly until he spotted Angela's house. He cut the headlights as he pulled into the yard. I got out and stayed behind him just as he'd instructed. The house was dark as we eased up the steps.

Dad raised his fist and rapped on the door.

"Who is it?" Angela's voice called out.

"Sheriff Holliday."

"Is Doc Holliday with you?"

I answered, "I'm here, Angela."

"Just a minute."

Dad stood to one side. He motioned for me to stand behind him. As we listened to feet shuffling, he spoke into his collar mic telling Deputy Goodbody we were good. I watched Tiny's car pull away from the curb. My heart skittered.

The door eased open, with Angela huddled behind it. I said, "We came as quickly as we could."

"Thank you." Her voice was weak. "Come in. I shouldn't have bothered you, Doc Holliday. I should have waited until the sheriff returned my call."

"Your timing was perfect, Angela. Dad was just leaving for his office. I'm glad you reached out to me."

She opened the door barely wide enough for us to enter. The inside of the house was dimly lit. I thought she was about to cry, but her reservoir of tears seemed to be empty. All that emerged from her were dry gasps. I waited until that spasm had passed before saying, "Do you want to tell us what happened?"

Dad pulled a mini-recorder from his pocket. "It's customary to record these sessions. You are not legally obligated to answer any questions or make any statements without counsel present."

Angela shrugged. "I understand." She directed us to a small dining table and indicated we should sit. Dad set the tape recorder on the table. "Please state your full name and today's date."

She leaned forward. "My name is Angela Teasdale, and today is Friday. I'm making these statements voluntarily."

She mopped her eyes with a napkin. I said, "Take a deep breath, and begin at the beginning."

She nodded. "After school, I drove to the extension center. I walked inside to sign in. Today is the day I meet with my 4-Hers on their plant projects. Before I entered the meeting room, the receptionist handed me a note stating that Mrs. Trowbridge wanted to meet with me."

A fresh well of tears sprang forward. Dad and I waited for Angela to calm herself. She explained that Liz Trowbridge had ripped her a new one because of the two toxic plants found in the greenhouse. "I tried to explain that I had no idea how those flowers got there. I certainly hadn't ordered them. And then she accused me of being irresponsible for not carefully checking the shipment when it arrived from the nursery."

"What happened then?" I asked.

Angela's voice grew resentful. "Trowbridge said she had reported the incident to my principal." The tears came again. She blew her nose. "I suppose he'll call me in Monday morning. If I lose my job over this, I'm afraid it'll go on my record."

I saw the panic in her eyes and asked, "What does all of this have to do with the box of donuts and a note?"

"Oh, they're in the kitchen."

Dad pulled a pair of disposable gloves from his pocket. "Do you have a fresh trash bag?"

She rose and we followed her to the kitchen, where she pointed to a white box sitting on a counter. The lid was up, revealing six round donuts similar to the ones I had received. Dad said, "I suppose you touched the box and the note?"

Her eyes widened in dismay, her tone a bit sarcastic. "Well, of course, how was I to know any different? I've made no bones about how much I love Patty Sweet's donuts. I thought perhaps one of my colleagues had left them for me."

I said, "Angela, do you mind if I use one of your

knives? I'd like to look inside one of the donuts."

She pointed to a drawer.

I removed a sharp-bladed knife and sliced through the pastry and laid it open. I looked at Dad and nodded. He said, "Ms. Teasdale, it's a good thing you didn't eat any of these."

"Why? Is something wrong with them?"

I used the tip of the blade to point at multiple flakes. "I'm a hundred percent certain this is dried Autumn Crocus. I'll know for sure when I test them."

Angela's face paled. She leaned against the counter for support. "Oh, my God."

I read the typed note aloud. *"You know why you must die."*

"Does this mean anything to you?" I asked.

She shook her head. "I can't imagine what it means."

Dad closed the lid and set the box inside the plastic bag. He indicated we should return to the living room, where we resumed our seats.

I said, "Why were you so upset at Forest Rakestraw's memorial? And don't tell me you were suffering from an allergy attack. I know crying when I see it."

She nodded, her sobs coming out in hiccups. "He was the best and the worst thing that ever happened to me. All he gave me was heartache."

We gave Angela time to compose herself. Her smile was tense. "He made me feel beautiful, and he said he loved me, and even pseudo-proposed."

I gathered my eyebrows into a frown. "What the heck is pseudo-proposed?"

Angela twiddled with her thumbs. "Forest was

honest and upfront about the pre-nup agreement he'd signed. There was no way he'd ever divorce Beverly. He enjoyed living in the lap of luxury too much." She shrugged. "And there was no way we could live off my teaching salary. I'm single and barely eke by on what I make. So Forest bought me a ring—diamonds and emeralds—and we were happy with our secret rendezvous...our pretend engagement. At least, I thought we were."

I responded in a low voice, "What changed?"

Angela twisted her hands together. "This is humiliating. It was the eve of our first anniversary. Forest owns...owned a cabin in a place called Cozy Cove. He said he bought it especially for me. It was our forever honeymoon home." She stared off into space. I touched her hand, encouraging her to continue. "Like I said, it was the eve of our first anniversary, and I decided to stock the cabin with champagne, caviar, and other special goodies for our celebration. When I walked in, the place smelled of inexpensive musk cologne. Forest would never wear a cheap brand. He wore cologne that equaled my monthly salary. I told myself maybe he'd let a buddy use the cabin, which angered me because this was supposed to be our special place.

"A strange sensation wafted over me...suspicion, I suppose. You see, I'd heard rumors about his other women. I once asked him about it." She laughed. "Oh, he was such a convincing liar. I believed him. Well, I'd never plundered before. Of course, I'd never been there alone, either. So I decided to search the rooms. The place was clean, and I felt totally ashamed of my doubts. I sat down to enjoy a glass of wine and noticed the wall clock had stopped and decided to put a new battery in it. We kept extras. It's large and round, like a man's pocket watch. I didn't know it had a secret compartment until I lifted it off the wall and the back opened."

She squeezed her eyes tightly shut, either because her thoughts were painful or because she was trying to recall what she had already said. Either way, she opened them and said, "I found a small black zipper case filled with flash drives. You've heard the saying curiosity killed the cat...I wish to heaven I'd never looked at any of them, because I'll never be able to un-see the images of Forest and Alma Tackett naked, him and Bambi Crandall, him doing perverted things with men..." She buried her face in her hands and sobbed. "...and with me. I was so humiliated."

I exchanged an incredulous look with Dad. I tried to keep the astonishment from my voice. "He was filming you and saving it to flash drives? Is that why you killed Forest?"

She shifted her position in the chair, diverting her eyes from mine. I waited for her reply. When she did, her voice was flat. "Oh, you can believe I thought of all kinds of ingenious ways to make him suffer." She looked at me, her voice matter-of-fact. "I didn't kill Forest."

Dad said, "What did you do with the flash drives?"

"I drank the entire bottle of champagne and passed out. Forest found me the next morning asleep on the sofa. I scooped up the devices from the table and threw them at him. I said some horrible things. He slapped me, and then he laughed. He said I should be grateful to him for even giving me the time of day, that I was just another easy lay, and not a very good one at that.

"I pulled off the ring and ran outside and threw it in the lake." She hugged herself as if warding off a chill. "If I'd known about the other women and...and...men, I'd have broken off our relationship much sooner. I got in my car, and that's the last time I saw him alive."

I asked yet another question. "Was that before or after the night of his scheduled debate with Mayor Tackett?"

The sobs burst forth again. "The day after her death." Angela drew in a deep breath. "Now that I think about it, Forest didn't look well. His forehead was sweaty, and he complained of chest pains, but with my fury over the revolting movies and his slapping me, I didn't give his health a second thought."

Dad asked, "Do you think Mrs. Rakestraw knew about her husband's pastime activities?"

Angela released a long, resigned sigh. "If she did, why didn't she kick him out? I mean, a pre-nuptial agreement protected her from a costly divorce settlement."

"What about the flash drives? Do you know what happened to them?"

Angela shook her head. "It's anybody's guess. I don't know."

I hadn't prepared for this turn of events and tried to gather my thoughts. Angela wiped her eyes with the backs of her hands. "Sheriff, I'm afraid to stay here tonight. Afraid that whoever sent the donuts might be lurking outside."

I could see Dad's mind working, as if he were putting all the facts together. He said, "Keep your doors and windows locked. Don't open for anyone. However,

I don't think you have anything to worry about. Whoever sent the donuts is probably certain you've eaten them and is sitting back waiting to read the headlines about your demise."

He handed her his business card. "Call me if you think someone is trying to break in."

She managed a weak smile. "Just so you know, and because I don't have anything to hide, I've decided to tender my resignation. My sister has been after me to return home. As soon as the school year is over, I'm heading back to Colorado."

Angela's tale was wrenching, but I believed her.

Chapter Twenty-One

I'd been silent for the past few minutes. Dad finally said, "What's your inner sense telling you, Punkin?"

"It's frustrating, for sure. This is a case where the suspects are plentiful. Angela Teasdale certainly had plenty of reason to kill Forest. My instinct says she's telling the truth."

"That puts us back to square one with Sue West and Beverly as the prime suspects. And I haven't altogether ruled out Evelyn March."

"What about Talmadge Crandall?"

"Nah, Crandall would've lived up to his promise of castration, or have used his fists to beat Forest to a pulp. Poison is often used in crimes of passion—a woman's weapon."

Dad reached over and patted my shoulder. "You look beat. How about a cup of coffee before I take you home?"

I suppressed a yawn. "If you don't mind, I'd like to go home and straight to bed."

"You got it."

It's odd how silence can be a mutual agreement. I leaned my head against the window while Dad kept his eyes on the road. It seemed that neither of us wanted to talk. Words swam through my head, matching themselves up like the answer to a crossword puzzle. This happens sometimes. Grandmother calls it my secret sense. She says it's a rare gift.

"Lunatic!" The word spilled from my mouth in a shout.

The truck swerved, and Dad gripped the steering wheel. "Holy crap, Tullah. You want to give me a heart attack?"

I apologized for my sudden outburst. "I've got it, Dad. The killer is Luanne Sterns."

He glanced over at me, his expression serious in the darkness. "Explain."

"Remember this afternoon when Patty said you needed to catch the *lunatic* that was doing this?"

"Yeah, sure, although I don't get the connection."

I told him about sending Cindi to the Sterns' house on the pretext of checking on Gigi and the puppies, and to check the yard for crocuses. "Cindi said the house was loaded with cardboard boxes and that Father Sterns related he'd requested an assignment in Africa." I filled in all the details about Luanne being bullied, and her promiscuousness. "Cindi said Father Sterns went on to explain that Luanne had suffered a nervous breakdown. He's concerned because he's receiving complaints about Luanne's display of erratic and aggressive behavior."

I also reminded Dad of her impromptu confession to Grandmother about her involvement with Forest, and about Luanne's display of hostility at his memorial. "It has to be Luanne."

"It's a sound theory, Punkin." He huffed. "I hadn't heard about Jerry's resignation. Too bad, because he's one of the good guys." He suppressed a yawn. "It's late. We'll check out your theory tomorrow. Let's get you home."

Dad's police radio crackled. "Henry?"

Static.

He reached forward for the mic. "Go ahead, Joyce."

Static. "How far are you from the hospital?" Static.

"About eight minutes. What's up?"

"Dr. Gannon's nurse called. She said a patient was brought in and is now in ICU. He's critical and asking for you."

"Did she give a name?"

Static. "No, just that Dr. Gannon doesn't expect the guy to live through the night."

The siren wailed. Dad gunned the engine. I pressed my boots against the floorboard, thanking my lucky stars for almost no traffic. The route took us through the center of town. Dad hung a left on a back road past the public park and then skidded into the hospital's front parking lot in a space reserved for law enforcement.

I followed close on his heels as he sprinted toward the elevator. He punched the ICU button. The doors opened. He flashed his badge. A nurse said, "Follow me, Sheriff Holliday." She pointed her finger at me. "Sorry, not you."

Dad's tone was authoritative. "She's with me."

We entered the small cell-like room. Machines whirred and clicked, a monitor charted the patient's heart rhythm. Dr. Gannon's glance toward me was less than welcoming, and I was sure he hadn't fully recovered from his traumatic experience of sinking ankle-deep in horse manure. He directed his comment to my dad. "The patient's heart is failing fast. In fact, his entire system is rapidly shutting down."

I stepped forward. "Dad, its Father Sterns." I noted

the redness around the priest's mouth. I lifted his eyelids, and the pupils were severely constricted. "Doctor, have you tested for flora toxicity, specifically Autumn Crocus?"

He shot me a glare and replied, "We've drawn blood and are waiting for lab reports."

Dad said, "Toxicology from the autopsies proves that Autumn Crocus is what killed Alma and Forest."

Dr. Gannon snapped at the nurse to contact the CDC. "Tell them we need to know what antibody to use to reverse the effects of Autumn Crocus toxicity. Stat!"

Dad lifted Father Sterns' hand and leaned over the bedrail. "Jerry, it's Henry. Can you hear me?"

The priest's eyes fluttered open. His voice was barely audible. "My fault...donuts not for me...didn't know." His chest heaved as if breathing was difficult. He tried to lift his head and failed. "T-tullah, you were getting too close."

Dad said, "Jerry, did your sister poison Alma and Forest?"

His eyes closed. Dad beseeched, "Jerry...stay alert. Dr. Gannon is getting a serum to counteract the poison."

"No...too late. I can't help her anymore. God forgive me, I've tried."

"Jerry, tell me, did Luanne poison Alma and Forest, and did she send the donuts to Angela Teasdale and my daughter?"

Only the machines whirred and clicked.

Dr. Gannon bent forward. He put a stethoscope to Father Sterns' chest. "He's barely hanging on."

I stepped forward and took his hand, and schooled my voice into quiet compassion. "Father Sterns, we'll get Luanne the help she needs. Please try to answer my dad's question."

His eyes opened, and he rolled them around as if trying to focus. His brow furrowed in concentration. "I found her diary. She flew into a..." The word "rage" seeped out like air escaping a balloon. The heart monitor beep-beeped and then flat lined.

I laid Father Jerry Sterns' hand across his chest and stepped back. "Are you calling for a crash cart?"

Dr. Gannon said, "It's in his living will—no resuscitation."

Dad said, "We'll need an autopsy."

Dr. Gannon merely nodded. "I'll fax the report to you as soon as the lab gets it to me." He heaved a sigh. "Father Jerry Sterns died way before his time."

The three of us stood together at the elevator doors. Dr. Gannon said, "If proven guilty, Luanne Sterns will never go to prison. You know that, Sheriff."

The metal doors slid open. I stepped inside. Dad followed. He squinted at the doctor. "There are different kinds of prisons, Doctor. I'm sure that somewhere in your career you visited sanatoriums for the insane."

The elevator doors closed before Dr. Gannon could answer. Dad removed his cowboy hat and ran a hand through his thick brown hair. "That man rubs me the wrong way."

****

The trip took us twenty minutes. Dad called Tiny for backup, and we found Father Sterns' car was parked in the driveway. A dim light was visible through the front room curtains. Small pots of red geraniums lined the sidewalk. A black iron numeral twenty-three hung on a porch post. Two wicker rockers flanked a street-facing window. Dad climbed the five steps to the porch, followed by Tiny, and then me. He motioned his deputy to stand next to the screened door. I stood behind Dad. He opened the screened door and knocked on the solid wooden door. No response.

He knocked again louder and more prolonged this time. "Luanne Sterns," he called out in his deep bass voice, "Sheriff Holliday. Are you home?"

There was silence, aside from a train whistle in the far distance. Dad motioned me forward. I called her name, even louder, and knocked with force while I tried the doorknob. To my surprise, the door creaked open a little. I looked at Dad. He motioned me back behind him. He pushed the door farther and called Luanne's name one more time. When he didn't get an answer, he motioned us inside and flipped on a light. Boxes and articles of clothing littered the room.

I called out, "Luanne, it's Doc Holliday. I've come to check on Gigi and the puppies." At that thought, I wondered why Gigi hadn't barked. A chill slithered over me, and I prayed that in her depravity Luanne hadn't harmed the Chihuahua and her puppies.

Dad instructed Tiny to check outside and in the back yard for the dogs, and possibly a body. I circumvented the maze of cardboard boxes and pointed to the hallway. "Maybe she's in the bedroom."

A bathroom was on the right, in a partial state of being cleaned. The next door revealed a bedroom. Men's clothing draped across a bed stripped of its sheets. I stepped to the next door. "This has to be her room."

I knocked. "Luanne, it's Doc Holliday. Are you ill?

I've brought my dad, if you need help." I gasped when I turned the knob and opened the door. Luanne Sterns sat propped against the bed's headboard, completely naked, her eyes bulging and her mouth open as if she were gasping for breath. A plate with the remains of a partially eaten donut lay on top of her lap. One arm hung off the side of the bed and in her hand she clutched a leather-bound book.

Dad reached into his pocket and handed me a pair of gloves. I put them on, set the plate aside, and checked the side of her neck for a pulse. I shook my head. "Her body's still warm. Death could've happened anywhere from an hour to three hours ago."

"Go ahead and take pictures, Tullah, then cover her up." Dad removed the book from her hand and opened it. He leafed through the pages. "It's a diary."

I clicked several photos of Luanne and the room, then covered her with a sheet. "Does she make any confessions?"

He shifted his weight from one foot to the other. "In detail." He shook his head. "I'm sure as a priest Jerry tried to do all he could to save his sister. I don't understand why, as her brother, he didn't keep her in a sanatorium. She apparently had problems beyond his expertise."

I finished with photographing the room. Dad handed me the diary. I flipped to a page and read, "I did it. I killed them all. They were evil and deserved to die." I turned another page, and said, "Dad, in another life, Luanne was a florist. She details how she dried the flowers." I continued to read silently.

"What else does she say?"

"It says she took cooking classes at the extension

center to learn how to make donuts. She also tells how she accumulated the boxes from Patty's bakery." I'd be lying if I didn't admit I was revolted. How was it we'd been in Luanne's presence and mistaken her insanity for quirkiness?

I turned the next page. The handwriting was almost illegible. It took several seconds before I completely deciphered what she had written. "Dad, you'd better read this."

"Go ahead, Punkin. I'm listening."

I drew in a series of breaths. Emotions constricted my throat. I blinked back tears, and swallowed. It felt as if I had to push the words up my throat and out of my mouth. "The demons are back and stronger than ever. Looking to win. And this time I'll let them."

She also writes, "Why should I apologize for the monster I've become? No one ever apologized for making me this way."

I turned another page and held it forward for Dad to see. Scrawled in capital brownish-red letters that resembled blood were the words "Fatal Passion!" And a hand-drawn picture of six donuts, a bite taken out of each one.

Dad's eyes met mine. He forced a sad smile. We disposed of our gloves. He wrapped me in his strong arms. "Death is never pretty. I hope Luanne is finally at peace."

Tiny called out. "Sheriff?"

"In here."

The burly deputy entered, holding a crate. The sight of Luanne's covered body stopped him. "Miss Sterns?"

Dad nodded.

Inside the wire crate Tiny held, Gigi snarled as she guarded her babies. "I found them in this. No water—no food."

Dad relieved the burly deputy of the dog carrier. "Tullah's already taken a few pictures. Go ahead and photograph the entire house, and bag up the remains of that donut, as well as this diary. I'll leave it to you to cordon off the perimeter with crime scene tape, and to call Bubba and Rita to come pick up the body. As soon as I get Tullah home, I'll see you back at the office."

"Yes, sir, Sheriff." Tiny tipped his hat. "Tullah, you get some rest."

Chapter Twenty-Two

I never imagined I'd attend four funerals in less than ten days: Mayor Alma Tackett, Forest Rakestraw, Father Jerry Sterns, and Luanne. It's been a week since the double service for the brother and sister. The turnout was large, I suspect more for Father Sterns than for Luanne. Once I had time to recuperate from the beating Earl Redfern gave me, and the shock of discovering three dead bodies, I concluded that I still liked animals far more than people.

On Friday evening, Cindi and I strolled into the Whitehorse Saloon. I wondered what all the cloak-and-dagger suspense was with Grandmother's text to meet her and Patty here. I blinked, allowing my eyes to adjust to the interior. Grandmother waved. Dad and Charlie sat at the table also.

Cindi said, "What's going on, Tullah? Did I forget your birthday?"

I shrugged. "Your guess is as good as mine. My birthday isn't until September."

Flora walked over and set chilled glasses of wine in front of Cindi and me. Wearing a huge smile, Flora said, "Congratulations, Tanti. You and Patty will—" and then as if she had caught herself she said, "Oops! I almost spilled the beans. I'd better go check on your hamburgers."

I sat down. "Okay, out with it. What's all this

clandestine stuff about?"

Patty laughed. Grandmother laughed, too. "With all the mud brought out in the news about Forest's life, Sam dropped his bid for mayor. Also, it's my understanding from a reliable source that Beverly has severed ties with him both personally and financially. His only income will generate from his feed store."

"That's interesting. Is this why we're celebrating?"

Grandmother reached over and tweaked my cheek. "Remember when you suggested I run for mayor?"

My eyes widened, and the glumness I'd been feeling melted away. "No—way?"

"Yes—way. And since Enigma is without a mayor, the city council received special approval from the governor to go ahead and swear me in as interim mayor. Since we are now way past the deadline for candidates to qualify and submit their paperwork, come November, I will officially become Madam Mayor Tanti Crow." With great flourish she turned to Patty. "And Mrs. Patricia Sweet aka Patty accepted the position of vice mayor. The ceremony is Monday. You and Cindi will attend, won't you?"

I stood and hugged her and then Patty. "Wild horses couldn't keep me away."

Cindi clapped her hands like an excited teenager.

Around the table voices ebbed and flowed much like the ocean tides. Gigi and her pups had found a loving home with Cindi. My grandmother and her best friend were setting precedents for older women, my clinic was flourishing, and Cindi decided it was time to get her degree in veterinary science. I was happy for her to be moving forward with her life.

Someone put money in the old-fashioned jukebox

that sits in the corner of Charlie's saloon. My favorite song was playing. I glanced around the table at the people who meant so much to me. Life was back to normal, I hoped.

Recipe for Easy Donuts

As a busy mother and a middle school teacher, I rarely had time to make donuts that were light and fluffy like those of the story character, Patty Sweet. However, my children and I enjoyed making these quick and easy donuts together. They were a favorite for Saturday morning breakfast or any occasion. Enjoy!

Ingredients:

1 container of refrigerated biscuits (I prefer Pillsbury Southern Original Grands, but any brand will do.)
1 cup shortening for frying (canola, Crisco, safflower, etc.)

Directions:

1. Separate the biscuits. Use the heel of your hand to press each biscuit flat.

2. Use the lid from a milk jug or a cookie ring to punch out the center of the dough to create a hole. (Don't forget to fry the holes, too.)

3. Place oil in an iron skillet or a frying pan.

4. Heat oil. (An easy way to test the oil to see if it's hot is to drop a bead of water on the surface. If the oil spits or crackles, then it's ready. **Be Careful not to stand over the frying pan when you do this**)

5. Lay 2-3 donuts in the hot oil; let cook for approximately 1 minute, then turn to brown the other side.

6. Remove and place on a cookie rack to drain excess grease.

7. Repeat the process until all donuts and holes are finished.

Toppings:

Choose your favorite topping to coat each donut:

1. Cinnamon sugar: In a bowl place 2 cups of granulated sugar, 2 tablespoons cinnamon, and ¼ teaspoon nutmeg. Use a fork to blend ingredients together. Dip the donuts in the mixture and coat well.

2. Powdered sugar: Put 1 or 2 cups of powdered sugar in a bowl. Dip each donut until covered with powdered sugar.

3. Glazed: In a bowl place 2 cups of powdered sugar, ¼ cup milk, and a pinch of salt. Whisk together until blended. If the glaze is too thick, add ¼ teaspoon of milk. Pour over donuts or dip to coat both sides.

4. Chocolate: Personally, I use a quick short cut for the chocolate-covered donuts. I use chocolate syrup that you use to top ice cream. Lay each donut on a sheet pan. Coat each donut with as much or as little chocolate syrup as desired (add sprinkles or nuts, if you like). Place the pan in the refrigerator until the syrup sets.

Enjoy!

*A Grisly Find
in a Reputedly Haunted Swamp—
Eleven Female Skeletons
Who...Is...The...Killer?*

Enjoy a preview chapter of

The Bone Yard

Another
Loretta C. Rogers

Doc Holliday Mystery

Chapter One

The early Greeks and Romans believed the sultry dog days of August was a time of evil and bad luck because of unexpected thunderstorms and lethargy. Maybe I believe this. Maybe not.

My name is Tullah Crow Holliday. I am a doctor of veterinary medicine with secondary degrees in both human and animal forensics. I am licensed to practice in the state of Kentucky, operating an animal clinic in the small rural town of Enigma, where I have lived my entire twenty-nine years, not counting the years I attended the University of Georgia. And before you ask, yes, I do get kidded a lot about being someone's huckleberry, and yes, the infamous outlaw, Doc Holliday, is my ancestor on my father's side. By the way, it just so happens that my father, John Henry Holliday, is the sheriff of Enigma.

I don't consider myself an amateur sleuth. Rather, trouble seems to find me. My grandmother, Tanti Crow, who is full-blooded Cherokee, says it's because of my empathic abilities that lost souls seek me out to find their killers and bring them to justice.

Today the scorching air feels like it's sucking the breath right out of my body. There isn't a hint of a breeze. I'm glad I had the foresight to install fans in the barn. Even now my horses prefer to stand in their stalls instead of grazing in the pasture.

In spite of the heat, Grandmother and I sit in the porch swing sipping iced tea and watching the sun slide below the horizon. Occasionally we swat a horsefly seeking to feast on our blood. It will be dark soon. Lightning bugs blink across the pasture like tiny bobbing lanterns. We inhale the sweet scent of night-blooming jasmine.

Grandmother lifts her face to catch the ceiling fan's cool air. "How much longer does Cindi have before she graduates with her degree in veterinary medicine?"

Too long, I thought. Not only did I miss my friend, it's tough trying to run a busy animal clinic without a good assistant. "Two more very long years."

We resumed our swinging, and then Grandmother asked, "Now that she's reconnected with her mother, do you suppose Cindi will return to Enigma?"

I sipped the last of my tea. "With Earl in prison, there's no reason for Cindi and Annie to stay away. Here's the thing, Grandmother. Annie has a good job at a bank in Lexington. I've offered Cindi a partnership in the clinic. She'll run the small animal side while I take care of the large animals."

"That sounds like a deal not to be passed up. What did she say?"

I sighed and gazed out at the fireflies blinking their lights. "She appreciated the offer, but this early in her education she'd rather not commit." I shifted to look at my grandmother. "Honestly, my gut instinct is telling me Cindi will never return to Enigma."

Grandmother made a pfff sound. "After all you've done for that girl. Took her in when no one else would give her the time of day because of who her daddy is, gave her a good paying job, even supplied her with a house, and paid her first semester's tuition...why..."

I held up my hand. "Stop. You're getting yourself all worked up over nothing. Whatever decision Cindi makes will be because it's right for her."

Grandmother lifted my hand to her cheek. "You are just like my Josie, may she rest in peace—you have a good soul."

The mention of my mother sent a painful twang through my heart. I reminded myself that someday...someday when the time is right...I will find the monster that murdered my mother and left her like a heap of trash in a New York back alley.

We rock back and forth in the swing in silence.

Grandmother shifts. "It's about time I gather up my dishes and head home. I have a busy day tomorrow."

"What new project are you presenting to the council this time?"

As the newly elected and overly enthusiastic mayor of Enigma, Kentucky, my grandmother's ideas aren't always met with exuberance from the city council.

She clapped her hands together. "I've contacted Premier Entertainment Productions, and they are interested. What better place to make a movie than our beautiful countryside?" Tanti Crow spread her hands to indicate all of our rural community. "And not to speak of the tourism dollars PEP would bring."

"That's a worthy idea, Grandmother. The council is foolish if they vote against it. "

An unexpected shiver slithers over me, prickling the hairs on my arms. I use my bare toes to abruptly halt the swing's back-and-forth motion. A vibration starts in my chest, and I have the feeling something unexpected is about to happen. Grandmother calls this my inner sense. She says only special people are blessed with this secret sagacity. She also says it's because of my Cherokee heritage. Whatever *it* is, most of the time I consider it a curse.

"You're as pale as a ghost. Have you taken ill…Tullah…speak to me…what ails you?"

I clutch my wrist. The pain is almost unbearable. Tears flood my eyes. The knot in my gut twists tighter with the tingling premonition that something unusual is about to happen.

"I'm not sure." My heartbeat quickens and I take a deep breath to calm the nerves that want to come.

Grandmother scoots closer and wraps her arms around me. She says, "You are trembling like the weather just turned cold."

It's true. Shivers slither up and down my spine. I look at her and say, "My instinct is telling me to be watchful. For what, I don't know."

I gaze out at the open pasture, searching. Something about the evening and Grandmother's mention of death has awakened my inner sense.

Grandmother rubs her hand up and down my arm as if trying to warm me. She says, "For those who are blessed with the secret sense, it is the wisest part of them. It knows when the stars are out of kilter and steers us clear of what's bad for us. It also guides us toward what is right, and sometimes it's difficult to tell which is which."

"Whatever *it* is, I wish someone other than me had inherited *it*."

As quickly as it came, the feeling of unease fluttered away, leaving me to sigh a breath of relief. Grandmother and I sit in solitude, allowing the songs of the night creatures, blending with the creaking of the swing, to serenade us.

In the waning light, River, my black Labrador Retriever, dances up the porch steps and happily lays his trophy at my feet. Grandmother gasps. "Oh, my lands, is that…is that a…hand?"

River sits with his long pink tongue hanging from his mouth. He actually looks as if he's smiling. I reach forward and reward him with a pat. "Good boy, River." And then I lean down and carefully lift the bony skeleton of a hand.

Whatever *it* is—the inner sense—has joined River in opening the door to a mystery I feel compelled to solve.

Grandmother's eyes are wide when she asks, "Is it human?"

I handle the skeletal remains as if it were a fragile piece of china. "Maybe, but it could also be primate. They look similar."

A word about the author…

A native Floridian and proud of her Scots-Irish heritage, Loretta C. Rogers is a bestselling author. She writes in all sub-genres of romance. There is always a little bit of mystery and suspense in her novels. Her books are in libraries throughout the USA and Europe. When not writing, she is an avid traveler, and enjoys researching her family genealogy.

HAPPY!

If you enjoyed reading *FATAL PASSION*,

your review is highly appreciated.

www.lorettacrogersnovels.com

Thank you for purchasing
this publication of The Wild Rose Press, Inc.

For questions or more information
contact us at
info@thewildrosepress.com.

The Wild Rose Press, Inc.
www.thewildrosepress.com